Risk Aware

SAUGATUCK BOOK 2

AMELIA C. GORMLEY

ACG Publications
www.ameliacgormley.com

Risk Aware (Saugatuck, Book 2)
Copyright © 2016 by Amelia C. Gormley

Cover Art by Samantha Santana
https://www.amaidesigns.com/
Editor: Kate De Groot

ISBN: 978-1-62622-614-2

First edition
May, 2016

Second edition
September, 2018

PRAISE FOR AMELIA C. GORMLEY

SAUGATUCK SUMMER

… a wonderful [book to read.] It will pull you in, involve you emotionally and mentally. It will tear you up as you watch Topher breaking on the shoals of his illness and family history. And finally it will move you to tears and happiness as Topher finds his way to love and a future.

— MELANIE MARSHALL, SCATTERED THOUGHTS AND
ROGUE WORDS

I can think of quite a few of these guys that have stayed with me long after I finished their book. Topher will be one of those guys!

— VANESSA, THE JEEP DIVA

This hurricane of emotion is a category five recommendation.

— TINA, THE NOVEL APPROACH

STRAIN

…dystopian fantasy at its finest…devastatingly beautiful.

— JENNI LEA, BOY MEETS BOY REVIEWS

Strain is a well written and absorbing novel. The further into the novel the reader gets, the deeper the reader sinks emotionally. It grabs onto your heart or should I say Rhys does, and, refuses to let go. Trust me when I say you will be sobbing at certain junctures within this story. Rhys will break your heart over and over.

— MELANIE MARSHALL, SCATTERED THOUGHTS AND
ROGUE WORDS

Amelia Gormley has created a really excellently drawn post-apocalyptic world

— AUTHOR LETA BLAKE

A LIFE HALF-LIVED NO MORE . . .

Hemophiliac Geoff Gilchrest has lived his entire life swaddled in figurative bubble wrap, thanks to his overprotective mother. Now he's free of everything except the prison of his own mind, where forbidden desires war against crippling self-doubt.

Geoff is a masochist. He craves his sex with a side of pain and degradation. But when getting shoved against a wall could result in catastrophic brain injury and even a moderate flogging could leave him paralyzed—or worse—it's hard to find a dom willing to step up and give Geoff the experiences he's been longing for.

Robin Brady has doubts of his own. Still stinging from massive violations of trust on the part of his drug-addicted ex, he has retreated to Saugatuck to start a new life. But the yearning in Geoff's eyes calls to him, and he knows that, armed with a deft hand and foreknowledge, he can give Geoff what he's been seeking, without putting Geoff's safety at risk.

First, though, he's got to convince Geoff to trust him—not just with his well-being, but with his pride. Geoff's injured self-esteem and trouble with communicating what he perceives as weaknesses, could end them before they have a chance to begin.

READER DISCRETION ADVISED

Each reader is unique in their tolerance for graphic material. As such, please be aware that this novel may contain material or references which may be triggering for some readers. If you worry that this might be an issue, the author whole-heartedly encourages you take the time to read some of the reviews others have left at Goodreads and various ebook retailers to see if it contains subject matter you may find disturbing. Thank you.

For Paul and Tristan, whose love and support keep me going.

And for Leta, Tristina, and Chris, who helped me whip this thing into shape after almost two years of bashing my head against it.

CHAPTER ONE

Geoff

"Is that the last of them?" my sister asked, helping Jace stack boxes. She dusted off her hands as I glanced around the crowded self-storage room. Funny, they always sounded bigger than they were. When Ling and I decided to move everything from Colorado to Chicago in a U-Haul, a ten-by-ten space had seemed like plenty of room for storing the stuff we weren't able to bring ourselves to part with.

"Almost." I slipped an arm around her waist and kissed the crown of her head as she obligingly tucked herself under my chin. It had been nearly a month since we'd gotten the call from our mom's neighbor that our mom had passed away, and we were still feeling a little shaky about all the changes. "Guess it's pretty much over now."

She squeezed me harder. "Yeah. The inscription on the urn will be done tomorrow. We can pick it up in the morning, before my flight back to Philly."

"Sounds good. When does your plane leave?"

"One thirty. I should be at the airport no later than noon." She snorted and shook her head. "Part of me wishes this had happened a few weeks later, so I could have taken care of it while I was on vacation. But then, I wouldn't want to be traveling in spring break traffic."

"Nah." I kissed her temple. "Be glad for it. Now you can still have something of a vacation."

"What about you?" She drew back and smiled at me. "What are you going to do now that you're in Chicago to stay?"

I shrugged. "I don't know. I'm still a little shell-shocked that I decided to leave LA at all." In a spur-of-the-moment decision that was fueled by grief more than logic.

"Is Rogier still leaving you scathing messages?"

That was enough to brighten my mood. I grinned. "They've gone from scathing to positively blistering now that he's noticed I took all my designs with me."

Jace clapped me on the shoulder as he squeezed past us toward the van for another load. "Good boy."

"Well, it was about fucking time he stopped passing my work off as his own." I released Ling and followed him.

"I still don't get why you stayed with him for a year after your apprenticeship ended." Ling's voice echoed down the stairway from behind me, bouncing off cinder-block walls, heavy with disapproval.

I emerged into daylight and scrambled up into the back of the truck to grab another load. "Because no one else reputable wanted to hire me. I'm pretty sure he spread a rumor that I lied about my HIV status so none of the other studios would poach me."

"Fucking asshole," Ling hissed, lifting the final box, then called out to me as I started down the ramp with my own, "Careful!"

I gave her a flat look, more determined than ever to carry that box no matter what it cost me. "I'm *fine*."

It would have been nice to see some contrition, because she knew how I felt about that shit, but Ling arched an eyebrow. Jace stood by with his own armful. He didn't speak a word, though his bland expression made it clear what he thought of my rejection of Ling's concern.

After a moment, Ling shook her head with a wry quirk of her lips. "They're your joints," she muttered as she carefully walked down the ramp.

Now I was the one feeling contrite. She was the last person on Earth who deserved my grousing, and while it wasn't in her nature not to occasionally be concerned for my health, she was never over-bearing. We'd both been a little off since Mom's death, and I think I, in particular, kept wondering when Mom was going to reappear, inserting herself into the middle of everything in a well-intentioned but carried-way-too-far effort to protect me from life's bumps and bruises.

"Sorry." I offered Ling a sheepish look as she passed.

Her eyes softened. "Forgiven. Now, back to Rogier. You might have been better off going home to do your apprenticeship. There was that great tattoo studio—"

"Oh, *please*. Like I was going to spend three more years than I had to in that town."

She gave me an iffy smile. "It wasn't really a bad town. You just had bad experiences there for a rather unique set of reasons. I'm kinda gonna miss it."

"I guess," I conceded grudgingly. As things went, our hometown actually *hadn't* been that bad a place. My issues had been due to a lot of bad luck: unfortunate genes, public ignorance, family and social dynamics. Still . . . "There was no way I was going to move back that close to Mom."

"Hmm, good point." Ling shifted her box higher and turned toward the building. "So, did you hear from the realtor?"

"Yeah. He says the new buyers are ready to close on the house. The money will be in your account well in time to pay next year's tuition." I rolled my eyes when Ling grimaced. "Don't give me that look. That was the deal. I got the life insurance policies, you got the real estate. It's done, so quit arguing about it."

"But you need it more than me."

"Oh, so you're *not* planning to go for your PhD now?" Our foot-falls made twangy echoes in the stairwell until we reached the unit. I heaved my box onto the nearest stack, wincing at the strain in my arthritic elbow. Then I wiped the expression off my face before Ling caught sight of it.

"I am, but I can get loans—"

"Absolutely not."

"But your medical expenses . . ."

It always came back to that, didn't it? Once they began to grasp the reality of the expense and potential for disability that would come with my health issues, my parents had cut back our household expenditures to a bare minimum in order to afford the largest life insurance policies they could. The legalities of adopting Ling had been their last major splurge. We'd been well within the comfortable middle-class income bracket, but we'd lived like we subsisted at poverty level. Dad had worked a weekend job as well as his full-time job. All so they could be certain my health wouldn't bankrupt me.

I sighed and crossed my arms, pressing my back against the wall to make room for Jace to squeeze in and offload his armful.

"Ling, my sweet baby sister, you know as well as I do that the proceeds from the sale of that cheap little bungalow on the wrong side of the tracks at the ass end of Nowhere, Colorado, aren't a drop in the bucket where my medical expenses are concerned. So, with all due adoration, shut the fuck up and take the money."

Jace chortled. Ling narrowed her eyes at me, another argument blossoming on her tongue. It died unspoken.

She *tsked* once. "Fine. You're right." With a sad smile, she hugged me again. "No sense wasting our last afternoon arguing."

"You can lighten the burden of your unwanted wealth by taking me out to lunch," I offered.

"It's a deal." She lingered with her arm around my waist. I laid mine across her shoulders, closing my eyes as I pressed my nose against her temple. Dad and Mom were gone, and it was just the two of us. I wasn't proud to admit that I found that as much a relief as a cause for sorrow, but it was what it was. Maybe now I could live my life rather than holding back to spare others stress and worry.

It would be different from here on, I vowed to myself, hugging her tighter. This was me leaving the old behind and beginning anew. The only thing that could drag me down now was myself.

FUNNY THING ABOUT GRIEF: we're led to believe that all our other needs simply stop while we're dealing with it, but they don't. It makes us feel guilty, like it's disrespectful, like we should have more appropriate matters on our minds while we're mourning, but it's true. Which was why, an hour after Ling called to let me know her flight had landed safely and Jace left to go work out, I strolled into an adult video store and selected a booth. I settled in on the semen-stained sofa to watch my movie and wait.

While I might still need time to process everything that had happened in the last month, that didn't mean I wasn't craving a release to take my mind off things. This trip was a very uncomplicated solution to that problem. Here, at least, I wouldn't have to deal with crowded clubs and the meat markets full of shallow tops cruising for only the cutest, fittest bottoms—of which I'd never be one. My body was too thin and untoned, because I couldn't do the sort of intensive working out required to build a lot of muscle definition. My nose nearly required its own zip code.

I'd seen the video before, but I'd enjoyed it. Big, mean leather daddies and a cum-slut bottom filled the screen, covered in straps and riveted harnesses. The first segment had the willowy, brainy-looking twink strapped to a Saint Andrew's cross, the apparent victim of an abduction by a group of massive, muscle-bound men decked out in leather. He pleaded for his life, for mercy, for *more*, as they whipped him with a heavy, braided cat-o'-nine-tails until his back was striped, until he sobbed and screamed, his pale skin looking *this close* to breaking. Some of those welts were fucking *livid*.

I groaned and opened my jeans.

Then they cut him loose and grabbed him by his hair, forcing him to his knees. One of them pushed him over on all fours and rammed a ginormous dildo up his ass while the rest of them took turns jerking him around and skull-fucking him until he gagged. One drew out only long enough to let him cough up thick strands of spittle that oozed down his chin before another one stepped up to shove his cock so deep in the bottom's throat I could see it moving, shifting the musculature of the guy's thin neck.

Jesus. I stroked myself slowly, not in any rush to get off yet. I envisioned myself in that bottom's place, whimpering, sore, welted, bruised, stuffed full of cock. I wanted it. I wanted it so fucking bad.

A sound and movement in the next booth drew my attention. My dick hanging out of my fly, I practically jumped off the sofa to sit on the convenient stool next to the hole in the wall. That stool was a nice touch and not something I found everywhere. At least I'd be able to walk in the morning.

I laid my glasses aside and wriggled my finger in the elongated vertical hole. A moment later, a dick appeared, covered in loose, sliding skin so dark a brown it was nearly purple, hard and good to go. Fuck, yeah. I hated it when they arrived semisoft and expected me to get them up. With him at the ready, all I had to do was open my mouth, lean in, and go to town, licking and sucking like it was my favorite flavor popsicle.

It didn't matter who was on the other end of that cock. Didn't matter what he looked like, what his story was, whether he was married or single, out or on the DL. As far as I was concerned, he had no issues, and as far as he was concerned, I was likewise issue-free. For all he knew, I was capable of taking the brutal things that bottom in the video was taking. I liked the idea of someone thinking of me that way.

He was clean and warm, just musky and salty enough to reward my senses, and thick and long enough to be a little challenging. I sucked actively and pulled back when he tried to push deeper, to signal that I didn't want him to fuck my mouth. Which was a lie, because I totally did, but even now the worry-filled voice telling me what I could and couldn't safely do never quite went away.

The stranger rewarded me with a low moan. My ears might as well have been attached to my dick for the way it leaped at the sound. I grasped myself, stroking slowly enough to draw it out a bit.

A deep, gruff voice muttered, "Yeah, suck it, whore."

I would have smiled if my mouth hadn't been otherwise engaged. I'd gotten a talker, the kind who said exactly what I wanted to hear. There was enough of an inquiring note in the words to let me know that if I backed off or indicated disinterest, he would stop. Some guys wanted total silence, a complete lack of interaction, but words worked better for me. I made an encouraging sound and sucked harder. Yes, that would be quite agreeable, please and thank you. My hand pumped faster on my cock.

He sighed after a minute. "Fuck, that's good. You been here waiting for me all night, you little slut?"

I agreed wordlessly and willingly. Oh yes, yes, I had.

"Fuckin' little liar. Bet you've been gobbling every dick that's gone through here for hours, just a cum dump waiting for another load."

A whimper rose from my occupied throat, distressed and caught out. It didn't matter that it was fiction. It was what I wished were the truth. I wished he was the latest in a nonstop line of strangers who had used my mouth and left, coating my throat with their spunk.

I couldn't have that, couldn't seek out the physical roughness I craved. No matter how badly I wanted it, hard hands wouldn't seize my hair, damn near pulling it from my scalp as merciless cocks battered my throat. These cruel words were the harshest treatment I could get. At least, without a lot of hassle I didn't want to deal with.

"Suck me harder, whore," he snapped. "Cram it down that slutty throat."

I made a discouraging sound and drew back a little. No, sorry, I would not be taking him that deep, despite his persistence. But I didn't stop sucking, swirling my tongue around the head, teasing the frenulum, moving as fast as I could without going so deep I bruised my palate or throat. He gave a dissatisfied grunt.

The dirty talk stopped after that exchange. Perhaps my refusal to deep-throat had displeased him enough that he'd lost interest in the game, or perhaps he was getting close enough to popping that he'd dropped the thread. My dented self-esteem feared it was the former, but the sounds he was making told me it might be the latter. Sure enough, he grew more rigid, and I was about to pull away when he choked out a warning.

"You gonna swallow my load, cum bucket?"

I drew off to whisper, "On my face. Let me have it on my face."

He groaned loudly, like this was a perfectly acceptable alternative.

"Fuck yeah. Won't even let me fuck your throat. You don't deserve to swallow my load, slut."

I shuddered, lost in a fantasy. My hand curled around the head of my cock and fuck, I was *this close* from the dirty talk alone.

I wrapped my other hand around him and jacked him hard and fast, leaning close enough that the thick crown of his cock brushed my cheek with each stroke. Two more soft groans and he swelled. I closed my eyes in anticipation. Hot, thick splashes of cum streaked across my face, hanging from my lashes, even splattering my hair. I jerked him until the pulsing stopped and he resumed breathing, then leaned forward and wiped the last drops clinging to the tip of his dick on my clean cheek.

After pulling his cock out of my grasp and back through the hole, the stranger reached through and tapped my lips in thanks.

7

"If you wanna come over here, help me get it up again, I'll ream that slutty ass open until you explode."

God, that sounded like a good offer. I was so hard. Aching, quivering with the need to be *handled*. Pre-cum had drizzled down the side of my cock, drying sticky and cool, and I knew I'd have to jerk off soon but—

I withdrew from the hole. He didn't say another word. When I turned back to the video, that poor, mistreated bottom was wearing the cum of a half-dozen brutes, licking it from his lips like cake frosting. My tongue darted out in a sympathetic gesture.

I moved to the sofa and began stroking myself once more, too caught up in need to heed the ominous tingle that had begun in my elbow. Covered in a stranger's congealing cum, I jerked hard and fast, panting. The orgasm stayed at bay, though, and I had to work for it, groaning and thrusting into my fist, squeezing and twisting. Finally, I blew with a gasp and sank into the sofa, panting and dazed. I fished out some tissues to wipe the back of my hand, then cleaned up the spooge painting my face.

Once I was presentable in my graduate-student-of-library-sciences way, I left the booth and made my way home. As the high of orgasm faded, the sharp ache and sickening *bubbling* sensation in my left elbow grew.

Fuck. I hadn't managed to give myself an elbow bleed by jerking off in quite a while; it had become a considerably less frequent event in the years since adolescence. But then, I'd spent the day before moving heavy boxes as well. Stupid. I should have seen it coming.

Grimacing, I put my foot down on the accelerator and hurried back to Jace's apartment and the clotting factor I kept in the refrigerator.

CHAPTER TWO

Robin

After nearly fifteen years of living in New York City, I didn't think I was ever going to get used to the quiet. Saugatuck, Michigan, was downright comatose in comparison to other popular gay vacation destinations like Fire Island or Provincetown. Which, I supposed, was *why* I was in Saugatuck rather than Fire Island or P-Town. Also, the lack of proximity to NYC could only be a good thing. I often reminded myself of that as I lay in the narrow berth of my vintage Chris-Craft Commander, the weight of the silence nearly crushing me. I'd come to this spartan marina on Kalamazoo Lake to get away from everything familiar and start over again. New surroundings, new business, new perspective. A whole new life.

Of course, it didn't help that it was early summer. The shores of Lake Michigan were a little too chilly to see a lot of action yet. I imagined July and August would be busier. But "not a lot of action" didn't equal "no action," which was why I found myself stepping from the balmy June night into the sweltering nightclub at the Dunes Resort. It was also the weekend of the Dunes' annual Buns & Baskets Benefit, a fundraiser to aid with expenses for various Mr. Michigan Leather events. I might have been new to the Michigan gay and leather communities, but I felt obliged to attend and support the

MML. I was also rather enjoying the prospect of being in such proximity to Chicago for the International Mr. Leather competition in May.

Relocating to the Midwest did have *some* advantages.

The scent of leather and man-sweat greeted me, raising an instant prickle of perspiration on my arms where they were bared by my leather vest. The full brunt of the music crashed against me like a tidal wave, and for the first time in nearly a year, I found myself wanting to move with it, wanting to dive into the sea of gyrating male bodies and ride the rise and fall of the rhythm with them. I had missed this, however much I had tried to convince myself I hadn't. I'd thought I'd left the scene for good, but one glance at a couple of rounded and welted butt cheeks revealed by assless chaps and I knew it was never going to happen. I loved it all too much.

At one end of the crowded room, I could see the current Mr. Michigan Leather holding court, and the throng was rife with everything from lithe, collared subs in leather jocks to harness-bound bears. It was rather more kink than the resort had had on display at the New Year's Eve party I'd attended. That had been mostly casually dressed (or club-wear dressed) vacationers and locals.

Tonight I could see the vacationers who hadn't known about the special occasion—standing out in the crowd, dots of color in a monochromatic sea of black leather and silver rivets. One such pair walked in the door as I leaned against the bar. The shorter, dark-haired one in the red silk shirt I dismissed immediately. He was adorable, but the furrow between his brows and the strained edge of his smile said he was vanilla and caught completely unprepared for what he was seeing. The other one, though . . .

Honestly, I wasn't sure what caught my eye about him. He wasn't gorgeous. Fairly ordinary, in fact. String-bean thin, maybe a little taller than I was. Pale and unmuscled. Dishwater-blond hair. Blue-gray eyes in a face with high cheekbones, a long, protuberant nose, and lips that managed to be both thin and lush looking. Above average, I guess I'd have rated him. But skinny had always been my type.

What really got my attention, though, was when he turned around to say something to his friend. I nearly swallowed my tongue. Visible through his black mesh shirt was some of the most amazing tattoo work I'd ever seen. It was, like, the Botticelli or Monet of body art. A mural that covered his back from neck to waist and shoulder to shoulder, full of vibrant colors. The thought of the time and dedication it must have taken for him to get that ink, the discomfort he must have endured, made me wonder just how much of a masochistic bent he had.

I watched him more closely, enough that I could see none of his friend's disinterest in the kink scene applied to him. He kept to himself, quiet, talking only to his friend. He didn't flirt, didn't make any inviting eye contact. But once in a while I saw him stare, from under his lashes, at one of the dominants when the guy wasn't paying attention. The looks he gave them were hungry, full of yearning.

Why was he here with a totally vanilla companion? Why wasn't he half-naked and kneeling with someone's leash around his neck?

The other doms didn't seem to be picking up the signals he was giving off. It was like his vibes were being carried on a frequency only I could receive. The others saw a vanilla tourist and didn't approach. Some of the vacationers did, and he danced with them, but his attention wasn't on them. Eventually his boredom communicated itself and his would-be partners drifted away, until he was left leaning on the bar, his eyes still full of longing.

I was intrigued enough to decide I needed a new beer. Which meant that when his friend joined him, I was still by the bar and got to listen in.

"I can't believe this." There was a note of derision in the friend's voice that said his disbelief was not of the favorable kind.

"I want it known, for the record, that I'm not laughing with you, I'm laughing at you," he teased. I smiled around the mouth of my beer bottle at the rejoinder. "I, personally, have no complaints with the scenery."

"It's the start of summer, dude. I thought this place would be crawling with twinks fresh out of college."

"Seriously? Have you *seen* this town? Not exactly somewhere college kids are going to come to party. Also, last I checked, most kids fresh out of college are trying to find jobs, not vacationing at resorts catering to middle-aged bears. Or have you forgotten already what that's like?" He took a long draw from his bottle and shook his head. "You could have checked the website. I'm sure they have a calendar of some sort."

"Thanks. Your sympathy unmans me. What about you? Picked out anyone interesting yet?"

"Eh, you know me better than that. 'Water, water, everywhere . . .'"

I paused with my beer halfway to my lips. He wasn't on the prowl? He wasn't even *trying*?

"So, lemme get this straight," his friend huffed. "Here we are, in the middle of what has to be a waking wet dream for you with all these leathermen around, and you're saying you can't score?"

"Wouldn't be a good idea." The mutter was so reluctant I had to strain to hear it.

"Seriously? Dude—"

Whatever his response was, I missed it because he and his friend took their drinks and disappeared into the crowd.

Fuck. Now I wanted to know what this guy's deal was, and why he didn't think he could get any action.

But I hadn't come here to find someone to play with. I'd sworn I was leaving it behind with Kyle and New York.

I wanted that guy on the business end of a whip in the worst possible way, though. I wanted to see him bound and screaming and afterward, muzzy and content, coming down from the high I could give him, that hungry look a thing of the past.

I must have watched him at least another hour, slowly nursing my beers so that I wouldn't be inebriated if and when I made my move. There was activity on the stage. A drag queen was MCing the night's festivities and gave a speech about the benefit and the MML competition before introducing Mr. Michigan Leather himself. The crowd roared for him. I couldn't have cared less, except that the guy with the ink was watching him like a starving man might stare at a banquet table. I wanted to be the one he stared at that way.

When Mr. Michigan Leather was done speaking, the music resumed. The object of my fascination danced again, starting with his friend. Someone else approached, but he was as uninterested in that one as he had been in all the others. Which wasn't to say he was rude; he smiled politely, occasionally leaned in to speak next to a partner's ear in order to be heard over the music, did all the things you're supposed to do at a club when you're looking for someone to take back to your room for the night. But it wasn't clicking; I could just *tell*.

When his next partner was just about ready to move on, I finished the last of my beer and made my way through the crowd to come up behind him. I put an arm around him and spread my palm across his chest, pulling him back against my body. The guy dancing with him gave me a surprised glance, then turned away and searched for other companionship.

"You look bored," I said, speaking low beside his ear. I began to sway, grinding a little against his ass without making it seem crude. I didn't let him stop dancing. He stiffened. Then his body damn near melted into mine, and I knew I'd been dead-on about what he needed.

"Are you here to help me with that?" he asked, peering over his shoulder. He couldn't quite make eye contact or get a good look at me from that angle, but he didn't seem to be trying to. As though what I looked like didn't matter nearly as much as what I was saying. He just wanted to be heard better. I got a good whiff of his hair when his head moved. He smelled woodsy and sweet.

He fell into rhythm with me, his ass brushing my hips. My hand glided down to his midriff. "Absolutely," I said, making less effort to be subtle in the way I was rubbing against his ass. "I'm Robin."

"Geoff." He sounded breathless, and I liked that sound a lot. I let my hand wander, bunching up his mesh shirt. Up to his ribs, then back down, until my fingers were touching bare skin.

"Nice to meet you, Geoff. Gorgeous tats."

He stilled, and I could see the way his lips curved. He must have heard that compliment a lot, but for some reason, it thrilled him. Then he rocked against me again. One of his arms came up and snaked over his shoulder, reaching to curl his fingers around the back of my neck and hold me closer. He cleared his throat twice before he spoke. "Thank you."

"I haven't been able to stop staring since you came in." I let my lips brush his earlobe. "I keep wondering what they'd look like without the shirt distorting them. Think I might be able to find out?"

Geoff chuckled. "You're direct."

I grinned, accepting the charge. "You were bored to tears by the dudes taking their time, so I thought I would cut through the bullshit. I want you to take me to your room when we're done dancing and show your tats to me."

"Why wait?" In one movement, he stepped away from me and began pulling his shirt up over his head. Eager to get my hands on his flesh, I aided in the endeavor, my fingers brushing his lean ribs. He wasn't muscular. He didn't have the lithe beauty of a twink or the unabashed bulk of a bear. He was just this side of scrawny—toned in the upper arms, but his abs were unsculpted. He was the kind of guy who usually tried to hide his skinniness, but whether Geoff was that proud of his ink or didn't care how his body measured up to others, he went for it.

The tattoos were even more breathtaking without the haze of the mesh shirt covering them.

"Nice." I hummed, my fingers itching to explore the skin he'd bared. I let myself trace the lines, puzzled by the strange texture of them. Was it only the fact that they were a solid, continuous work that made them feel different from others? I heard him moan softly, and the sound went straight to my dick. "But does this mean you won't be taking me back to your room? Because honestly, I'd still like a crack at that."

Geoff flicked a flirtatious glance over his shoulder. "Not making any promises, but what would you do if I did?"

I smiled. He might be the most eager-to-submit bottom I'd ever laid eyes on, but he had sass. I liked that. "I suppose that depends on how delicate you are."

I don't know what the fuck I said wrong, but the effect was instantaneous. He stiffened and began to withdraw, snarling at me over his shoulder. "I'm not *delicate*."

The only thing that stopped him from leveling that irritation directly at me was my hand on his torso, holding him in place. Trying to recover quickly and get our groove back, I pulled him against me and refused to let him turn, grinding harder against his ass.

"Oh, good. Guess I don't have to worry about being gentle, then, do I?" He didn't yield as effortlessly as he had when I first approached him. Jesus, what the hell button had I pushed there? "See, I think the reason you looked bored was because those guys were all being too polite." I moved my hand up, letting my thumb rub against his nipple, offering friction. He gasped, his spine arching. "Something tells me you don't like *nice* all that much."

"Close." His mutter still sounded grudging, even if his body was sending the right signals. "It's more that I don't like *safe* all that much. At least, not in the way someone approaches me."

Hmm. Any number of ways to interpret that. The qualifier made it clear he wasn't talking about condom usage, which was definitely a good thing.

"Ah." I chuckled, nuzzling the back of his neck. "You want danger, baby?"

"*Yeah.*" He spoke the word with a sigh, like a prayer, and went pliant against me. I brushed my lips against his neck a moment longer, toying with his nipple while I did so, before moving back to his ear and adding an edge of teeth. Just like that, he tensed and pulled away again. "No biting."

My rhythm faltered. No biting? Seriously? He tells me he doesn't want me to play it safe in one breath and then in the next rules out something as innocuous as teeth? ". . . Okay."

"Tell me more," he urged, swaying against me, coaxing me to begin dancing again. Now there was something sheepish, almost self-conscious in the way he tried to pick up the thread of our flirtation. Like it was on the tip of his tongue to apologize, but he couldn't quite manage it.

After a pause, I let my hands wander again, thumbing his nipples, my lips ghosting down his neck. "First, I suppose I'd have to start by taking my time admiring the tats. Just touch. And taste. Spread you out in front of me, pin you down, and follow them with my tongue, from your shoulders to your ass."

The music changed, and our rhythm altered with it. There was a heavier pulse to this song, and we could feel it in our hips, which drove together more firmly, more suggestively. The fly of my tight, well-worn jeans was feeling far more snug, because the word picture I'd painted was making me hot. I suspected I wasn't the only one.

"Why pin me down? Are you afraid I'll run away?" There was a slight breathy slur to his voice, and I recognized it. It was the sound of a guy transitioning from independent thought to the surrender of subspace. He wasn't there yet, of course. Wouldn't be there until I could push him harder, restrict him with my body or bondage, offer him a taste of pain, and get those endorphins flowing. But psychologically and hormonally he was primed. So very ready to lay it all down for me.

I smiled. Whatever that thing with the biting was, the rest of his responses were still screaming to the top in me. "No, I just think it would be fun. Or are you going to tell me you wouldn't *love* to be helpless underneath me while I did whatever I wanted to you?"

Was that a whimper I heard? I was sure it was, but there was also a challenge in his words, like he was fighting his own inclination toward surrender. Why?

"You're assuming an awful lot just from watching a few dances."

"Then correct me if I'm wrong," I said easily, because I wasn't, damn it. I knew it with absolute certainty. He wanted to yield to me.

"I didn't say you were wrong. Just presumptuous."

I laughed against the sweaty skin of his neck. "Guilty as charged. I've never been subtle. But you're not exactly telling me to fuck off, so I think there must be something about me you like."

"I haven't told you to fuck off *so far*." There was a smile in his tone, softening the correction to make it a tease, and his body remained relaxed. "Keep talking."

Oh yeah, I had him. I knew I had him. "You know, I'm really more of an action guy." I kissed his neck again, opening my lips to suck on that fluttering pulse point.

Suddenly, though, there was nothing beneath my mouth as he jerked away. "No hickeys," he said shortly.

Okay, what the hell? I stopped dancing and planted my hands on his shoulders, turning him forcibly around. He resisted at first, then yielded. I gave him a moment to take in his first real look at me.

"Next you're going to tell me I can't pinch you." I brushed my thumbs over both his nipples at once, and his breath stuttered to a halt, his eyes sliding shut. When he opened them again, I could see something behind them, something he wasn't letting himself say. Half-frustrated, half-fearful.

I decided rather than give it time to reach the verbal stage, I'd press my advantage. I kept his attention locked on me with eye contact and the touch of my fingers: gently tweaking his nipples, steering him until we were near the door and his back was against the wall. I dipped my head to let my lips and teeth graze along his neck without sucking or biting. I gripped his ass possessively when he tried to grind against me.

"Invite me back to your room," I murmured. "Let me give you what you want. I swear, baby, I'll fuck you so hard you won't be able to walk in the morning. I'll leave marks on every inch of you. You won't be able to look at yourself for a week without remembering how good it was."

Geoff groaned, a pleading, desperate sound, but I could feel something in him still struggling. He wanted to give in, his body was trying to give in, but his brain was holding him back. I felt it in the shuddering of his body, the way relaxation and tension pulled at him in turns.

"Okay," he panted when my fingers tried to wedge their way down the back of his jeans. "But . . ."

"Yeah?" I tongued the shell of his ear. "Tell me."

"We have to—" I tightened my hand on his ass and his words stumbled. Then his resolve rallied, and he opened his eyes. "Can we step outside, where it's quieter?"

"Sure." I nudged him those final steps toward the door. The cool air hit our fevered, sweat-damp skin like a blast out of a meat locker. I saw him shudder, his useless shirt still hanging from his back pocket, and I caught his body against mine, rubbing my hands over his arms. I pressed my erection against his hip. "Talk. You've got sixty seconds before I drag you back to your room."

His mouth opened and closed, his forehead creasing with that inner battle I sensed but couldn't quite understand. Seconds ticked by. Then he gave one decisive shake of his head and turned to mash his lips against mine.

Well. Okay then. So much for talking. I gripped his upper arms and yanked him closer, my tongue stroking deep inside his mouth.

He tasted as sweet and smoky as he smelled, and I thought I could devour him. Then the copper tang of pennies hit my tongue. I drew back in alarm, wondering if I'd forgotten myself and bitten him after he'd told me not to.

Realization dawned in his eyes at the same instant mine made sense of the dark streak beginning to flow from his nostril. It was . . . weird. He didn't look surprised by it. Just resigned, and weary, and disgusted. He actually rolled his eyes.

"*Fuck*," he hissed, letting his head fall back.

CHAPTER THREE

Geoff

"Stay right there." My would-be one-night stand dashed back into the bar. Furious at myself and my fucking body, I turned and followed the paths around the pool area that led back to the cottage with long, angry strides. Robin caught up with me before I'd gone fifty yards.

"I said to stay put," he scolded. He thrust a bar towel at me, which I accepted, pinching the bridge of my nose through it. I imagined him watching the nearly black stains spread through the terry cloth, stripped of their color by the darkness. Between the dancing and the arousal, my blood pressure had probably been surging and dropping all evening. Along with the change in humidity and barometric pressure that came with traveling, and the fact that I wasn't doing my prophy as often as I should, of course I was ripe for a nosebleed. I growled softly, too pissed off even to be self-conscious.

"Let me help you to your room." He slipped an arm around my waist.

"I'm not an invalid."

His eyes widened and an insulted expression settled on his face. I immediately regretted snapping, even if my voice was probably far too nasal with my nose pinched off for my rebuke to be taken very seriously. My issues weren't his fault. He wasn't aware of how irritated I got when someone hovered. "I'm sorry. That was rude. I didn't mean to snap. It's just— I've got this. It's only a nosebleed."

Robin dropped his hand from my waist, but he didn't step back. Instead, he folded his arms and regarded me with a lifted eyebrow. "I'm aware of that. But there are dark walkways between here and the cottages. I thought it might be harder to navigate if you're trying to keep your head tipped back."

Shit. He was right. Perhaps even more importantly, his voice didn't have that hint of concerned condescension I hated so much. He was simply being . . . logical. With a sigh, I conceded. "Right. Yeah, thanks. That would be good."

His hand came around my waist again. I let him keep an eye out for ground-level hazards since I couldn't really see much beyond my hand and the bulk of the bar towel. I directed him to our cottage. I could hear voices rising from the hot tub the two two-bedroom cottages shared. Sounded like Jace had found companions after all.

Not surprising. His vanilla inclination aside, there was never a time when he wasn't determined to wring every ounce of fun out of life and share it with anyone within speaking distance. Being aware of his history as I was, I thought Jace's way of handling his issues was about a thousand times better than some of the alternatives.

I smiled underneath my towel, too amused to be envious.

"Sounds like someone's having a good time," Robin said, sotto voce.

"That would be my friend, Jace." I dug blindly for my room key, still trying to hold the towel to my nose. Robin pulled my hand out of my pocket and replaced it with his own. His fingers fished around right next to my dick for the card. *Jesus.* If not for the total unsexiness of the nosebleed, I would have been instantly hard.

"The one who wasn't thrilled with all the leathermen around this weekend?"

"How did you know that?"

"I overheard the two of you at the bar."

"Oh." I wasn't sure how I felt about that. But then, it wasn't as though we'd been trying to keep it private. He hadn't necessarily been eavesdropping.

Once inside the cottage, Robin sat me on the sofa and grabbed a clean towel from the kitchenette. I was going to have to keep pressure on my nose for at least another ten minutes while he sat there, waiting awkwardly as the seconds ticked by.

Hot. Real hot.

"Thanks, um, thanks for the help," I muttered, trying to rein in my annoyance at my body's betrayal so I didn't sound as resentful as I felt.

"It's not a problem." Robin perched on the arm of the sofa, watching me with a patience that belied his earlier aggression.

"I know, but you didn't have to. Especially after the way I nearly took your head off out there."

He huffed a soft laugh. "Eh, that's nothing. I've got a lot of practice dealing with people who get prickly because they would rather go on offense than play defense. I get it."

I frowned at him. "What do you think I'm defending myself against?"

"Being seen as weak, obviously." He shrugged. "First you got your back up when I used the word 'delicate,' and then you protested the idea that you might be an invalid. Pretty simple math to conclude that it's a hot-button subject with you."

"Right. You know, it's just . . . baggage. Didn't mean to take it out on you." I drew the towel away from my face. The bleeding had slowed but hadn't completely stopped.

Robin shook his head, brushing the apology off. Unsure what I could possibly say next, I looked away.

"You get nosebleeds a lot?" he asked after a moment.

I nodded, seizing on part of the truth to avoid explaining the whole of it. "Um, yeah. Sometimes."

He studied me, his eyes searching. "It's not uncommon. Why does it bother you so much?"

I wet my lips, tasting blood, as I tried to figure out how to make him understand. I tipped my head back farther and pinched the top of my nose harder. "When I was a young kid—God, I don't remember when, maybe in the late eighties or early nineties?—I saw this movie. One of those athletic, coming-of-age things about a high school wrestler."

"I think I saw that one. Had Matthew Modine in it, right?"

"Uh-huh, that's the one. Anyway, you know, at one point he got a nosebleed. And after that, whenever his archrival was trying to rattle

Modine's character, he'd call the guy a bleeder. Like, having a nose-bleed meant he was weak or something. So whenever something like this—" I waved my hand at the bloodstained cloth still pressed to my face "—happens, that's the thing that comes to mind. That if you bleed, you're weak."

"I can see that." Robin's eyes were sympathetic but not pitying. Like he really got it. He slid off the arm of the sofa to sit beside me. "You know it's bullshit, right?"

"Sure, I guess." I looked away, because giving a more concrete answer would require details I didn't want to share. I *was* more easily injured than most people, and it *did* make me feel weak, or at least prone to being perceived that way. "But there's knowing and then there's *knowing*, you know?"

He chuckled and nodded. "I know. Why hang so much weight on such a meaningless word, though?"

Fuck it. After oh-so-suavely bleeding all over him, I wasn't getting any tonight anyway.

"Because for me it's not meaningless. 'Bleeder' is a word the hemophiliac community uses to refer to themselves."

I saw a wrinkle of confusion form between his brows before the pieces clicked together. "So, you're a hemophiliac."

I nodded, my eyes sliding away from his gaze to stare at the wall past his shoulder.

"Okay. Umm, aside from the whole business with Ryan White when I was a kid, and some movie that said a woman would die from a paper cut, I don't know much about that."

"We don't die from paper cuts," I growled between clenched teeth. "Hollywood idiots."

"All right. Then how does it work?"

I had to hand it to him: he was being cooler than I thought he would be about it. Some people immediately freaked or went all super-sympathetic, as if I'd told them I was dying. Or they got all uncom-fortable and didn't want to be around me any longer than it took to make an excuse to get out. Or they got morbidly curious and—

Never mind. "It means that when I bleed, internally or externally, it takes longer for me to heal. I don't bleed any *more* than anyone else. Small surface injuries can heal up with basic first aid, especially if I keep up on my prophy—sorry, prophylaxis, which supplements my clotting factor to reduce the number of spontaneous bleeds I get—but major wounds can be a problem. The real worry is internal injuries. The stuff that can't be bandaged up."

He nodded slowly. "Like?"

I sighed. "Well, my joints are a problem. Bumping an elbow, banging a knee—hell, just overworking a joint can cause a bleed. Or it can happen spontaneously. Bleeds injure the joint a little more each time, so eventually you're dealing with arthritis. Even worse are the deep-muscle bleeds. They can pinch off nerves and cause paralysis. Don't get me started on head injuries."

"No, please, let's do get started on head injuries. I'd like to know."

"Why?"

"So I know what your limits are. I'm assuming this is why you were declaring biting and sucking verboten. What else might I accidentally trip over?"

I blinked at him. Repeatedly. Was he saying he still wanted to get with me? I pulled the bloodstained towel away from my face, relieved to see the bleeding had stopped. Though my face probably looked like something out of a slasher film. I stared at the towel, not sure what to make of that possibility. Robin hopped up and disappeared into the bathroom, then returned with a wet washcloth.

"Your face—"

"Right." I accepted the cloth, trying to wipe away any traces of blood around my nose and mouth without a mirror. Robin took it back from me, gripped my chin gently with his other hand, and began cleaning me himself.

It should have felt patronizing and like all the oversolicitous crap I hated, but it didn't. For the life of me, I couldn't figure out the difference.

"Tell me about head injuries."

"Fine. Okay. True story." If he still thought he wanted to fuck me, I was going to let him know exactly how inconvenient it could get. "A couple years ago, I picked up a guy at a bar and went home with him. He was hot, I was horny, we were having fun. Then he pushed me against the wall to kiss me. Sexy, right?"

Robin's eyes had darkened. "I'm a big fan of up against the wall."

"Yeah, me too. For a couple seconds, I was really into it. Then I stopped thinking with my dick long enough to realize I'd bumped my head when he did it. Not badly. *You* wouldn't have had to think twice about it. But I had to leave him blue-balled so I could rush home for a dose of factor, and I spent the night afraid I would wake up in the produce aisle of the neurological care unit."

I watched the reactions slide across his face: arousal transitioning to humor and then to disbelief.

Bitterness was starting to creep in again, bringing up my not-so-inner asshole. I decided to lay another slice of my reality on him. "I just came out of the closet a couple of years ago. Want to know why?"

His eyebrows lifted, his expression sobering. I think he was starting to get it. "Why?"

"When I was seventeen, I told my mom I was gay, and she had a complete breakdown. Like, she had to be hospitalized and sedated. Not because she had a problem with me being gay, as such, but because she was terrified I might get bashed. She spent the better part of a year having panic attacks about it, until I finally promised her I wouldn't let anyone know."

I could tell by his thoughtful frown that he was taking it in, pondering. "You were going to tell me about this outside the club, and then you stopped yourself."

Licking my lips, I looked away. Fuck. That had only been, what? Twenty, thirty minutes ago? I'd been so damn hot for him, so ready to toss it all aside and take my chances.

If only I could go back to that moment and replay it without the nosebleed putting the brakes on everything.

"I gotta say, that pisses me off," he said so mildly that the anger indicated by his words was almost lost—or maybe being held in check. I lifted my head to stare. "When we got back to your room, I was planning to get rough because that seemed to be what you were into."

"I am. That's what I wanted."

"But you weren't going to tell me."

"Because I didn't want you to think I was—"

"Fragile?"

"Exactly. I didn't want you to hold back."

"Wow." He rubbed his forehead, like a headache was blooming. The line of his mouth was tightening, his lips bloodless. "How many guys have you played with, Geoff? I mean, not just hooked up with, but done BDSM scenes with? Or at least had sex rough enough to require a safeword?"

"Umm—" Damn it, now I was blushing. "I've never—" I cleared my throat. "None."

"Oh, good. At least you've never put anyone else in the position of being responsible for your well-being without knowing your physical limits."

"What?" I bristled, my all-too-easily-wounded pride snarling. "Excuse me, but I'm responsible for my own fucking well-being, thank you very much."

"Then act like it! And while you're at it, don't bullshit a stranger into accidentally *killing* you without even the courtesy of a heads-up."

I scoffed and glared at him. "Yeah, great, thanks. Ever think that this is *exactly* why I didn't want to tell you?"

"So your answer to that is to put me in a risky situation without my consent?"

"It's *my* risk to take!"

Robin threw his hands up in the air. His fury seemed excessive and somewhat misplaced. "Sure, until they fucking *arrest* me for reckless endangerment or assault or whatever grounds they want to use to charge me for your homicide. You think maybe, *just maybe*, I ought to have the right to decide if or how to deal with that issue?"

He deflated suddenly. "It's about consent, Geoff. Yours and mine. RACK: risk-aware consensual kink. That acronym does actually mean something. If I don't know all the facts, I can't give meaningful consent."

Okay, so there was some validity to that, but Jesus. "Wow. Dramatic much? I didn't want you handling me any differently than you would handle someone else. Is that really so much to expect?"

His eyes narrowed. "You don't get it, do you?" In an instant, he'd closed the distance between us, gripping my hair hard enough to command my gaze, keep me focused on his face right up in front of mine. His voice was a low, angry growl that spoke as strongly to my dick as his words did my ears. "You want to sub, baby, but you've got no idea what it means. When you give someone the power to do what they want to you, you also give them the responsibility of keeping you safe. Otherwise, you can't ever really give in and let go."

Oh God. His face swam before me, and my heart thundered, my pulse pounding with surge after surge of wanting. *Yes*, every nerve in my body screamed. *Do that. Hurt me. Control me. Take what you want from me.*

He let me go before I could become a whimpering, pleading mass of longing.

"Until you can give that up, Geoff, you're never going to get what you want."

It took me a moment to pull myself back together, and then I started to get angry again. "So, what, you're telling me if I'd been up-front with you about it, you wouldn't have held back?"

"I'm telling you the decision of whether or not I hold back, or how much—within any negotiated limits, of course—belongs to me, not you. And if you can't trust me to make that decision and still give you what you need while keeping you safe, then we've got no business playing together."

He pressed the damp washcloth, now marred with pinkish stains, into my hand. I stared at it while he pushed himself up off the sofa and strode for the door. "Think about that for a while before you go on the prowl again," he said, gripping the knob. "Good night."

I sat there for some time after he'd closed the door behind him, trying to wrangle my disappointment into something manageable. Then I growled in disgust at myself and went to dig some ointment out of my travel kit to keep my nose moist. I knew I should probably infuse to prevent another nosebleed, but if the prospect of unrestrained sex was off the table, doing my prophy was no longer imperative. It sounded like too much bother now, and too big a reminder of all the things that were complicated for me.

Instead, I threw the linens into a corner of the bathroom and went to my room.

CHAPTER FOUR

Geoff

I hid out when Jace and his companions came inside and retreated into his room, but the walls weren't soundproofed. I might not have been able to see what caused those groans and shouts, and the hard smack of skin against skin, but I could imagine well enough.

Sighing, I hauled out my laptop and earbuds, pulling up one of my preferred amateur porn sites and checking my bookmarks to see if my favorite poster had added any new videos. He hadn't updated, so I selected one I'd already seen from his channel. I stripped off my T-shirt and pajama bottoms while the top (always hooded and anonymous for some reason) cuffed the bottom to the cross and pushed a fat dildo into his ass. Without my earbuds in, it was soundless, but I knew the bottom's groan by heart.

Grabbing a prostate massager and lube out of my suitcase, I climbed onto the bed beside my laptop and put the earbuds in my ears as the top was warming up the bottom with a heavy flogger. God, I loved that sound, the meaty *thud* of the thick falls that could no doubt be felt in the deep muscles of his back. That literally could be deadly for me, but I bet it felt amazing. Rolling onto my side to face the screen, I squeezed some lube onto my fingertips and reached back, slipping them into my ass.

"Oh, fuck yeah . . ." I groaned in unison with the sub.

The top worked his way through a number of implements. Paddles and straps, tawses and cats, and even a cane, leaving welts in parallel stripes across the bottom's lovely, round butt. I lubed the prostate massager and worked it in to the point where my body took over, drawing it inside until the crosspiece caught against my taint, offering pressure there as well.

In my ears, the bottom's cries grew more and more pained, his back covered in the blotchy red of overheated skin broken up by deeper scarlet welts. Then, as I clenched and relaxed to help the massager do its work, and took my cock in hand, the top stepped back and grabbed another implement.

A completely unassuming implement. A thin, flexible rod with a short length of cord attached that was knotted at the end. I'd had to research to find out what it was called.

A dressage whip.

It barely made a sound cutting through the air, just the quietest whistle, even though it was obvious from the top's grunt that he was throwing it with all his strength. It was almost silent on impact, but the bottom cried out. A purple stripe so dark it was nearly black appeared. As I watched, the subsequent stripes got more livid and the bottom's screams escalated. Finally a line of crimson could be seen, a bead of blood seeping down the skin.

I groaned and began to pull on my cock with intent, the prostate massager pressing on me inside and out. The bottom had no tattoos, but he had permanent marks, oh yes. Shining white lines of healed tissue on his tan skin. I'd seen this couple do whippings before, draw blood before. I knew where those crisscrossed scars had come from. Single-tails, bullwhips, willow switches. But it was this one, with that harmless-looking whip, that kept me coming back.

It sliced into his skin neatly, in controlled cuts. Ruby droplets welled and slid down his shoulders, but they were contained.

The horrible irony was that this was something I could have—if I could ever find a partner to give it to me. A heavy flogger along my spine could paralyze or even kill me, but that little whip could be safe with a bit of first aid.

I closed my eyes, the bottom's moans filling my ears, and pictured myself bound to that cross, thin trickles of blood working their way down my skin. I could only imagine how it must hurt. Not the deep agony of joint pain, which I was intimately familiar with, but something else entirely. A pain freely chosen. I envisioned my own skin marked with the scars left by a man who spoke the language of passion not only with kisses and caresses, but with lashes and torment. The hooded top was replaced by a broad-shouldered, muscular blond who etched his signature into my flesh with a few inches of knotted cord.

The bottom's cries sharpened and accelerated. I knew the lashes were coming hard and fast across his shoulders, the whistling of that thin whip nearly constant. My orgasm built, pushed to the crisis point by the smooth toy within me, by the pressure of the handle against my perineum, by my own hand tugging it up from my balls along my cock, until I cried out, and it burst free, splattering my torso to my shoulders. In my ears, the cries receded to whimpers, the top's voice muffled through the mask but still tender as he soothed his sub. Next he'd let the bottom down and sponge off the blood before covering the stripes in antiseptic ointment. He'd turn the camera off as he took his sub in his arms, murmuring more comfort and devotion.

I lay there panting for a long moment, still frustrated and unfulfilled despite getting off. Porn was a flimsy substitute for what I really wanted. I sighed and cleaned myself up and put away my toy and computer before crawling into bed. I stared at the ceiling and listened to the party going on in Jace's room, my mind pacing back and forth over a well-worn path, until I finally managed to sleep.

THE NEXT DAY was unseasonably warm for early June. Jace and I both dragged ourselves out of bed late, though for very different reasons. Jace looked far too satisfied with himself, at least until he saw the bloody linens on the bathroom floor.

"Hey, you okay?" he asked when he'd emerged from the shower.

"Everything except my ego." I offered him a wry smile, pouring two cups of coffee. "Worst timing for a nosebleed ever."

"Oh, man, seriously? Right while you were getting busy?"

"God no! That really would be the worst timing. No, we never got to that point. The mood was already sort of ruined."

Jace's forehead creased. "He was *that* put off by a nosebleed?"

"No. I was." I heard the clipped, abrupt sound of my own words, knew I was starting to get—what had Robin called it?—prickly, and looked away, hiding behind my cup of coffee.

"So, wait. Let me read between the lines. You had a guy here and you sent him packing because you were embarrassed?"

"Not exactly, no." I wasn't about to tell Jace that the evening had ended with Robin putting me in my place for holding back critical information about my hemophilia. According to Robin, I didn't get it, so Jace certainly wouldn't. All he'd know was that my hang-ups over being a bleeder had lost me an opportunity to start living my life the way I'd promised I was going to, and I really didn't need the *I told you so*.

When I looked back, Jace was still staring askance at me.

"Forget about it." I set my coffee aside, then rubbed my forehead. "It was stupid."

Jace's lips tightened for a moment. Then he blew out a breath. "Well, I thought I'd go out to take some photo references of the beaches and dunes. Want to go with? You can find someone else to get laid by."

"Thanks, but I think I'll hang out by the pool. This place is still wall-to-wall leathermen." I grinned, but Jace's look said he wasn't buying it. I was staying behind because I was moody, and he knew it. Shrugging, he left, his camera bag over his shoulder. With my nostrils conscientiously lubed with petroleum jelly, I spent the afternoon under an umbrella beside the pool, sketch pad in hand. I wanted to have a much bigger catalog of designs to offer when I opened my own studio. I didn't want to rely on the ones Rogier had already used on A-list celebs, taking credit for my work while he stuck me with the D-listers and porn stars.

By the time dinner was over and I'd turned down Jace's invitation to check out a bar in Saugatuck, I had to admit that I'd gone beyond moody and progressed to sulking. The arousal of last night, followed by the spectacularly unsexy resolution, had hit all my buttons.

We lived in a world where the more physically able you were, the more desirable you were. The cult of masculinity reigns supreme. A lifetime of finding myself sidelined in ways large and small had done a number on my self-esteem, and I was tired of it. My twenties had almost completely passed me by. I wanted more, if only in this one realm. I wanted everything Robin had claimed he had to offer.

God, did I want it.

But aside from the glaring self-image issues, there were the actual problems I faced as a result of my hemophilia. Not just injury. Joint pain and depression could take their toll on sex drive and sexual performance. My sex drive seemed to be doing okay, but my performance hadn't been put to the test all that much, aside from acquiring some champion cocksucking skills at glory holes.

I was still spinning these thoughts around in my head, endlessly fixated on a puzzle with no apparent answers, as night fell outside. I put away my sketch pad and lay on the sofa, restless and apathetic. Finally the reckless streak that occasionally popped up to say "fuck this shit" took the reins. I grabbed a light jacket and slammed out of the cottage, striding across the resort grounds toward some woods Jace had told me about the night before.

CHAPTER FIVE

Robin

I spent the rest of the night after the Buns & Baskets party trying to convince myself that I'd done the right thing by walking away from Geoff. As captivated as I was by his gorgeous body art and the hunger in his eyes and the dry wit that came out even in his anger, it was better this way.

It wasn't that the hemophilia was a huge stumbling block for me; every sub has boundaries and limits. Sure, usually they're a matter of comfort or psychological health, but I wasn't going to dismiss him just because his were the product of a disability. I was awake long into that night after walking out on him, mulling the countless ways I could give him what he was looking for without affecting his deep tissues or joints. In fact, it sounded like a pretty fun challenge.

So there it was. If my reaction when I saw him was any indication, I obviously hadn't left the leather scene behind, but I'd damn sure left behind the evasions of a sub who didn't want to come clean. And I'd left behind my own arrogance that I couldn't possibly miss problems I should have spotted in my sub if I were as good a top as I liked to think I was. The last thing I needed was to hook up with a bottom with massive communication issues and not the slightest clue about risk-aware consensual kink. Emphasis on *aware*.

I wasn't about to play with another sub I couldn't trust. I'd more than learned my lesson there. It didn't matter how badly I was itching to give Geoff a taste of what he was so blatantly craving.

By morning, the altruist in me had taken over. *That* particular inner voice was chiding me for missing a golden opportunity to teach Geoff how to play safely. He was going to get himself seriously hurt if he kept fumbling around cluelessly. He needed a mentor, and to get involved with the leather community.

Had he ever been to a munch, or any gathering of kinksters? Done any research? Or was he acting on an uninformed instinct to seek out the things he saw in porn? He seemed to be under the impression that he needed pure brute force to get what he wanted. While I certainly wasn't opposed to delivering those things, there were also ways to meet his needs without jeopardizing his well-being.

That voice got louder throughout the day as I met with my realtor and teleconferenced with my parents regarding when I would take possession of their remaining inventory. By evening, the altruistic inner voice (urged on by the frustrated, wanna-give-him-his-first-scene inner voice) had drowned out the ambivalent inner voice and emerged the victor in my psychological tug-o'-war.

No way in hell was I gonna analyze whether having so many inner voices was healthy.

I went back to the Dunes that night on a mission to find Geoff and sit him down for an earnest conversation. If his disability came with the sort of limitations he said it did, it would be reprehensible of me not to help him, right?

Right.

There was no answer at the door to his cottage, which I should have expected. He was a fledgling sub in a resort full of leathermen. That should have been a relief; the chances of him running into a careless or clueless top here on this particular weekend were no doubt considerably lower than if he were randomly trolling for a hookup in clubs. Chances were good that if he found someone to play with, he'd be in skilled hands.

Skilled hands that, nonetheless, he might not inform about his physical condition and its potential pitfalls. Not to mention that even here, the leather community wasn't immune to predators who thought safewords and negotiation were a joke.

Fuck.

I considered heading to the club, which was no doubt packed by this time of night, but I remembered how bored Geoff had been with the scene the night before. No, I was sure he was cruising, but not there.

Where, then?

Rumor had it the basement level of the hotel complex was, for all intents and purposes, a bathhouse, though the website referred to these low-budget rooms as "dorm-style." But it was apparent that Geoff and his friend hadn't done much research before booking their vacation here, so Geoff might not know to check that out. The more obvious cruising spot would be the woods behind the resort.

Only the well-trodden footpaths through the trees made it at all safe to navigate at night. There was barely enough moonlight to see where I was going. Occasionally I passed other men on the prowl. I'm sure they thought I was checking them out when I gave them the once-over to see if they were Geoff. Certainly I got some welcoming smiles, but I shook my head and continued on my way.

Not far off the trails, I occasionally heard gasps, sighs, moans, and, despite the chill in the June air, the slick, wet sound of kissing and sucking, the slap of flesh on flesh. I got hard in my jeans, which really wasn't a good thing considering I was supposed to be running an intervention here. All I could think of was Geoff making those noises, Geoff melting against me the way he had in the club, and it was fucking distracting me from my purpose.

I heard the crunch of gravel ahead of me, and I knew even before he came into view that it was him. I felt his presence like a pulse through my body, and oh, fuck, that was so not a good thing. But it was him, despite the fact that he wore glasses today and wasn't dressed for clubbing. That hunger in his eyes was still there, burning hotter than ever. Everything inside me *throbbed* with the urge to give him what he *had* to have. I'd never exactly been a service top, but his need spoke to me on a whole other level.

I didn't just want to be sure that, whoever he played with, he knew how to do so safely.

I wanted to be the one to give him what he needed.

God, how I wanted that.

Something flickered in his eyes. Then he swallowed visibly, grabbed my wrist, and tugged me off the path.

Right. Okay. Time to stop pretending I just wanted to talk to him. Time to deal with the reality that, despite last night's epic failure, I still fucking *wanted* him.

As soon as we were out of sight of the trail, I backed him against a tree trunk—stopping short of slamming him into it, enough to give him the feel of force without hurting him—and picked up where we'd been interrupted the night before.

There was no beer on his breath this time, and though I missed the taste and smell of it, this was better. His fingers scrabbled over my shoulders and grappled with the back of my jacket while I set about filling every square millimeter of his mouth with my tongue and breath. No biting? Fine. I nipped at his lips firmly enough to toe that line, teasing him with danger, with the possibility that I *could* bite. I could feel the struggle in his body as he debated with himself whether to slow me down and remind me of the limits, or to throw caution to the wind and accept whatever consequences or injuries might arise if I overstepped the bounds.

He didn't realize there was a third option, something between overcautiousness and willful recklessness. He didn't realize he could trust me to safely take him right up to the limit and then bring him back.

But he would. I'd show him.

He hooked one of his long legs around me, his knee riding my hip as he ground on my thigh. "Jesus. Oh Jesus!" he gasped, tearing his mouth away from mine when I wedged a hand between our bodies to cup his erection firmly. I tangled my other hand in his hair, keeping his awareness on the tug of my fingers in his waves instead of on the fact that I was also cushioning his head while I sucked at his lips.

I remained mindful of all his cautions from the night before, but I pushed at each of them, deliberately giving him the sense that I could overstep the boundary at any time. I felt him yield the struggle and resign himself to the fact that there might be a price to pay for this indulgence. That wasn't what I wanted. I didn't want him to just give in to the momentum, telling himself it didn't matter if I injured him so long as he got what he needed.

I wanted him to *give himself over to me*, to trust that he didn't have to police me, that I could deliver what he needed without harming him in the process. It was a totally different thing, and I knew he didn't get it. Not yet.

He smelled good. I wanted his scent covering me, saturating my clothes, my hair, my very skin. I accidentally knocked his glasses askew, then fumbled to take them off and stuff them in one of the pockets of my jacket, where they had less chance of being damaged. I gripped his ass, first through his jeans, then wedged inside to feel the soft, downy hairs on his narrow backside. My finger slid into his crack. I found that wrinkled skin and knotted muscle and pushed at it. Not too firmly. I just wanted him to feel the pressure, the fear that I might try to force my way inside. I kept it there to taunt him with the uncertainty.

I was hotter for him than I could remember ever being for anyone as he humped against me. I pushed my thigh between his, butting it up nice and firm under his nuts, and he *rode* that fucker until I was ready to cream my pants. From his sounds, he wasn't far behind.

"Take me to your room." I drew back long enough to speak before fucking his mouth with my tongue.

I could practically read the decision-making process in the split second it took him to comprehend that request. If we stopped, something might interfere. If we stopped, he might have to do something that would remind me of his condition. If we stopped, he might lose sight of his resolve to just go with it, heedless of the consequences, and begin policing me again.

He wanted to let go *so fucking badly*, and he didn't know how to do it safely.

"No, this is hot, being out here." He ground against me harder. I let go of his hair and growled my irritation that he'd come down on the dangerous side of the fence. I planted my hand on his chest—the other still delving into the back of his jeans—and pressed him hard against the tree. It took a second of me not moving for him to open his eyes, but I wasn't going to do a damn thing more until he did.

When I had his attention, I asked, "Is there anything you need back in your room to keep you from being hurt?"

I could feel his frustration, but I wasn't going to back down.

Finally he pressed his lips together and shook his head. "No. Unless I get injured, I'm fine here."

I didn't double-check. If I wanted him to trust me, I needed to show some trust in turn. "Good," I gritted, and pulled my hand out of the back of his jeans to rip at his belt and fly, roughly jerking them open.

"Fuck," he groaned when I wrapped my hand around his cock and began to stroke. "Yeah, like that. Oh God, *please . . .*"

"Christ, I could come just listening to you beg. Don't think I've ever had anyone who wanted it as bad as you, even when you're holding back. Turns me on. Tell me what you want, baby," I muttered, panting against his ear.

"Just . . . God, please don't stop . . . Please. Please." He was already quivering. For my own part, I could feel tension pulling everything taut, drawing my balls up and making my ass clench as he pushed into my grip. I rolled his foreskin over the flaring ridge of his cock, rubbing past his frenulum. The look on his face was sublime. That look told me it felt good. Incredible. Agonizingly intense. I had to eat the sounds he was making.

My mouth covered his the second before he began spurting into my hand, staining his clothing and mine. I swallowed his shout, groaning an encouraging response. Afterward, I held him up until his knees were willing to support him again, sucking and nibbling on his lips while he caught his breath.

"Jesus, you're every bit as hot as I knew you'd be," I whispered beside his ear. His hands skimmed over the shirt covering my back—and I wanted them on my skin—while I plunged my hand into the back of his jeans again, groping freely. I wriggled a finger down his crack, teasing at the wrinkles around his hole. "Take me back to your room. I want to fuck you."

"No. No." He wrapped his hand around the back of my neck, drawing me into another hard kiss. His lips were swollen and hot. "Don't want to ruin this. Just let me . . . let me . . ."

He sank to his knees, and I felt him flinch. Something had happened, and he wasn't going to tell me.

This was it. This was my chance to show him I could look after him and keep him safe without destroying the heat and momentum we had going.

He was already leaning in, nuzzling at my crotch, fumbling with my fly, but I pulled him back by his hair far enough that I could see all the way to the ground. Beside one of his knees, half-hidden by last autumn's decaying leaves and crispy pine needles, there was a sharp stone. I was willing to bet he'd come down on it when he knelt. Ouch. That would have hurt like a bitch even for someone whose joints weren't in danger.

I swept it aside with my foot, safely away from any possibility of him landing on it again, and cupped his face, working my thumb between his lips. His eyes fluttered shut while I controlled his mouth, invading it.

"Yes or no," I murmured, fucking his mouth with my thumb. "Does that knee need attention right now?"

I drew my finger back long enough for him to answer, trailing saliva down his chin. A flash of indecision flickered across his face, but I thought he landed on the side of truth. Or at least I was going to treat him like he had, trying to build that trust we needed.

"No," he said levelly. "I'll just need to infuse later."

I wasn't sure what that meant, but since the second objective here was to demonstrate that we didn't need to lose the heat and intensity, I didn't inquire. I reached down and jerked my fly open.

"Good. Then suck my dick." I thrust my jeans and briefs down my hips with one hand, and gripped the back of his head to pull him in toward me with the other. Oh God, his mouth was as hot and eager as I knew it would be, like he couldn't live without the weight of my cock on his tongue. He slid back and grasped me, moaning, stroking firmly. I slid my hands through his hair as he rubbed the head of my dick against his face. My pre-cum smeared his cheek while he breathed deeply, like he was trying to wallow in my scent.

"Talk to me," he pleaded. He licked a wet stripe up the length of my cock, and I moaned.

Words? What are words?

Then he backed off and rolled his eyes to look up at me. I saw the reflection of the moonlight shining on his tongue when it darted out to flick the head of my cock. "And say what?"

Another stroke of his tongue while he considered the question. There was too much intensity behind his request for me to assume he just had a thing for dirty talk. He'd wanted me to talk to him last night as well, on the dance floor. That meant something, and maybe I could get an idea of what he was after if I pushed him on it.

Of course, thought was getting harder the longer he had his mouth on my cock.

"What do you want me to say?" I prompted again.

"All the not-nice, dangerous things you had in mind for me last night." He wriggled the tip of his tongue against my slit, collecting a salty droplet. "Please."

I closed my eyes to block out the sight of him with my dick to his lips, or I'd never be able to make sense of what he was asking for. The sensations were almost more than I could handle as it was. He worked up and down the sides of my cock, licking and wetting it, doing everything *except* taking me into his mouth. Teasing.

He wanted rough. Dangerous. Brutal, even. But clearly he thought he couldn't have it with someone who knew about his physical condition. He was both right and wrong, but that was beside the point.

Did he want the words to supply the brutality he didn't think he could get physically? Was that what he needed?

That, I could do. I tightened my hand in his hair.

"Suck it." I didn't quite pull on him, but I definitely applied some pressure. "Suck it, you bitch."

"*Fuck, yes.*" His moan was so grateful, I almost shot off right there. He obeyed, plunging down eagerly, taking me deep and sucking hard. His response was so ardent I knew I'd unlocked an important element to figuring out what he needed.

"Oh, is that why you've been holding out on me?" I panted, thrusting until he grabbed my hips to stop me. He wasn't okay with letting me fuck his throat. All right. Noted. But the verbal humiliation? He was *all over* that. "You didn't want me to bend you over and drill you in the ass until you'd gobbled it like a back-alley whore first."

He nodded, groaning around me.

"I can do both," I scoffed, which made him suck even more enthusiastically. His face was a study in rapture, trapped somewhere between humiliation and exultation. "I can do things to you that you can't even imagine. I can stuff you with a dildo the size of your forearm, lock your cock in a cage, and fuck your face until I come down your throat. Then I can bend you over, whip you till you scream, and shoot another load up your ass. You'd pass out with my cum in both ends and my marks on your skin, and then I'd wake you up in the middle of the night and do it all over again."

Okay, so I wouldn't be doing some of that without a fuck-ton of negotiation first, but right now the fantasy was what mattered. Geoff moaned abjectly, the sound vibrating around my cock. God, I wanted him to take me deeper, so fucking deep. And he seemed to want to; he was pushing himself right to the edge of deep-throating me before backing off, like he wanted to choke on my dick. We'd be having a conversation later about what was and wasn't safe in that regard.

But now wasn't the time, not when he was moving frantically, sucking and licking as hard and fast and deep as he could. His hands rested on my thighs, where a tremor settled into my muscles the longer he worked. It didn't matter that the fantasy I was spinning for him was unsafe. It was just that: fantasy. He loved it, I could tell. He wanted to lose himself in it.

"You want that, don't you? You want me to mark every inch of you with bruises and welts, to feed you my cum every chance I get. You want me to make you beg and scream and cry, and then mark you again. Don't you?"

He hollowed his cheeks, sucking hard, and whimpered an agreement. I pulled on his hair, jerking his head back. My cock slipped from his mouth with the *pop* of a vacuum seal breaking.

"*Don't you?*"

His pale eyes glittered as he looked up at me, and I wished I could make out his expression better. I wanted to read all his most desperate desires, and promise to give him all the things he thought he couldn't have. I gave him a slight shake by his hair. "Answer me, you whore."

"Yes." He resisted my grip on his hair, yearning toward my dick again. "I want that. Want all of it."

I let him suck me down, working frantically, words failing as my groans got louder and my trembling got stronger. My body started to lock up, my cock swelling until Geoff's jaw was stretched as far as it would go. I felt the pressure of his tongue against the vein on the underside of my cock as he refused to pull away, and I fell into it.

"Fuck!" I shouted and flooded his mouth with my spunk. He swallowed, moaning like it was fucking ambrosia.

When I began to soften, he tucked me away and rose, grimacing. As much as I wanted to slump there against the tree and enjoy the afterglow, he was favoring that knee.

I kissed him again, gently this time, my tongue stroking inside his mouth and tasting myself. I lingered at making out with him, not wanting to break the spell prematurely or too abruptly. But I subtly held him so that he was off-balance, putting more of his weight on the leg he hadn't hurt and on the support of my arms.

Finally I eased out of the kiss, gentled him through his breathless panting before I helped him right his clothing.

"Come on," I said quietly, going for calm and matter-of-fact. Something that wouldn't make him feel fussed over, but would make it clear that I wouldn't tolerate him neglecting his well-being just to get off. "Let's go check out that knee."

CHAPTER SIX

Geoff

The last thing I wanted was to end this hookup with Robin watching me infuse. I bent to pick up my jacket, feeling a sense of genuine regret. The knee that had hit the rock was really hurting. It was a bruise rather than a joint bleed, but I'd have to do my prophy as soon as I got back to the room, just in case.

I could only imagine what I'd look like if he got me into the light. His kisses hadn't been gentle there in the beginning, and I hadn't infused in days. I could disregard caution, but not self-consciousness. There was no way I could leave these woods without him seeing. And yeah, I'd told him about my hemophilia, but while he knew it in the abstract, I wasn't ready for him to see the reality.

"I can handle it." I caught my lip between my teeth, feeling how puffy it was. Fuck. "Look, I've got some boundaries about this shit, you know? I don't blame you for being frustrated. Honestly, I'm not sure why you keep trying."

"Why?" He pulled me to him, and I swear, the moment our bodies made contact, it was like an electric current arced between us. "Because of this. Because from the very first time I touched you, I knew I had what you wanted, and you sure as hell have something I want. Don't think I can put a name to it—chemistry, I guess?—but it's there. Can't you feel it?"

"Yeah, I can." I'd known the instant he'd pressed up against me the night before. If I could stop feeling like a freak about my hemophilia, I could have him. "But tonight's not a good night for it. Can't we enjoy what happened without going into that now? Please? Give me your number. I'll call you, I promise. I *will*. I've got plans with Jace during the day tomorrow, but maybe after?" I gave him a questioning look.

He looked back, giving me a long, level stare, then shook his head. "No deal. I can walk you back to your room, or I can carry you, but I'm not leaving until I've seen that knee for myself. That's *my* boundary. If a mishap happens to someone I'm hooking up with, I don't bail until I know it's handled."

I gritted my teeth. "That is the most autocratic, heavy-handed, domineering—"

Robin shrugged casually. "Not so much a dom thing as a decent-person thing, if you ask me."

He wasn't moving, and the night was getting colder the longer we stood there. Finally I sighed and stomped (as best I could, because, you know, knee) back toward the trail. "Fine. Let's go."

"Listen," he said, falling into stride beside me. "There are certain responsibilities I take seriously. I make sure the people I play with are safe and healthy. All your particular medical issues do is redefine what that means. But I'd do it no matter who you were. You want to be treated like anyone else? Well, guess what? This is how I treat *everyone* I play with."

His words were brusque, but he said them with a shrug and a smile. He was a bull in a china shop, yeah, but he was a good-natured one. And, damn him, it did help to hear that he wasn't treating me differently than he would anyone else.

That didn't mean I was going to let him watch me infuse. I stopped him at the door to my cottage. "Jace is inside, or he will be soon if he's not back yet. I'll be okay from here."

Robin looked like he wanted to argue, but he didn't. Oddly, though, the way he chose not to argue said he wasn't surrendering so much as he was picking his battles, and that felt good. Like I didn't *want* to win this fight. What the fuck was that about?

"I'm going. But you and I need to sit down and have a talk." He held out his hand. "Give me your phone. If you don't call me, I'm going to come find you."

I dug my phone out of my pocket and passed it to him. "I will. I swear I will. Tomorrow." Hell, if he'd wanted, I'd have called him tonight. As long as it was sometime *after* I'd infused. Hopefully the bruises from our tryst in the woods wouldn't be too shocking. "Thank you. Have a good night."

He nodded and returned my phone, stepping away from the door. "Yeah, you too."

I backed into the cottage, hesitating, so damn tempted to issue the invitation he wanted. I wanted to believe this reluctance was the voice of my injured self-esteem talking, and that if I did ask him in, it wouldn't be as bad as I feared.

In the end, I chickened out and closed the door.

And immediately had second and third and even fourth thoughts. I stared at my phone and the name he had entered. *Robin Brady*. He probably hadn't even reached his car yet. I could still call him back . . .

No. I needed to infuse and I wasn't ready for him to see that. I tucked my phone in my pocket and gave up on the idea of inviting him to return.

I had pushed my knee to the limit, but it hadn't turned into a bleed, thank God. I gathered up my supplies: the factor in the refrigerator, the sterile water, the alcohol swabs and tourniquet and butterfly needles. It was a lengthy process, gently mixing the factor with the water, filling the syringe, locating a vein without too much scarring, and inserting the needle with practiced ease.

Jace returned to the room, flushed and sweaty but alone, as I was putting everything away and cleaning up. He took one look at my face and blinked.

"Have a good time?" I asked mildly.

He snorted, his dark eyes dancing. "Not as good as you, apparently. How long since you did your prophy?"

I closed my eyes and hung my head, laughing softly at myself. "Um, I think it's been three days. Maybe four."

Jace sighed. "Okay, I'm not your fucking babysitter, but come on, dude."

"I know. I just can't seem to get into the habit of remembering to do it every other day. Hemo kids nowadays grow up with that routine, but I didn't." I was courting a lot more trouble than I needed to by forgetting. The reduction in spontaneous bleeds that came with having factor levels approaching normal meant, among other things, far less joint damage early in life, less arthritis later on. But acquiring the habit and following it with diligence was only part of my problem.

I was tired enough of my own bullshit to admit that was an excuse. The fact was, each time I infused, I was conceding that I was different. That I couldn't function normally without my medication. Instead of accommodating that reality, I lived like I had when I was a kid—restricting my activities, favoring injury prevention over prophylaxis.

I crossed over to the sofa and stretched out on it, curled up on my side. After watching me for a beat, Jace urged me up and sat down, letting me lay my head on his lap. He smelled like sex, but then I probably did too. I was tired, both from the sex and the sleepless night before, and I was feeling absurdly fragile. I'm not ashamed to admit I can be a cuddler when I get to that place, and Jace is mellow enough to indulge me. For all that he was younger than me, in some ways he felt like the doting older brother I could pour out my heart to. Maybe because he always saw so much and nothing seemed to put him off, so there was nothing I couldn't say to him.

"What's going on?" He stroked my hair. A moment's hesitation as he examined my part told me I had a bruise on my scalp where Robin had pulled. He hadn't even been that rough.

"Same shit." I sighed. "How do you stop being humiliated by the fact that you can't do what everyone else can, at least not without a lot more hassle? More importantly, how do you convince people not to see you as broken or defective because you can't?"

"Looks like you solved that one at least."

I flicked a glance over my shoulder to see him grinning.

"The dark of night hides many sins." I smiled ruefully. "If he were to see me now, he'd run screaming for the hills."

"You don't know that."

"Yeah, I do. Past experience. Should I regale you with tales of some of the ridiculous boo-boos that got me sidelined in gym class as a kid because my mother put the fear of God—or at least a lawsuit —into my school principal?"

"There are always exceptions to every rule." Jace shrugged. "How will you ever find them unless you keep testing it?"

"I dunno. Sometimes I'm not sure the letdown is worth it."

"Yeah, but is the potential reward?"

"Maybe?" I rolled onto my back, elevating my legs on the arm of the sofa, stretching out. "If I ever find one of those exceptions, I'll let you know."

He tapped once on the bruise on my scalp.

"*Ow*! Jesus!"

"Why not start here?" he asked. "Clearly there's already someone out there whose default position is that you won't break."

I touched my lips, feeling the swelling there. "And if he is turned off by the reality?"

"Well." He shrugged again. "What do you have at present that you'll have lost, in that case?"

"Just my pride." I sighed and closed my eyes, falling silent until Jace nudged me out of my half sleep and urged me to bed.

MY KNEE APPEARED to be doing fine the next day. Bruised as hell, but fine. Jace and I decided to stick to our plan to walk around Saugatuck and visit some of the craft shops and art galleries. It was a gorgeous, sunny June afternoon, perfect for strolling around a lake-side town. I assumed Robin was staying at the Dunes somewhere, which meant my chances of running into him were a lot better hanging around the resort than playing tourist. After getting a look at myself in the mirror this morning, I'd decided that I'd keep my promise to call him tonight—but when I did so, I'd schedule any hookup for the next day at the very earliest.

Of course, thinking that bumping into him *couldn't* happen ensured it absolutely *had* to happen. Which it did, as we were heading down the street from the paradise known as Saugatuck Spice Merchants (I walked away with several blends of tea that smelled incredible), full from lunch and debating which of the intriguing nearby restaurants to have dinner at this evening.

Robin practically ran right into us as he stepped out of an empty building, never noticing because his attention was on the professionally dressed woman with whom he was speaking. A glance at the name tag the woman wore identified her as being from a realtor, and a sign in the window of the building revealed that it was for lease.

Robin was looking at properties in the area? I blinked, adjusting my assumption that he was a vacationer.

Before I could wonder about it any further, though, he finally saw us and stopped short, staring at me. It took me a moment to remember what I looked like.

"I'll be in touch with you, Vita," he said abruptly, his attention fixed on me. I could see the consternation wrinkling his forehead and braced myself for the inevitable.

The realtor clearly picked up on a vibe of some sort and accepted the dismissal without protest. "Of course, Mr. Brady."

When she'd gone, I jumped in before he could speak.

"Jace, Robin. Robin, my friend, Joscelin Sieger. I'm crashing at his place in Chicago."

It was too much to hope that he'd let himself be diverted. He gave Jace a distracted nod, but his eyes never left me.

"Wow. Did I do that?"

How the fuck was I supposed to answer that? He'd been nibbling and sucking on my lips like they were his favorite candy, and I hadn't infused in days. "It looks worse than it is."

"I didn't—" His mouth tightened, and for the first time since we'd met each other, he looked well and truly disconcerted. Even upset. "Did I go too far?"

"Don't worry about it. You just got a little nippy, and I bruise easily, for obvious reasons. It's not your fault I look like I got punched in the mouth." I rolled my eyes and gave him a wry smile, because fuck it, you had to laugh at that shit sometimes.

Or I might have been trying to use humor to defuse the whole thing before Robin freaked out. I felt Jace's eyes on me as I shrugged. "It's no big deal."

I glanced at Jace, pleading for some backup, and he came through for me like the true friend he was. "It's true. He gets a shiner if you cuss him out."

Robin stared at me another moment, then nodded slowly. "Okay."

Jace really needed to quit looking at me quite so intently.

"So, you're local?" I asked in a desperate bid to turn the conversation. "I'd thought you were a vacationer."

"No, I just moved here. I'm still looking for a house and a space for the gallery I plan to open." He snorted and shook his head, though he was smiling as he looked around the street. "Because, of course, another art gallery is *just* what this town needs."

Jace's eyes lit up. "You're an artist?"

"No." Robin ducked his head. "I can't draw a stick figure. My parents were art dealers, and they recently retired, so I've inherited their contact list and inventory."

"Jace is a painter. We went to art school together. You should check out his work." I tossed Jace a grin.

"What about you? What do you do?" Robin's pale-blue eyes fixed on me.

"Tattoos. I'm a tattoo artist."

"Ah. That explains the gorgeous ink." I smiled and ducked my head under his perusal. His admiration felt *good*. "Where are you two headed this afternoon?"

I looked up and down the street. "Just sightseeing."

"Have you made it out to Oval Beach yet?"

Jace grinned broadly. "Not yet, but it's on the agenda. I've heard interesting things."

"Oh, really?" I flicked a sideways glance at him.

Judging from the way Robin was mirroring that grin, I suspected at least some of those interesting things might even be true. His gaze zeroed in on me. "I'd be happy to play tour guide."

Fuck. If he got me in the light of day mostly undressed, he'd see the *other* bruises he'd left. Not to mention the fact that the temporary tattoo paints Jace had applied were beginning to fade. And then there was that conversation he was determined we were going to have . . .

"We don't have our suits." I felt Jace's eyes on me again and silently begged him to keep backing me up.

"Where we're going, you won't need them. Unless you plan to

hang out by the water and swim. Which would be insane this time of year."

Oh great. Scratch the "mostly" bit. I'd be fucking nude.

"Uh, we had plans to—" I began to stammer, but Jace cut me off.

"Sounds fun. We're in."

Fucking traitor.

WE STOPPED by Robin's place for blankets and sunblock, which was how we learned Robin's place wasn't exactly a place.

"You live on a boat?"

"For now." Robin shrugged. "There's not a lot of space, but I didn't want to leave her behind in Connecticut, so I took her through New York on the Hudson River and then along the Great Lakes, up one side of Michigan and down the other to get here."

He jogged down the steps to the cabin or whatever you called the area below deck to grab what we needed. As far as personal boats went, it was large, but I didn't think it would quite qualify as a yacht. Not that I would have known. I had to imagine whatever living space he had down there was cramped.

While he was out of sight, I took advantage of the opportunity to give Jace a death glare. "Want to tell me what that was about?"

"What?" He pulled off innocent and bewildered well. "I wanted to go to the beach."

"Is this your way of telling me something?"

He crossed his arms over his chest, leaning against a tall piling on the dock. "What message do you think I might be sending you?"

"You're deliberately maneuvering me into a position so he can see all my bruises," I accused. "Are you afraid I haven't told him the truth? I have."

"*Pfft.* Not my business." He rolled his eyes at me. "Dude, last time I checked, I wasn't a cricket with a top hat and cane. If your first assumption is that I think you should be more forthcoming, then it probably says more about what you *are* holding back."

He had a point there. Robin was interested in another go, and so was I. Especially given the sort of stuff he kept promising to do to me, if he made good on even a fraction of his dirty talk. But he wanted to *have a conversation* first, and that could lead to nothing but disappointment. He'd hold back, or he'd decide it was too risky and he wanted nothing to do with me. I wanted to go with it and damn the consequences, and Robin wasn't going to allow it to go down like that.

Robin drove us from the little marina on Kalamazoo Lake to the beach on Lake Michigan, north of the town. At first glance, the beach was like any other. On a warm June day like this, families with children were everywhere, building sand castles and swimming despite the chill of the lake, and everyone in a bathing suit. The only thing unusual was that the proportion of same-sex couples was somewhat higher than you would normally see.

Robin gestured. "Head north, toward those dunes up there."

It was a long trudge through the sand, but the farther north we got, the more apparent a trail became, heading out of sight of the shore. Some ways in, there was a booth where Robin paid a fee.

"It's private land," he explained. "Not part of the state park, so there's a separate admission fee."

Past the booth, the trail ended. The sand was dotted with blankets and towels and men lying nude in the afternoon sun. There was plenty of cruising going on and no small amount of public groping; many of those who weren't sunbathing were engaged in a variety of not-family-friendly activities. No wonder this place was off the beaten path. On public land, these guys would end up in jail.

Jace, a shameless, self-professed voyeur and connoisseur of every sort of man, grinned with delight, peeling his shirt over his head. I wouldn't put money on Robin and me enjoying his company for long.

"Holy shit," Robin breathed, pausing in spreading the blanket. I stopped undressing, smiling with pride. I knew exactly what had caught his attention. Robin's eyes slid to me, then back to Jace. "Did you do those?"

Jace presented his back more fully to let Robin admire. "He did."

I shrugged. "Jace helped with the design. He really is an incredible artist."

"I've never seen anything like it."

The concept for Jace's tats had evolved from a trip we took when we were in art school together, when he'd come home to Colorado with me for spring break. I'd taken him to see a number of natural attractions, and he'd been particularly moved by the Garden of the Gods.

Crawling up his back and shoulders were images that called to mind the red sandstone formations that tower over the landscape there, without being a literal depiction of them. An *interpretation* of the impression they had left, if you would. Careful shading gave the illusion that they were in 3-D, rocky spires rising in relief against the surface of his skin. Greenery filled the space between the formations and curled around his upper arms, like the forests that grew between the mounds. The rocks towered over a river that ran from his lower right ribs to his waist on the left side, and a coyote stood on its banks, drinking. Other animals were worked in, mostly hidden by the trees. It had taken countless hours to do the piece, and we still added to it on occasion. I liked the design because it was earthy, very much like Jace himself. Nature at its most beautiful.

"This is even better than the ones I admired on you," Robin enthused. I smiled, unable to disagree with him there. The design frankly made the one I'd drawn for Jace to paint on my back look downright amateur. I wondered if I'd ever do another work equal to it.

"That's because Geoff hasn't found anyone as talented as he is to ink him, so he's got to make do with shoddy substitutes," Jace said cheerfully, drawing away from Robin to finish stripping.

"Shoddy substitutes?" Robin gave me a confused look.

I chucked a thumb over my shoulder at the fading marks on my back. "They're not real. They're paints, the expensive, long-lasting ones they use for fake tattoos in movies. I'm still looking for someone qualified to do the kind of work I want done." In one-hour increments, for months on end, with healing time in between, and with the risk that even if I properly infuse, excessive bleeding could still push the ink out and make it look shabby. Sure. No problem finding someone willing to take *that* job on. There had been a guy in my hometown who had the talent—and probably the availability—to do it, the one I would have tried to do my apprenticeship with if I'd been willing to live that close to my mother. But unless I moved back, having him do the work wasn't an option.

My perfectionism and my disorder conspired to keep me from turning my body into the canvas I'd always wanted it to be.

Robin tilted his head at me. Curious, not judgmental. "You're a tattoo artist and you're not inked yourself?"

I gestured to the small image of a blood drop on my ankle, the one that had made my mother freak the fuck out when I was eighteen. "Aside from this? Like I said, not yet. The amount of time and effort that will go into the design I made is intensive." I shrugged self-consciously, dropping onto the blanket to finish undressing. "It made it hard to find an apprenticeship, actually, since most tattoo artists won't take you seriously if you're not tattooed yourself. I had to rely on my designs to get me in."

Nude, Jace stretched and looked around. "While you two bond about body art, I think I'm going to introduce myself to some people. Catch you later."

My self-bet turned out to be prophetic. Within minutes, he was chatting up a couple of very femme twinks nearby. I smiled at his predictability, basking in the warm sunlight. Jace's tastes might be eclectic, and I might be just as likely to find him bidding farewell to a grizzled bear as a drag queen in the morning, but beyond all else, he adored the willowy princesses.

"Sunblock?" Robin cast a shadow over me, interrupting my musings, and I smiled and nodded. I had to admit, his active pursuit was nice, and not something I'd gotten to enjoy much in my life.

"Sure." I rolled over and offered him my back.

He paused in drizzling sunblock down my spine. His large hands practically covered me from rib to rib. "I'm trying to figure you out."

"Why?" I buried my face in my arms, wondering if he would notice the bruises his fingers had left on my upper arms and ass the night before.

"Because nothing about you adds up." I felt his finger, greasy with sunblock, trace the point where my hip curved around to my buttock. Yeah, he'd noticed the bruises.

"Those aren't a problem," I gritted, lifting my head and getting ready to turn and glare if he started fretting.

"I know," Robin said equitably. "Or at least, that's what I assumed from everything you told me."

"So you're not freaking out?"

I watched his shadow on the sand shrug. "I won't say the first glance didn't startle me, but only because it was unexpected. If you say they're not a problem, I'll believe you."

His tendency to prove me wrong when I assumed he would react badly was frustrating. "They're only a problem when someone who doesn't understand sees them. Parents can catch shit when the neighbors see their hemo kid with a bloody nose or a bunch of bruises and jump to conclusions. More than one family has had social services called on them."

"Ouch." Robin's fingers tightened a moment, then relaxed, like he might have clamped his hands down on me hard if he hadn't remembered not to. "Believe it or not, I know what that's like."

"Oh?"

He resumed working the sunblock into my skin. "People can misinterpret bruises on a sub too," he murmured, so softly it was almost inaudible beneath the breeze off the lake. "How's your knee?"

"Bruised, but the joint didn't bleed." If he could be straightforward about this and not freak out, I guess I could stop trying to downplay everything. "I infused after I got back to the room. Honestly, the bruising you see wouldn't be as bad as it is, except I hadn't done my prophylaxis in a few days."

"I did some research last night and this morning. Infusing, now, that's dosing yourself with clotting factors, right?"

I shot him a startled glance over my shoulder. "You did research?"

"Of course I did." He looked surprised by the question, as if I was being ridiculous for not knowing he would. "Tell me more about infusing."

Which was how I ended up sitting nude on the sand, surrounded by dunes and similarly nude men, filling Robin in on infusing for injuries and bleeds versus prophylaxis. And no matter how many times I tried to change the subject, he kept bringing it back to my hemophilia.

"You don't want to hear all this," I protested.

"I need to hear this. This is stuff I have to know if I'm going to play responsibly with you." He said it simply. Just a matter of fact.

Then uncertainty creased his brow and made him frown. "Unless —am I reading this wrong? Are you actually not interested in playing with me?"

"No, I am, I am. It's just—" I waved my hands around in a vague, confused way that probably told him nothing except that I was a flighty neurotic who made no sense. "I'm only going to be here for a few days. This is more trouble than a hookup is worth."

"A hookup? Is that what you think I'm offering?" The amused lift at the corner of his mouth was way sexier than it had any business being.

Sitting up, I grabbed the sunblock from him. "Your turn. Wouldn't want all that pale skin to burn." There were freckles covering his shoulders, suggesting what happened when he got too much sun. Aside from those, however, he was so pale I imagined he nearly glowed in the dark. Unfazed, he turned around and let me have his back. "If we're not talking about hooking up, what are we talking about?"

"At the risk of sounding completely arrogant, let me give you my read on you. You don't just want sex, you want a *scene*. You've never really played before, at least not beyond a couple one-night stands that got rowdy, and that was unsafe enough to frighten you." He peered back over his shoulder and smirked. "How am I doing so far?"

"Pfft." I flapped my sunblock-smeared hand dismissively, grinning back. "Amateur hour. I pretty much told you all of that."

"True. Somewhere along the way, someone taught you that having your condition meant you could never do or be or have anything *but* that condition, that it's always *you can't* and never *you can*. So now you think you can't really get what you want, which is to forget about your health for a while so you can submit."

That was way too fucking close to home. Literally. I seized on the one inaccuracy I could find, trying to keep my tone light. My chuckle rang hollow. "Hello, have you met me? I'm really not submissive."

He waved that off, the muscles of his back moving under my hands with each motion. "Blanket term. Keeping it basic. You're a masochist, definitely. You might not need to *serve*, but you do want the freedom of giving over control. Also, what better way to demonstrate that the person you're with isn't hung up on your hemophilia than for them to feel comfortable hurting you?"

I swallowed thickly. His insight would have been creepy if not for the fact that it relieved me of the burden of coming up with words for things I couldn't explain. "Okay. You're still on track." My voice was more subdued, and he clearly picked up on that when my hands stopped rubbing sunblock into his skin. He looked back at me again.

He blinked and the offhanded tone fell away, replaced by something far more gentle. Compassionate. "You're *tired* of it. So you keep running up to the edge, determined that one of these days you're just going to say 'fuck the fallout' and jump, but you can't quite do it because you're neither suicidal nor stupid." He gave me a soft smile. "So instead you step back and you keep holding on and you only get a fraction of the things you want. Don't you get it, baby?"

He faced me fully, and I had to duck my head. Otherwise he was going to see that he had me dead to rights. I was covered in goose bumps and my eyes were burning. Just by virtue of his presence and insight, he was giving definition to all my nebulous desires. The yearning that evoked was so strong I ached with it.

"You need someone you can trust. But you can't trust anyone who doesn't have the whole picture. Problem is, you also don't trust anyone enough to let them have the whole picture." He released a long, wistful sigh, the sort of sound that suggested maybe he'd surprised himself with that outpouring of words, or that he worried he'd said too much.

That compelled me to look back up at him as he licked his lips—nervously, I think.

"So that's what I'm putting on the table. I can give you that, but only if you're *totally* fucking honest with me. No downplaying shit, no holding back. If you want it, you gotta trust me to give it to you *and* look after you in the process. And in order to do that, I gotta learn everything I can, or neither of us is going to feel safe."

The whole afternoon might have passed us by while I sat there, staring into his ice-blue eyes and weighing my options. I wanted everything he'd offered so much that I was quivering with it, but—

"That seems like a big order for a vacation fling," I said at last, picking at my thumbnail with a singular focus. "Maybe we should just start with fucking. See how that works for us?"

"No problem." His growly drawl brought my attention back up to his face, and he gave me a lazy smile. "I can make you scream without ever leaving a mark."

My mouth went dry and my brain forgot how to make those things. What were they called?

Oh. Yeah. Words.

It took me a moment to recover. "If I weren't concerned about sand where sand don't belong, I'd tell you to take me off into the dunes right now."

Next thing I knew, I was on my back and he was above me, pinning me to the blanket. "I'm going to hold you to that," he rumbled before his mouth crashed down on mine.

CHAPTER SEVEN

Robin

W hen I woke up that morning on my boat, I hadn't imagined that by late afternoon, I'd have Geoff beneath me, making out on a beach blanket, much less that he'd have already agreed to give me a chance to show him what I had to offer.

I definitely wasn't in any damn rush to let him up. He tasted good, and his body felt amazing beneath mine. Given the numerous and obvious black marks on his self-esteem, I would have thought he'd be too self-conscious to enjoy himself, but the fact that we weren't doing anything that people around us weren't doing far more explicitly no doubt offered reassurance. Or maybe he had a thing for public displays of debauchery. I, personally, might have been more self-conscious *not* fooling around, with so many others going at it around us.

"God, you feel good," I muttered, sliding my erection against his. There was a grit of sand between us, but it was worth it. "Your body—Jesus."

He stilled at that, suggesting that maybe I'd dinged one of those bruises on his ego. Suddenly I was glad we were in Saugatuck, which was geared toward the everyman gays instead of the underwear models you found in a lot of big-city meat markets. Geoff had no reason to worry about how he rated in comparison to everyone around him.

I tried to keep his attention off it by offering him a much more tangible distraction. Each time he got desperate enough to reach for his cock or grind up against me, I backed off, leaving him frustrated and desperate for more.

"The hell are you doing?" he finally growled.

"No way am I giving you a reason to duck out again when it's time to go back to your room." I scraped his neck with my teeth without biting. He didn't flinch. Already he was starting to trust that I knew where to stop. "Or my boat. Or on the hood of the car. Or wherever the first convenient place to bend you over and drill you might be."

Geoff chuckled breathlessly. "Gotta say, the determined pursuit is good for my ego."

Excellent. Mission accomplished.

When we couldn't frot against each other anymore without either coming or going crazy, I rolled off him.

"Start talking before I make a liar of myself," I panted.

Geoff smirked, reaching up for me. "Not exactly an inducement."

I evaded his hands and pulled him up to sit with me. "Talk."

It took him a moment. "So, you came from Connecticut?" he finally asked. I suppressed a smile that this awkward conversational sally was the best he could manage.

"Yeah. Darien. Typical case of using Connecticut as a bedroom community when your family works in New York."

"Because your parents were art dealers."

"Exactly."

"What about your family? Any brothers or sisters?"

I smiled, leaning back on my elbows. The sheen of sweat and sunblock on Geoff's skin made me want to lick him. "Nope. I am the quintessential rich, spoiled, only child. My mom says by the time I was old enough for them to consider having another one, I'd just worn them out."

"You were that bad?" He stretched out on his side, curling his arm under his head as a pillow. The sunlight beating down was almost too warm, but at least this early in the summer, the humidity wasn't bad.

"I'm sure the existence of God is proven by the fact that I survived to hit puberty."

That made him laugh. "You and me both."

"You had a lot of problems when you were young?"

"If you listened to my mother, you would have thought so." He plucked at the blanket. "Mostly she was just overprotective. I *couldn't* have had many problems because she pretty much tried to swaddle me in bubble wrap until I hit puberty."

"No siblings to keep her distracted?"

"Well, yes, but that was part of the issue. Not with Ling, of course —that's my sister. They adopted her when I was three years old. It was more because, um—" He grimaced, then took a deep breath, like he was bracing himself. "Well, because of my older brother."

Something about his change in attitude sobered me right up. "He died?"

"Yeah." I watched him visibly suppress the urge to skirt the truth. "He nearly bled to death at a day old, when he was circumcised."

"Wow, seriously? That can happen?"

Geoff nodded. "Yeah. It's one of the ways you can discover a baby has hemophilia right off the bat. But this was 1980, back before anyone knew much about HIV and AIDS, much less considered the possibility of contaminated blood supplies. David passed away not long after they finally came up with a name for what was killing him."

I swallowed hard and sat up straighter. "Jesus."

Geoff shook his head impatiently. "Anyway, that's beside the point. I was saying my mom was overprotective. Which she was. I told you why I stayed in the closet."

"Yeah, you did." I tacked a helicopter parent onto the mental image I was building of what he'd been like as a kid. I reached over, combing my fingers through his hair, massaging light circles on his scalp. He closed his eyes and sighed. "What about your dad?"

"Dad . . . I don't think Dad ever got over David's death. I mean, he tried, he really did. He went through all the motions, did all the right things, but there was always something detached about him, you know? Like he couldn't let himself care too much. I think it's because he was sure he'd lose me too. He didn't have that problem with Ling." His eyes grew distant for a long moment before he came back to me.

"Anyway. Dad passed on when I was in art school, and Mom died a few months ago, so now there's just me and Ling. We've got a really great relationship. She was younger than me, but for a long time, she was the best friend I had growing up."

"Not a lot of friends?"

"No." He bit his lip, something I was learning to read as him stopping himself from speaking.

"What?"

Geoff squirmed. "You mentioned the whole Ryan White thing the other night. Let's just say I caught some of the fallout from that sort of ignorance too. I mean, we weren't like the Ray brothers' family. They didn't burn our house down or drive us into hiding. But it was the eighties. A lot of people assumed that because I had hemophilia, I was infected—which, statistically, there was a good chance I might have been. I got really lucky."

"How lucky?" Okay, this was a subject of significant relevance for multiple reasons.

"Well, I was born in eighty-two, and by the time they got HIV out of blood supply in the US in 1985, ninety percent of severe hemophiliacs—which is my kind of hemophilia—had been infected. Seventy-five percent of the total hemo population."

I blew out an astonished breath. "That many? Holy shit."

"Yeah." He smiled wanly. "If my mom's overprotectiveness accomplished one thing, it was that I didn't have as many bleeds as most little kids, which might have made the difference. Still, a lot of parents didn't want their kids around me, and they managed to keep me out of school until junior high. My parents had to sue to let me attend, and then some of the kids reverse-engineered the assumption of HIV infection to an assumption of queerness." He scoffed. "The logical contortion there is amazing, don't you think? Because I had hemophilia, I *must have* HIV, and because I *must have* HIV, I must be gay. Well. They had two out of three right."

The way he veered off on that tangent was telling. Something in my chest ached as I imagined what that must have been like, struggling through puberty against a backdrop of bullying for a disease he didn't have and a sexual orientation he was just coming to understand he did have.

God, no wonder I'd homed in on him from the very start. It was a minor miracle that I wasn't rolling around on him like he was catnip. His issues were pretty much my kryptonite.

That chain of thought, however, would lead to all sorts of uncomfortable speculations about whether I was falling back into destructive patterns, and I really didn't want to go there. He was only here for a few days. I could indulge in him without worrying about the long-term significance.

Thankfully, Geoff gave me an out and shifted the conversation.

"So, dude, what's with all the questions?"

"Sorry." I ducked my head. "I guess I like trying to figure out what makes people tick. I can't remember a time when I didn't do it."

He shrugged. "I guess I don't mind. It's somewhat less morbid than the curiosity I get from a lot of people."

He said it breezily, like it didn't really matter. In fact, he'd delivered a lot of his biographical information the same way. But now that I'd seen his art on Jace's skin, I felt like I'd seen into him well enough to suss out all the little wounds that were buried not all that deep under his prickly shell. A sensitive soul cut by things he'd been too young to understand until indifference crusted over the injuries like scabs.

Jesus. I was waxing poetic. Time to change it up.

I had him on his back with very little maneuvering, tracing my tongue along his collarbone. "Trust me, my interest in you is anything but morbid."

Not a lot of conversation followed. I stuck to my resolve—barely —and didn't let us get off. The resulting make-out session was lazy and unpressured.

Weird. How was it that between adolescence and adulthood, people lost sight of the idea that necking doesn't have to be just a means to an end?

Finally we were interrupted by a *thud* as Jace dropped onto the blanket beside us, his eyes heavy lidded and his smirk completely self-satisfied.

"If you guys have had enough sun, I'm starving. What are we doing for dinner?"

CHAPTER EIGHT

Geoff

R obin took us to dinner at an amazing Italian restaurant near
the marina in Saugatuck. It had a club attached, so we went
over, despite the fact that we hadn't intended to go clubbing. It was a
mixed club, not like the one at the Dunes. There were plenty of
straight people there, but also enough same-sex couples that we
weren't out of place.

I was glad for the distraction, because after our conversation had
gotten so heavy, I wasn't sure I could find the transition back to the
effortless sexual chemistry Robin and I had been enjoying. I was
more than ready to take Robin to the resort and let him fuck my
brains out, but something had shifted between us. A connection had
been made, which put the sexy hookup vibe on strange, unsteady
ground. Maybe hanging out and partying for a while would help us
get back into the flow.

Robin was in favor of the idea and helpfully pointed out that if we
wanted to leave before Jace was ready, Jace had his car still parked
there in town. Robin and I could go to the boat or take Robin's car to
the Dunes.

Once we got on the dance floor, it became apparent that if I was
having trouble slipping back into the sexy groove, he certainly
wasn't. Robin just wanted to torment me some more. Make me abso-

lutely desperate for him. Which, hello? It was already way too late for that.

The feeling of his body moving against mine—knowing that this time I really was going to go for it, no indecision, no angst—was incredible. Prolonged foreplay. Nerves strung taut and vibrating with anticipation. Hands grasping, hips brushing with deliberate intent to tease. Sweat and the lingering, sweet coconut scent of sunblock. Ice-blue eyes fixed on mine, searching for something.

A low growl next to my ear. "Tell me how you want it."

I managed a weak laugh. "As soon as possible, that's how."

"That's not what I meant." He spun me abruptly, pressing his chest to my back and grinding against my ass like he had the first time we danced, without ever missing a beat. "Still want it hard and brutal?"

"Yes." I hissed as his hand slid across my abdomen, lightly teasing above my groin. "That's how I want it."

"Good. Because I want to throw you down and pound you so hard you pass out."

It was just dirty talk, right? He knew he couldn't be careless. The nervous voice inside me, the voice that always reminded me to be cautious, to avoid any risk of injury, tried to pipe up. I squelched it without mercy. I was playing with fire and I *didn't fucking care.*

"Yes," I said again, letting my head fall forward, offering him the back of my neck. He nibbled without biting. Perfect.

"Stop it," he breathed against my ear.

"Stop what?"

"Stop second-guessing if you're safe with me. You are. I won't forget the boundaries. Let that shit go. It's my worry now."

"I'm trying."

"Good. Ready to get out of here?"

I paused before answering, because his hands and lips and teeth felt too amazing to interrupt. "Yeah. Just . . . let me find Jace, tell him we're going."

"I'll get the car, meet you outside."

I searched the crowded dance floor for Jace and finally spotted him, then pulled him aside with an apologetic look at his partner.

"I'm taking Robin back to the Dunes."

He smirked at me. "You know, his boat's closer."

"Yeah, but my factor's back at the resort if I end up needing it tonight."

"Ah, right." Jace nodded slowly. "Okay."

"Look, he knows, but I just . . ." I grimaced, hating that voice of caution that wouldn't let me leave without making sure of this. "Whatever you do tonight, bring it back to the cottage, would you?"

I couldn't bring myself to add "just in case." That seemed like a concession. Jace got the implication, though.

WE BARELY MADE it into my room before Robin was all over me, shoving me toward the bed.

"Careful," I gasped between kisses, stumbling as I tried to kick off my shoes. The hated word had escaped me unintentionally, and I cursed myself for it, but for a moment it had seemed like he might toss me onto the damn thing.

"Stop. Worrying," he growled again, emerging from the folds of the shirt he'd been peeling over his head. "We're just fucking for now. If you say stop or slow down, I'll do it."

Fuck. I hated that thought. I didn't want to be able to stop him. I wanted to do shit that would require a safeword.

"I'll try." I took the last few steps to the bed on my own, shucking my jeans and crawling onto it before I tossed my shirt aside.

He stared at me. Whatever he saw must have satisfied him, because his lips came down to meet mine again. His weight felt good on me, trapping me, pinning me down. We were both tacky with sunblock residue, gritty with sand. A shower should have been in order, but his tongue was in my mouth and the stretchy cotton covering his erection was rubbing against mine. Who the fuck cared about anything else?

This kiss wasn't frantic like all the ones before. It was slow, searching, as though he was feeling his way along cautiously. That wasn't okay. I pressed up against him harder, ground my mouth against his more firmly, and *Yes, there!* That was it. Perfect. His cock rocked against mine. His mouth twisted. The pull of his lips and thrusts of his tongue became demanding, and *fuck*, that was exactly what I needed. I tried to draw him closer, but he caught my wrists and wouldn't let me grab him.

I wanted to struggle against that grip. I wanted to make him force me down and take what he wanted, but I couldn't escalate it to that point. Not after we'd agreed that we'd just be fucking.

I lay pliant beneath him as he tongue-fucked my mouth. He jammed his hips between my thighs, humping against me until I was right there on the fucking edge. Then he backed off, leaning over to jerk open the drawer of the bedside table. My lube was in there from the other night, but not the condoms.

"On the dresser," I panted, so dazed and kiss-drunk I didn't think I could move. "In my shaving kit."

He practically launched himself off me to get to it, spilling razors and pill bottles to find the small package of condoms I carried in the largely vain hope of getting laid. He paused, staring at the mound of prescription bottles, then looked at me with a frown.

"These are some heavy-hitting painkillers. I didn't even know you could get Demerol outside a hospital."

Fuck.

"Joint bleeds can hurt pretty bad." I reached for him, rubbing my other hand over the bulge in my underwear before pushing them down my hips and shimmying out of them. "Come on."

He set the pill bottles aside and grabbed the condoms.

"Just to make sure: have you taken any today?" he asked as he strode back to the bed, losing his briefs along the way.

I shook my head and scooted back on the mattress. Then my leg was hanging over his arm and one of his slick hands was fisting my dick while the other worked lube into my ass. I was torn between the impulse to tell him to *hurry* because I didn't fucking care if it hurt—I *wanted* it to hurt—and the nagging voice of reality sawing at the back of my brain, reminding me what a bitch it would be if I tore.

I realized he probably had figured that out too. Hence the caution. Which, in some absurd, contradictory way that didn't even make sense in my head, was both a relief and an irritant. A relief, because it meant he really was being attentive to my safety. And an irritant because that nagging little voice insisted he was going to treat me differently, like I was made of spun glass. Fuck that sh—

His fingertips hooked up and found my prostate. Well, okay then.

There were at least some advantages to taking our time. I groaned and closed my eyes. He added another finger, fucking me harder with them. Edging that boundary without crossing it.

Oh God, yes.

"You want it?" His hand curled around the head of my cock, rolling the foreskin forward, then back down. I whimpered, my hips coming up off the bed, using my knee draped over his arm for leverage. It tightened me around his fingers.

"Fuck. Yeah." My higher brain functions had shorted out. I'd gone Neanderthal, monosyllabic, nothing but a tense ball of *wanting* humping the air in front of him as he wrung another drizzle of pre-cum from my dick.

He drew his fingers out of me, and his cock replaced them, wedging against my hole without pushing inside, applying only enough pressure to threaten penetration without actually doing it.

"Beg me for it."

"Wha—" My eyes opened, and I stared up at him, confused and panting. His hand pumped my dick without relenting.

He wanted me to *talk*?

Lube and all, his other hand fisted in my hair, jerking my head back, craning my neck hard while he glared down at me. "You're the one who likes words. So beg me for it, bitch."

Suddenly I was on my knees in those woods again, gobbling his cock while he rained filthy, vile words on me, offering verbal violence to substitute for the physical roughness I craved.

"*Please!*" I arched my spine, dislodging the head of his cock with my squirming. He pushed me back down and repositioned himself, putting more of his body over mine to keep me in place. Even in such dire need, I still couldn't manage more than fragmented, gasping syllables. "God. *Fuck!* Pluh—please! Fuck! *Please!*"

If he was expecting an eloquent monologue, he was going to have to deal with disappointment. Apparently what I managed was good enough, because in the next breath he was shoving into me, hard and fast. Harder and faster than any partner who knew about my hemophilia had ever penetrated me. He'd taken his hand off my dick to brace it on the pillow next to my head, which was probably a good thing. I was *way* too close to popping already, and I hadn't even had a chance to enjoy this yet.

He ground his mouth against mine, drinking in my half-pained groans while I adapted. Then he reared back and began to stroke. Steadily at first, building up a rhythm, drawing soft moans from me with consummate skill. And then more forcefully as the outer layer of his restraint began to crumble. That's when it went from good to fan-fucking-tastic. Not brutal, but not gentle either. He didn't try to hold back. Even better, he didn't seem to think he *had* to hold back, because he had taken the time to make sure he knew what he was doing. And Christ, he felt amazing in my ass. Each jolt of his hips jerked a sharp moan from my throat. Each press of his cock past my prostate made my balls draw up and my dick go even more rigid against my stomach, spreading a steady pool of fluid. Throwing his head back, Robin gasped and grunted, cursing between his teeth as he shuddered and drove deep one last time, twitching inside me and out.

I whimpered at the loss of stimulation, reaching for my cock, intending to give myself that last bit of sensation to make it over the top, but Robin caught my hand.

"Wait."

Kissing me, he carefully lowered my legs and pulled out, then made his way down my body. He lapped up the puddle of pre-cum on my abdomen before moving lower to suck me all the way down his throat.

"Oh *fuck*." I arched, thrusting until his hands pushed my hips back into the mattress. He didn't make me wait long, though, driving me headlong toward orgasm with beautifully skilled lips and tongue. I drilled the heels of my hands against my eyes until I saw sparkles, straining with the need to come, barking sharp cries until everything flashed white behind my eyelids, like a magnesium flare. It almost hurt, the force with which the orgasm ripped through me, starting in my nuts and racing up my dick and spine simultaneously. I pumped down his throat in one agonizingly good burst after another.

Afterward we sprawled in a messy tangle on the bed, slick with sweat that made the sheets damp and cooled rapidly in the air-conditioned room. I needed a shower in the worst fucking way, but my muscles didn't seem to want to work. I was sure my brain had melted and might even be dribbling out my ears.

"You said you're here for a few more days?" His blunt fingers traced idle patterns on my chest.

"Jace booked us for the whole week."

"Good." He shot me a toothy grin. "I would really like to do this again before you go."

"Well, I don't have any plans. Just lots of hanging around. Maybe checking out the galleries with Jace."

"Excellent." His pleased expression was enough to make me consider how soon I'd be ready for another round tonight. "That reminds me. Make sure I have Jace's contact information before he leaves. I'd like to see his work."

"I'll do that." Now we were getting to that awkward stage where we tried to figure out if this was an overnighter or if it was time for the other guy to leave. I hadn't had enough one-night stands to have that part worked out yet. That first night when I almost brought him back from the club, it wouldn't have been an issue, but this had evolved into something more than a simple hookup.

I was enjoying his company for its own sake.

I scratched my chest as I tried to figure out what to say next, grimacing at the tacky feel of my own skin. "I really need a shower."

"Want me to clear out so you can do that?" He propped himself up on an elbow. "I have an early meeting with my realtor tomorrow, and I didn't bring anything for overnight, so I'll need to go back to my boat at some point." He dragged his nails lightly up my thigh. "Which is not to say I wouldn't be more than happy to hang out for at least a while longer."

Inspiration struck and I smiled. "You know, we share a Jacuzzi with the cottage next door. I could see if it's unoccupied."

His grin mirrored mine, and my dick made it known that it would definitely be interested in another round in the not-so-distant future.

"I'm in."

CHAPTER NINE

Geoff

J ace and I had just gotten back from driving up to Grand Haven
the following afternoon, and I was hanging out by the pool
when my phone chimed with an incoming text message
from Robin.

Paperwork sucks.

I felt the corners of my mouth tug up into a smile.

What are you working on?

A pause. I lay half-dozing in the sun, my phone under one hand
on the chaise beside me.

Some stuff from my accountant. Boring stuff. Entertain me.

Jace peered at me from over the tops of his sunglasses as I chuckled, but soon ignored my texting. I chose to disregard his knowing
smirk.

What should I say to entertain you?

Tell me what you want me to do to you when I fuck you again tonight.

Oh Jesus. And here I was still sex-drunk and blissed-out from the
night before.

ARE you going to fuck me again tonight?

Damn straight.

Unf. I drew a towel discreetly across my lap before my swim
trunks had a chance to start tenting.

Wouldn't it be better if you told me what you plan to do to me?

Nope. You're still calling the shots. We're just fucking, not playing, right?

I grimaced, and the danger of springing wood by the poolside dropped dramatically. I wished my physical reality could be as wild and unfettered as my imagination.

But then, last night had been fine. He'd given me a hell of a ride—or three—and I was no worse for wear. Maybe I could see what he had to offer if we went beyond just fucking.

I stared at my phone for a long while, trying to figure out how to respond. It must have taken longer than I thought, because another text came in.

Something wrong?

I sighed.

No. It's just hard to say where the boundaries are. What I want doesn't bear much resemblance to what I can actually do.

Why's that?

Another pause as I pondered.

I want more than fucking. You know that already. But...

I expected him to come back asking for a better explanation, but he didn't.

What would you want to do if you didn't have to worry about anything?

Everything.

Everything?

Well, almost. No minors, animals, or bodily wastes. But beyond that, yeah.

Now I was getting hard, shifting on my chaise as I imagined how extreme *everything* could get and how badly I wanted all that it encompassed.

Give me an example.

I swallowed hard, thinking of that video I'd watched at the glory hole in Chicago, the twink being kidnapped and beaten and brutally gangbanged.

I had to get away from the pool. Draping my towel in front of me, I gathered my things and hurried back to the cottage. I was glad to be doing this via text. It kept me from stammering nervously.

I . . . think a lot about being forced.

I tried not to read too much hesitation into the pause that followed.

Forced. In the sense of just being pushed around a bit, taken forcefully? Or did you mean rape fantasies?

Oh thank God.

Yeah. That second one. Well, both, really.

What about being tied up?

Yeah.

Exhibitionism? Made to perform in public?

Gulp. *Yeah.*

Role-playing? Being ordered around? Beaten?

Oh Jesus. I was throbbing hard as I stretched out on my bed.

Yeah. But I'm not sure just how far we could go with the bondage or beating.

I know. I promise you, I won't forget that. So, mostly you want it to feel dangerous and for it to hurt?

God, yeah. I moaned, stroking myself inside my swim trunks. Then I pulled my hand out just long enough to send a quick follow-up.

A lot. I have a high tolerance for pain.

Ooh, a challenge. I could practically see his smirk. *What about drawing blood?*

I jolted and had to pinch my dick at the base to keep from coming. The mental image of myself like the bottom I'd seen in my favorite amateur video—shallow gashes slanting across my back, beads of the infuriating, faulty blood welling up and dripping down my skin, painting me in streaks of crimson . . .

Yes.

I grabbed my laptop and called up the URL and sent it to him.

Like the end of this.

The delay before he responded was long enough to make me wonder if he was somewhere he couldn't watch the video. Hopefully I hadn't sent him porn while he was sitting in a mortgage broker's office or something. With nothing better to do than wait for his response, I watched it myself, finding it every bit as stimulating as before. I had gotten to the part with the dressage whip when another text arrived.

Get your hand off your dick. Don't you dare come.

Oh, *Christ*. I jerked my hand out of my shorts as if I'd been burned. I watched the rest of the video with my heart racing and my breath coming in shallow pants.

What about fear play? Mind games?

I frowned, not entirely sure what he meant.

I think that would be okay.

So, making sure we're on the same page, this won't be just fucking anymore. We're going to be playing.

My mouth dry, I nodded stupidly before realizing he couldn't see it.

Right.

Another pause, the blinking ellipsis in my text app making it clear he was typing. And then:

Here's what we're going to do. I'm going to be there in two hours to pick you up for dinner. I want you clean, inside and out, lubed, and stretched. You'll wear the outfit you wore to the club the other night. You'll have a safeword chosen by the time I get there. Understood?

Everything in me clenched tightly. *God.* He was offering me all I ever wanted, if I could relax and trust him not to harm me. With a safeword, I could stop him if he seemed to be in danger of doing something that could injure me, right? And if I infused before he arrived, my factor levels would be fine for the evening.

Ok. Where are we going to eat, anyway, that a mesh shirt would be appropriate?

Did I give you permission to question me?

My heart thudded in my chest so hard I was sure it registered on the Richter scale. For all my professed disinterest in being submissive, those words grabbed my balls and squeezed until I worried I might come without even being touched.

No. Sorry.

If you have a thong or a jock to wear underneath, fine, otherwise, no underwear.

Oh shit. Jeans that tight, commando? I didn't have time to go shopping. As it was, I would have to rush to get through the preparations he required, especially since I would also have to do my prophy. I acknowledged the command and signed off to get to work.

By the time he picked me up, I was ready. Once I opened the door,

I promptly forgot all about Jace chilling on the sofa behind me, where he was no doubt hoping to get a glimpse of whatever show Robin had planned. Robin was wearing a suit that hadn't come off any rack. I had to be too conservative with the money I'd gotten from my parents' life insurance to ever consider buying high-end menswear, much less bespoke, but I'd admired enough to recognize it.

He even carried a briefcase, and he had glasses on. Brainy-yet-sexy light-rimmed specs that set off his blue eyes perfectly. Oh, fuck me.

And here I was in skintight jeans and a see-through shirt.

"What the fuck?" I demanded, going a bit googly-eyed. The situation might have been every sort of ridiculous, but damn if he didn't look amazing.

He smiled, folding his arms across the buttoned-down and immaculately tailored breast of his jacket. "Is there a problem?"

There was something coldly avid in his eyes that reminded me of his restriction on questioning him, so I bit my tongue. Then he leaned close, and his lips brushed my ear. "I thought you liked being treated like a whore."

My pulse staggered and tripped, jogging to catch up once it recovered. Or maybe it was just trying to keep up with the immediate demand for more blood south of the border.

"Up for a game of rentboy and demanding client?" he murmured, still tight in my personal space. When I turned my head to look at him, we practically kissed.

I had to clear my throat a few times before I could answer. Somewhere on the periphery of my awareness, I heard Jace stifle a laugh at how long it took me to come up with a response.

"Aren't I a little old to be a rentboy?" I whispered.

"It's called role-play for a reason, baby." He pulled a wad of bills out of his wallet—I'd have to make sure he got those back later, because there was only so far I was willing to go for role-play—and stuffed them in my tight front pocket, easily dropping back into character. "As a paying client, I call the shots. You wear what I want and do what I say. Are we clear?"

I knew I must be blushing to the very roots of my hair, in no small part because I could now hear Jace quite clearly behind me, damn near choking to death trying to contain his snickers. If he didn't stop, he was going to rupture something.

"Yes." I nodded, ducking my head.

Robin's voice took on a stern edge I was beginning to recognize all too well. "Yes, what?"

"Yes, sir, Mr. Client, sir," I shot back. Fuck it. If I was going to be a rentboy, I was going to be a fucking sassy one.

Robin's lips twitched, but I ignored him, leading the way out the door and adding some wriggle to my walk for the hell of it. I heard him ask Jace to stick something in the freezer, which made me stop and turn around. I hadn't seen anything in his hands but the briefcase. I supposed a bottle of wine or the like could have fit into the soft-sided bag, but why would that go in the freezer? Before I had a chance to figure it out, he murmured a courteous farewell to Jace, then closed the door and quickly caught up. His hand clamped roughly on my ass cheek as he fell into step alongside me.

"That was cute, but I warn you: I *will* make you regret it if you get too mouthy."

He wasn't doing that dangerous, chilly thing that froze me in my tracks. In fact, he seemed awfully damn cocky himself, as if daring me to try him.

Which was really rather annoying. If he wanted me to do it, that stripped all the satisfaction from attempting to provoke him.

The restaurant he took me to was nice: dark and cozy but not excessively elegant. Too conservative for my attire, not fancy enough for his, so we both stood out, which was all sorts of awkward. Especially with the way he kept one hand riding the small of my back and clutched a briefcase with the other. Suddenly I wasn't sure about this game. It felt like everyone's eyes were on me, even though the restaurant was dimly lit and maybe a third of the tables were occupied.

At Robin's request, they seated us at a booth in the far back corner. He urged me into the seat facing the wall, rather than the one facing the dining room. He slid in beside me instead of across. The dividers between booths were high enough that each was like its own little cubicle. No one except a person standing right beside the table could see us tucked in there. We might as well have been in a private room. The overhead light was low and an oil faux-candle burned beside a small vase, providing just enough light for us to see our menus and adding to the intimate atmosphere.

That was good, at least. No one could gawk at me.

"I'll be ordering for us tonight," Robin said.

The waitress appeared, cheerfully asking for our drink orders. He ordered two virgin margaritas, which made me cringe.

I stopped the waitress before she could leave. "Can I just have a water, please?"

She nodded and left. Robin turned to narrow his eyes at me. "Did you not understand the part about me ordering for both of us?"

"I don't order virgin drinks." I shifted uncomfortably, the lube I'd worked into myself slick between my bare cheeks.

His eyebrows lifted, and he wore that arrogant expression again. "Oh? I don't recall asking your preference, but do enlighten me as to why virgin drinks are beneath you."

"It's humiliating, that's why," I hissed. "If you order water, you might do it for any reason. Maybe the drinks don't appeal to you, or maybe you're just in the mood for water. No one knows. But if you order a virgin drink, you're advertising that you'd rather be having a real drink, but you're a candy-ass who can't handle booze."

If his eyebrows crept any higher, he would look like he'd had disastrous plastic surgery.

"Ah. Your issues with not wanting to be seen as weak are showing." Then a corner of his mouth quirked up. "You'll notice I ordered drinks for both of us. Am I a candy-ass who can't handle alcohol?"

"No, that's even worse." I shot him a baleful glare, wondering what I'd done to make him think I couldn't handle my liquor. "I don't even know why you ordered virgin. Hemophiliacs can drink, you know."

"Obviously, since you had a beer the other night. Thank you," Robin said to the waitress, who appeared with the drinks—my glass of water, but also the two margaritas Robin had ordered. He turned on the charm and handed her the menus we hadn't even glanced at. "We're going to have the marina dinner, and please make sure to space out the courses. We'd like to take our time and relax tonight."

"Of course!" She bounced away, and Robin gave me a long stare.

"The reason I'm not drinking—" he took a leisurely sip of his margarita; I had to admit, my mouth watered a bit at the thought of its tart lime bite "—is because I happen to like margaritas with seafood, but I need to be in full control of my faculties if we're going to play the way I intend to play. And so do you."

"Oh." Well, fuck. Now I felt like an idiot.

He tapped his finger against the base of his glass, then gave a nod. "I believe our agreement was that, as the client, I get what I want. I think you need a better understanding of who is in charge here tonight. Get up. We're taking a trip to the restroom."

He slid out of the booth, clearing the way for me to rise. I glanced around the sparsely populated dining room with more than a little anxiety.

I got to my feet and leaned close to him, hissing, "I am *not* going to let you fuck me in the men's room."

"As long as I'm the client, you'll let me do whatever the fuck I want." He reached over to the opposite bench and grabbed the briefcase, which I'd assumed he carried inside because he didn't want to risk it being stolen from his car. No one in their right mind would leave a case like that in the car in Boston, LA, or Chicago. "Go."

Trying not to appear conspicuous (yeah, right), I wove between the tables. I didn't dare look and see who might be staring. There were two restrooms, both unisex, and when I opened one, I saw they were single-room lavatories. No lines of stalls—and best of all, the door locked.

Robin slipped in behind me and flipped the latch. An instant later, the briefcase was on the floor and I was pinned against the wall, being kissed brutally.

Despite my resolution that we were not going to fuck in the john, I melted into it. Damn, but he tasted good, his lips and tongue tangy with lime. The spicy musk of his cologne was so subtle as to be practically subliminal, but he smelled absolutely delicious. His hands made quick work of my fly—being careful with the zipper, thank God—and reached inside to grasp me.

"*Fuck*," I whispered, biting my lips against a moan as my head fell gently back against the wall.

"Well, at least you've followed one of my instructions." Robin worked my dick until I was rigid and groaning. "You choose a safeword?"

I nodded, trying to focus my thoughts. "Bodysuit."

His eyebrow lifted, and I blushed. "Bodysuit?"

"Tattoos. Neck to wrist to ankle. It's called a bodysuit."

"Okay." He gave me a tight smile. "Turn around. Grab the railing there."

Panting, I obeyed, insensible of any objections I might have had. I needed him inside me now, and I didn't care where or how or who figured it out. Grasping the stainless-steel rail intended to assist customers with disabilities, I bent forward, pushing my ass back in offering. Robin slid my jeans down and caressed the taut halves of my ass, then pulled away.

I expected the sound of a zipper and the rustle of clothing. Instead, he bent to dig in the briefcase beside my feet. *Right. Condoms*, I reasoned, and closed my eyes.

After a moment, something slick pressed against my asshole. Too cold and unyielding to be human. Shit, was it—

"Whoa, wait." I tried to push myself up to standing, but he shoved me back down.

"Client, remember?" Robin said darkly, reminding me again of our roles, which frankly kept slipping my mind. "You're just a whore who'll do anything I say for money, and I say this plug's going up your ass. How long you have to keep it there depends on how well you adjust your attitude."

I whimpered, trying to relax, then blew out a slow breath and arched my spine to open myself a bit more. He worked that lubed plug in and out, going a millimeter deeper at a time. Jesus fucking Christ on a pogo stick, this was so incredibly bent. What did he intend to do, make me eat supper with that thing in there?

"Precisely." Robin's smug rejoinder brought my attention to the fact that I'd spoken aloud. Staying silent became more difficult the more intense the stretching became. He patiently worked until my ass allowed the plug to sink in. As it approached the widest portion, I gripped the bar with white knuckles and rested my head against the wall, shaking.

"Fuck. Oh, *fuck* . . ." God Almighty, how thick was that thing? If I hadn't lubed and stretched before I got dressed, it would have hurt.

"Just a little more." Another gentle push and it slipped inside, my body drawing it in, clamping down to squeeze that narrow stem before the flange.

"Christ!" I gasped, feeling my muscles clench, working to expel it.

Robin casually wiped some of the excess lube from where the plug was seated and turned away. "Go back to the table and sit. I'm sure the soup is already served, but wait for me before you begin to eat. I'll be there shortly."

Scarlet with humiliation, I did as I was told. I fastened my jeans with trembling fingers as he turned on the water and began to wash his hands.

"Yes, sir." Overwhelmed, I fled.

CHAPTER TEN

Geoff

If I thought I felt conspicuous before, it was nothing compared to trying to stroll casually through the restaurant without walking like I quite literally had something up my ass.

Then I sat down, and it was all I could do to keep from groaning loudly enough that the whole dining room would have heard. Jesus fuck, I was sweating—my hairline growing damp and beads rolling down my temples. It was a large plug, and I felt so fucking stretched and full. Each little shift sent a bolt of sensation through my cock. Every brush of denim was unendurable friction against the exposed head of my dick.

Our soup and salads were there, but I waited as I'd been told. There was no fucking way I was going to disobey anything Robin said ever again. Call me a wuss, but if he had worse than this up his sleeve tonight, I didn't want to test him. I really, really didn't.

Why was I putting up with this? I hadn't even considered using my safeword. Why wasn't I telling Robin that this was way over the line?

Maybe because I'd been more turned on these past couple of days by Robin than I had been by anyone in my life, ever. This shit might not have been what I'd intended, but it still felt. So. Damn. Good.

Robin was clearly no novice, but for me, having gone from *nothing* to *this* in the course of a couple of days was amazing.

Robin returned and set his briefcase on the opposite bench, sliding in next to me, pinning me in the booth. I stared at the leather case suspiciously, wondering what other methods of torment he might have stashed away.

"Please, help yourself." He picked up his role of magnanimous client easily as he gestured to my soup.

"You expect me to be able to eat like this?" I asked under my breath.

Robin's lips curled up at the corners, making him dimple. "You have no idea what I intend for the rest of the night. It might be advisable to keep your energy up."

With a frustrated sigh, I tried to focus my attention enough to eat.

As Robin had requested, they paced the meal so that I didn't eat so fast I felt stuffed after the first course. We had time to enjoy our soup and salad before the appetizers arrived, during which Robin seemed to break character to make conversation.

"So, you said you have an adopted sister?"

I nodded, smiling because I couldn't help but smile at the mention of Ling. "I do. She's amazing. We were close all through high school and even once I left for college. She chose to study art like I had. Well, she'll be the first to say she can't make art worth a damn—you and she are alike that way—but she has a good eye, and she's working on her graduate degree in art history. She might go into restoration and preservation, maybe become a curator."

Robin watched me as I spoke. My sappy smile never faded, except when I moved and thereby reminded myself of the plug up my ass.

"She sounds like a great sister," Robin said softly, mirroring my smile.

"She is." I looked down at the table, blushing. "She says if I decide I want kids with someone, she's going to be our surrogate, because she wants to make sure she gets to have a niece or nephew." I chuckled lightly. "Her heart's going to be broken if I end up with someone who doesn't want children."

"Wow. You miss her a lot?"

"Yeah, I do. We haven't lived near each other except for summer breaks for eight years now. We talk or email or text at least once a day most days. I hope someday we can settle down close to one another."

"And where is that going to be?"

"I have no idea." I sipped my margarita thoughtfully. "I don't think either of us is interested in returning to Colorado, but I'm not sure where I can really make it as a tattoo artist. I think in a large city like LA or Chicago, I'll get lost in the shuffle, no matter how good my work is. I don't fit most people's idea of a tattoo artist. I might have better luck going somewhere smaller and more conservative. I don't know."

Whatever Robin might have answered, it was interrupted by the arrival of a platter of deep-fried calamari, which I hadn't had in forever. But I barely had time to enjoy a few bites before Robin's hand slipped under the table to stroke the inside of my thigh and cup my crotch.

And just when I'd nearly forgotten my predicament, too. The erection that had slowly flagged began to swell back to life under my fly.

"I think you need a different appetizer." He had that smug look again. "Get down under the table."

"*What?*" I yelped loud enough for the closest tables behind our booth to hear. I couldn't help it. No. No fucking way did he expect me to—

"The waitress will be back one time in the next fifteen or twenty minutes before our main course arrives, to check on our drinks. She won't look down anyway, but even if she did, the tablecloth is long enough that there won't be anything to see." He arched an eyebrow at me. "I've been hard since I stuffed that plug up your ass, which I only did because you seemed to have forgotten our arrangement. Since it's your fault, you should be responsible for dealing with the problem. So get on the floor and deal with it."

"But—" I looked frantically around, searching for some excuse that he couldn't counter. "I can't—"

"You will." He continued to give me that calm, challenging stare, telling me without words that I had two choices: obey or safeword.

I was so close to choosing the second, but that taunting gaze mocked me. Damn it. I wasn't a submissive. I was too fucking moody and irascible to be submissive. But despite that, I was harder than I could ever remember being.

I was sure if I refused, we would go back to the hotel and have a perfectly satisfactory fuck. But that wasn't what I wanted. I wanted rough and dangerous. I could either take this chance while I had it, or give it up.

Robin leaned close enough to kiss, whispering, "Humiliation is just another brand of pain, isn't it?"

Fuck. Oh fuck, *yes*.

My dick was stiff and hot beneath the denim separating it from his stroking hand, and my ass was full, driving me slowly insane from the pressure. Finally, whatever it was within me that had been resisting this game threw up its hands and said *Fuck it*. I wanted to find out what he had brought to the table tonight, and the only way to do that was to go with it.

Moaning softly as the plug pressed against my prostate, I glanced around to make sure nobody could see, and slipped into the cramped space under the table.

Robin parted his legs to make room, and reached down to open his fly and pull out his cock. I grabbed for it, but he batted my hand away and threaded the fingers of his other hand through my hair, drawing me in and feeding his cock to me.

I don't know why that made it hotter than if I'd gone after his dick myself, but it did. That little loss of volition nearly had me moaning before I remembered not to. He slipped between my lips, deliciously salty, the heavy scent of musk surrounding me. I sucked with an eagerness that belied all my earlier protestations. As in the restroom, my reservations lasted only as long as it took for him to get his hands on me.

His fingers rested on my scalp, guiding me. I didn't even need that much pressure. Once I had him in my mouth, I was completely absorbed. I wished he would use more force, though I knew this wasn't the time or place for something that rough. I let him urge me up and down, his other hand above the table. I could envision him up there, eating calamari and pretending to be nonchalant while I worked myself into a sweat down here.

I nearly banged my head on the bottom of the table when the waitress spoke above me.

"How's the calamari?"

"Perfect, thank you."

"Your date doesn't care for it?" There was a smile in her voice.

"He's just in the mood for something else tonight," Robin answered casually. "I'm sure he'll finish it when he comes back to the table."

"Would either of you like another drink?"

"Absolutely, for both of us." I could imagine the charming smile Robin wore to brighten his tone in that way. Unable to resist the sudden surge of mischief that tickled me, I sucked harder and faster.

"All right, I'll get those out to you, and your entrées will be along shortly. Will you want to see the dessert menu tonight?"

"Please." Robin's hand tightened on my hair in warning, and I could hear a bit of strain entering his voice. "And we'll have some coffee after dinner as well."

"Of course. It's warm on this side of the restaurant, isn't it? Would you like me to check the thermostat for you?"

"No, no," he said quickly. "I'll take off my jacket if it gets uncomfortable."

If my mouth hadn't been otherwise occupied, I would have grinned in satisfaction. Robin's low grumble reached me under the table.

"You are in so much trouble when we leave."

He did not, however, stop me from picking up the pace, even though it meant his responses to the waitress were monosyllabic when she brought another round. His hand went slack on my hair when she left, letting me have my way, and I took the time to enjoy the control he ceded. I forgot, even, how uncomfortable I was, crammed under the table with a plug pressing against my prostate and my dick pinched by the folds of my fly.

I slid my tongue along the veins and tendon, and drew back to push it firmly against his slit until more salt tingled my taste buds. I thought I heard him groan at that.

Then his fingers pushed hard against my scalp again. His cock swelled, stretching my jaw, and his hips came off the bench two, three times before I felt the first surge. A moment later, thick fluid pulsed over my tongue and his entire body relaxed. His hand stroked my hair languidly.

"Coast is clear," he murmured as I swallowed. I crawled back up to my seat, suppressing a groan at the shifting of the plug. Then I licked my lips and gave him a satisfied smirk.

"Great appetizer." I popped a piece of calamari in my mouth, washing the residue of cum and squid alike down with my margarita.

Robin chuckled, his fair complexion flushed. I wasn't the only one with sweat darkening the edges of my hair.

He turned suddenly and hooked a hand around the back of my head, pulling me into a quick kiss. "It's going to be fun, trying to keep you on your toes."

"Think you're up for the task?"

"Maybe, maybe not." He drew away and grinned, reaching for his drink. "But it's the trying that's the fun part."

The rest of the dinner proceeded unremarkably, except for the plug driving me insane by steady but persistent measures. I enjoyed talking with Robin, which really wasn't something I'd tried with a hookup. He was interesting and funny and sexy, and he seemed to enjoy what I had to say. I was glad that we hadn't fucked that first night. If we had, it would have been hella enjoyable, yeah, but ultimately a one-night stand. What we were doing now couldn't have happened if we hadn't had to step back and get to know each other.

Nonetheless, I could have strangled him for making us dawdle over coffee and dessert. Walking to the car with his hand riding on the upper curve of my ass was enough to buckle my knees. I whimpered when I finally sank into the seat of his sporty BMW. As he drove, he continued to tease me. It wasn't far to get back to the resort, but by the time we arrived, I could barely walk.

"Please." I groaned as he slipped his arm around me for support. "Please tell me you're taking this fucking thing out soon."

"When I'm ready." Robin nipped the shell of my ear softly. "When we get inside, I want you to go straight to your room, get naked, pull the covers all the way down, stand in the corner, face the wall, and wait for me. Do *not* look around."

I nodded, rushing to do what he demanded. Anything that brought me closer to ending my torment. I didn't even bother to check if Jace was in his room as I hurried into my own and stripped, then peeled back the covers and stood as I'd been instructed. I heard Robin in the kitchen, though what he retrieved I couldn't say. He came in and closed the door. I heard him set something on the dresser. Then a bottle of water appeared on the table beside me.

Robin's hand caressed my back, making me shiver. His fingers moved on the nape of my neck, slowly creeping around to my throat. They brushed the upper edge of my collarbone, and I shivered again. I swayed, mesmerized by the light caresses, but for all he acknowledged, it might have been someone else's hand playing along my skin.

Then he was gone again, spreading another sheet over the bed with an efficient snap. I stared at it in confusion.

"What did I say about looking around?" Robin demanded, and I quickly turned my head away. "Guess we'll take care of that problem sooner rather than later."

There was more rustling behind me, and he laid a folded length of black fabric—silk?—across my eyes and tied it firmly behind my head. Only a sliver of light remained in my peripheral vision. Not enough to see what Robin was doing.

I heard a match strike behind me, the smell of burning sulfur hitting my nostrils. He struck several more in sequence, and the sliver of light I was able to discern dimmed and flickered. He'd turned off the lamps and set candles.

"Lie down." He pressed one hand to my back and, grasping my arm with the other, guided me the few steps toward the bed. "On your stomach."

It wasn't until I felt the roughness of terry cloth under me that I realized he'd also covered the bed in towels. What the fuck did he have planned? The fabric chafed my half-hard dick, and I humped against it, finding the friction delicious and frustrating. Robin's hands spread my ass, tugging at the plug lodged in my hole. Pushing, I helped him remove it before sinking back down with a relieved sigh. "Thank God."

I laid my cheek on the pillow and watched that sliver of wavering light. Robin barely gave me time to relax before he wiped away the leftover lube. Then he pushed my cheeks apart, and I felt his breath an instant before his tongue began stroking at the edges of my stretched hole. I gasped, my voice dropping to a breathless whisper. "Oh, sweet Jesus."

He took his time licking me, and I melted into it: warm and wet. I thought my asshole would be less sensitive after having that plug in for well over an hour, but that didn't seem to be the case. I moaned again and again, my hips lifting and wriggling as he pushed and prodded, kneading the halves of my ass.

"Don't get too comfortable." He drew away with a final lick, caressing up and down my spine. "I haven't gotten my money's worth out of you."

"Huh?" Lost in sensation, it took me a while to remember his game.

"Don't move." His fingers curled loosely around the front of my throat, crossing my larynx. He didn't squeeze or put any pressure into the touch at all, and yet their presence was like hitting a switch. I shuddered once, then went stock-still. I could feel the weight of his hand as I swallowed.

His other hand skimmed over my ribs, my shoulders, down my back to the upper curve of my ass. Goose bumps prickled my flesh, and I drew in a shaky breath. I wasn't sure what to make of the fact that, despite the demonstration with the plug and the safeword and everything, he was being so slow and careful. I'd hoped he would set upon me as savagely as he'd pushed me against that tree the other night, but for the moment what he was doing felt good.

"Roll over."

When I was on my back, his mouth brushed my lips. I sighed and opened to him, but he jerked back.

"I said don't move."

Jesus, but when his voice got chilly like that, I could feel it in my cock, having the exact opposite effect of cold. Of course, I was feeling just about everything in my cock right then.

Puzzled, I lay passive as he traced the outline of my lips with his tongue, and then the inside. Jesus, it felt good. I moaned softly, trying to press closer and deepen the kiss as his tongue nudged my teeth apart.

Once again he laid his hand across my throat, the web of his thumb hooked under my chin. He still didn't squeeze, but the positioning was full of menace. It froze me, left me lying there trembling.

"Do. Not. Move." He pulled me forward with a little pressure under the hinges of my jaw.

He then proceeded to fuck my mouth with his tongue. There was no other way to describe it. Holding my throat in a grip that commanded me to utter passivity, he pushed his tongue into my mouth, brushing it against my own, against my teeth, against the roof of my mouth, moving it in and out while I lay inactive. It wasn't a kiss; a kiss takes two, requires a response, but he wouldn't let me kiss him back. I had no word for what this was, except that it left me feeling rather like an inanimate object whose only purpose was to *receive*.

He was using me. As if I were a toy or doll. As if I weren't even real.

It should have been bizarre. Instead it was hot, and I had no idea why. It was unlike anything anyone had done with me before. Hell, I'd never even heard of someone doing this to someone else.

"Don't move." He shoved his other hand under my ass cheek, squeezing, fingering my crack while he resumed tongue-fucking my mouth.

I wanted to move. I wanted to open my mouth and seal that kiss. I wanted to wriggle or writhe with his caresses on my ass, to push back and greet the finger that wedged itself in my crevice, then retreated. Just as frustration was on the verge of overwhelming the strange fascination that kept me still, he withdrew.

"Onto your stomach again."

It was tempting to come back with something snappy and smart-assed now that he wasn't menacing me with the notion of strangling, but I obeyed, my body reacting before my mind was fully on board. And what was that about? He was barely touching me and not allowing me to touch him at all . . . and I was *permitting* it.

I frowned, some of the weird passivity falling away. I was freshly infused, able to do just about anything. I wanted it all, wanted rough and wild, dangerous and scary and painful. I didn't want a guy who thought he had to handle me like I was fragile. If that was what Robin thought he was going to do, I might as well stop.

The sound of Robin stripping rustled behind me, and then he rummaged in the bedside table. Something hit my hip. Lube and condoms, I thought. Something else clinked on the nightstand before Robin crawled onto the mattress beside me.

I debated whether to say something, to warn him that handling me delicately would torpedo this faster than anything. But I wanted to see where he intended to take this. I defied his admonition against moving long enough to fold my arms under my head and turn to watch the flicker of candlelight under the blindfold, my discontent building at this meticulous, almost disconnected encounter.

"Are you trying to look?" he asked, a note of censure in his voice, and he adjusted the blindfold, closing off even the sliver of light. I bit back an argument, thoroughly perplexed. If he was going to go all dom on me, surely he'd be doing it more roughly, so what the fuck was happening?

Troubled, I buried my head in my arms and tried to relax, tried to remember the arousal and fascination that had brought me this far. But inside, a voice was taunting that I'd known all along this was futile, that he could talk a good game, but in the end he wouldn't have the balls to play the way I wanted to play.

Robin's fingertips continued to explore me lightly, his lips trailing in their wake. His breath warmed my skin.

It didn't feel unpleasant, but it wasn't what I *wanted*. It wasn't what he'd implied with his talk of safewords. After waiting several minutes for him to pick up the pace, I finally pushed myself up with a low growl of annoyance, ripping off the blindfold.

"If I wanted a *safe, careful* fuck," I said, letting contempt hang on those hated words, "I wouldn't have told you all that shit earlier."

In an instant, his hand was on my throat once more, adding the smallest bit of pressure this time. He reached for the bedside table, and I saw something glint before his weight pressed me back down onto the mattress.

"You're mistaking being in control for being careful." His tone was stern. "If I want to take my time enjoying you, I'm going to take my fucking time. And *you*"—something hard, chilly, and flat whispered down my cheek toward my jaw, coming to a stop before it curved under to my neck—"are going to lie there and take it. Aren't you?"

Fear congealed in my chest. I realized what he held an instant before he pulled it back far enough for me to get a glimpse. A knife.

A large pocketknife. He caressed my cheek with the back of the blade, then let the very point rest against my skin.

"Aren't you?"

My heart raced at a jackrabbit pace, my breath suddenly short and shallow. A cold sweat prickled along my skin. He was holding a knife to my face. A knife! What the *fuck* was he thinking? I wanted to throw him off and run away. I wanted to shoot out of that bed and demand to know what the hell he thought he was doing. I didn't dare. Not with that knife touching me.

Then I understood why he was waiting for an answer.

Bodysuit.

I almost said it. It was right there on the tip of my tongue. My mind spun.

The very first night we met, there on the dance floor in the club, he'd asked me if I wanted danger. I had sighed wistfully and said I did. And I'd told him I wanted to be forced.

He was giving me *exactly* what I'd asked for; he was just doing it in a way I'd never come close to expecting.

"I can make you scream without ever leaving a mark."

Now I knew how easily he could keep that promise.

Then I was more turned on than I had ever been in my entire life. Even in the midst of my terror—and it *was* terror, sharp and primal, filling my throat with the metallic tang of adrenaline and bunching all my muscles in the instinctive drive toward flight or fight—I was ready to hump the bed. I would have done so if I'd dared to move. Hard, throbbing, aching, I would have exploded at the smallest brush.

The blade of the knife had stolen the warmth from my skin, and he was still waiting for an acknowledgment. Swallowing, I whispered, "Yes."

He caressed my cheek with the dull edge of the blade. "You gonna be good for me, baby? Or am I gonna have to hurt you?"

"I'll be good." I shuddered, my breath hitching. He laid the knife, still open, on the nightstand in front of my eyes, taunting me with it —or perhaps letting me know I had options if I really didn't feel safe and couldn't remember my safeword.

I stared at it, transfixed, while he pulled away. I was barely aware of his actions until his fingers slipped into the crack of my ass, dripping with lube. Then I moaned, my ass lifting, offering itself without my volition.

"Don't. Fucking. Move," Robin snarled, and his index finger nudged at my well-loosened and slightly sore hole. With a sigh, I let my hips drop back onto the towels, my cock rubbing against a cool smear of pre-cum.

Then he wrapped the blindfold across my eyes and blocked out everything again.

CHAPTER ELEVEN

Geoff

His hands were gone, and I heard a rustle and an ominously familiar crystalline clinking. "Wait—"

Before I could protest, though, a chilly drop of water splashed onto my taint, and he quickly pushed a melting ice cube into my ass.

"Oh *fuck!*" I yelped, my nerves having trouble deciding if I was being burned or frozen. I pushed myself up from the bed, ready to rip the blindfold off again and yell, but his hand between my shoulder blades forced me back down. "Stop—"

"Not yet," he growled in my ear. "I haven't gotten my money's worth *yet*. But I damn well mean to. Don't. Move."

I could feel that fucking thing *melting*, sending confused impulses through my prostate, which sped along my nerves to my cock. Cool water pooled inside me, gradually warming and then mingling with more cool water as the ice continued to dissolve.

"Fuck," I whispered, shivering. "Oh fuck."

More clinking against the glass on the table, and then there was another ice cube—not up my ass, but rubbing lightly along my balls and perineum. I yelped again, this time more loudly, bucking without meaning to. If there was one positive thing to say, it was that my erection—which had been plaguing me since the introduction of the plug—disappeared. All organs indigenous to that particular region tried to shrivel up into my abdomen. I trembled as if I were standing outside, naked in a blizzard, damn near quaking. Every part the ice touched became so cold it burned and ached, but never quite got cold enough to go completely numb.

The next ice cube trailed along my spine, melting in small rivulets that trickled down my ribs and waist. The one after that melted against the sensitive skin of my inner thighs.

"Jesus, stop. Please, stop."

"What the client wants, the client gets." He stroked another ice cube over my ass cheeks, and then one across my shoulders and even along the insides of my arms as I whimpered, not quite daring to try to get away. "I did warn you that there would be consequences for noncompliance, didn't I?"

"Yes, but—" I gasped as something freezing cold and heavy and much more substantial than an ice cube began to work its way into my wet ass. "Oh *Christ*! What the fuck is that?"

"Stainless steel." I could hear the smirk in Robin's voice. "Can be frozen, refrigerated, even dipped in or run under warm or hot water."

And ridged too. I felt each bump pass through my sphincter, and *oh Jesus* it was freezing me from the inside out.

"Please, I can't—"

"Would you like me to warm you up?"

"Please! Yes!" I panted, squirming, trying to get away from that relentless chill pervading me from the waist down.

"All right." Robin wiped the water that had run off my back. I felt his hands on me and smelled . . . olive oil?

"Please, take it out." I was damn near whining. The rational part of my mind knew that eventually the metal shaft would acquire the heat of my body and warm up, but I didn't think I could bear its icy presence inside me, pressed against my prostate, long enough for that to happen. It was, after all, a substantial dildo, which meant it would be slow to heat up.

"Not yet. I have other ways of warming you."

Robin's hands *were* warm, smoothing the oil over my back, massaging lightly. But then they were gone. His weight left the bed, returning a moment later.

"I recommend you hold quite still." I barely had an instant to shudder and go immobile before something hit my back. A *plop* at first, but the instant after it landed, it was hot enough to be startling. I don't know if it cooled or if my nerve endings adapted, but the spot of heat quickly became bearable.

"What—" And then a small stream of *plops*, light and brief, not painful at all for the first split second, then shockingly warm. The smell of burning wax reached me, and I realized what the *plops* were. "Oh *fuck* . . ."

I wanted to protest, but my muscles, even those of my vocal chords, locked up. The next drizzle was still light, but denser, hotter. The one after that was even more so, approaching the point of discomfort. The hotter they were when they landed, the longer they took to harden and cool, and the more painful they were.

"How does that feel?" Robin murmured, gently peeling up one of the early lines, which came off my skin easily thanks to the olive oil.

"How do you think it fucking feels?" I grated. "It's fucking burning."

"Not quite. If it were actually burning, you'd be yelling a lot more, not just gasping."

The next time the wax fell on my skin, it wasn't in a cluster of small drips, but in an actual stream—small, but thicker and heavier than before, and far hotter.

"Oh God!" I groaned, writhing as I waited for the layer on my back to cool and congeal. The wriggling moved the stainless-steel dildo in my ass, rubbing the cold ridges against my prostate, and then I groaned for another reason entirely. My nerves, still frayed from that session with the plug and from the ice skating across my skin, were approaching the point of overload. I was having trouble making sense of what was hot and what was cold, what hurt and what felt good. "I don't think I can—"

"You can." Robin's lips tugged at my earlobe, his voice dipping to a sexy murmur. "You want this, because you *need* to know if you can take it. If you can't endure this, how will you ever endure that whipping you want so badly, the one that makes you bleed?"

I shuddered and humped the bed, immediately caught up in the fantasy that had thrilled me time and again, imagining small lines of fire streaking down my back, slicing me open with shallow little cuts from which my defective blood would well and trickle. Robin took the opportunity to fuck me in slow, shallow strokes with the dildo, the ridges bumping back and forth through my twitching ring of muscle. Beginning to warm up now, it just felt good, and I lost myself in it, in the delicious fullness and pressure, the easy glide of those bumps.

"Fuck . . . Fuck, Robin . . ."

He tutted. "I didn't give you permission to call me by name, whore." He drew the dildo out abruptly. When it came back, it was freezing cold again, and thicker than before.

"There are two ends to it," Robin explained. "This one is fatter. Fucking huge, really. The size of cocks we usually only see in porn films and on the exceptionally gifted."

I wanted to make a quip about his own attributes, which were by no means insubstantial, but my brain had given up language as a losing proposition. He stuffed that fat dildo in me, filling me so full I thought I might burst with it and freezing me all over again. While I was gasping and groaning, trying to adapt to the new intensity, he poured another dense stream of wax down my shoulder.

"Jesus!" I yelped, bucking and twisting, which only made the presence of the steel sheathed in my ass all the more intense. The wax wasn't cooling, didn't feel like it would ever cool. It just sat, massed on my skin, hot and heavy, condensing. "Jesus, *fuck!*"

No sooner had it begun to cool than there was another, and another. Each time he seemed to pour more wax, or the wax itself seemed hotter, and I couldn't figure why it was getting hotter—

"I'm moving the candle closer to your skin," Robin answered, cluing me in to the fact that I'd gasped the question aloud. "The less time it has to travel through the air, the hotter it is when it arrives. Just how much will it take to make you scream, I wonder?"

"Please. God, please!" I didn't really know what I was begging for, but it didn't seem to matter, because Robin poured another stream of wax down my spine.

"You're to address me as 'sir.'"

"Please, sir! Take it off . . . Please . . ." No matter how I squirmed and wriggled, I couldn't seem to shake that line free. Worse, my movements made it spread, reaching across my skin in hot tendrils. It burned. He had to be burning me now . . .

"No." His voice was calm, implacable, and he did it again, moving to my as-yet-untouched lower back.

Moans turned to whimpers. Whimpers turned to quiet, keening wails. And the wails rapidly escalated to yells.

"I knew I could make you scream." By now it felt like my whole back had been burned, intense and persistent in some spots and slowly receding in others. Still he refused to relent, going back over territory he'd already seared, from which he'd peeled the wax away, and adding hotter, thicker rivulets. I danced against the surface of the bed with each new, scalding puddle that splashed onto my skin, and every motion stirred the dildo, over and over. I was rapidly approaching the point of insensibility.

"You look so fucking good, moving like that. And you sound even better." I could only imagine the words were meant to be encouragement. I trembled, limp and panting, waiting for the next assault on my nerve endings. But Robin merely drew the dildo out of my ass.

"If I had more time, I'd have you shave your ass and balls and thighs, and pour wax over them too. Ah well. Maybe another night. Roll over."

No sooner had I obeyed than there was ice again. The runoff pooled in my navel, chilling me until I was flaccid. Robin took me in his cool, wet hands and stroked me to fullness. That was better. I could cope with that. I moaned, sinking back into the bed and letting myself enjoy it.

Which was, of course, when he grabbed another ice cube and wrapped the hand holding it around the end of my dick, pressing it against my frenulum. I howled again and nearly came off the bed, shouting for him to *Stop, stop, take it away, please God, take it away.*

When he wiped off the water and started to massage olive oil over my chest and stomach, I began begging in earnest.

"Fuck . . . Oh, fuck no. Not the wax. Not there. Jesus, please . . ."

I checked out. Disconnected. Felt like I was having an out-of-body experience. Everything hurt, but it didn't seem to touch me, except to leave me strangely euphoric. Not like when my joints hurt *at all.* The fresh clumps of wax on the sensitive skin of my belly still scalded, and I could hear myself moaning and wailing, begging for mercy, but it felt like the words were coming from another person, one who didn't really matter because I was somewhere else.

There were no more streams, and his fingers were working more lube into me. I heard the sound of a condom being rolled on, and then he pushed my knees up and apart, and slid easily into my ass.

"*Fuck*." He panted, shuddering. "Even after all that, you're tighter than you were yesterday."

The cold and the pain *had* tightened me. With my muscles no longer numb from that freezing steel dildo, and sore from all the stretching, I felt every goddamned inch of him working in and out, rocking, pushing up against my prostate as he angled for the sweet spot.

I began to beg for something else entirely, for Robin to fuck me harder, to keep going. He obliged, releasing my knees and letting me hook them over his hips, my ankles riding his ass. But then there was another piece of ice, again chilling my nipples to hard, painful points. I cried out, clamping down on him, and he growled in response.

"Fuck, yeah, that's it. Squeeze harder, bitch. I wanna feel like mine's the only cock you've ever taken."

The ice cube melted, and I relaxed. He stroked in and out, pumping his hand up and down my dick until I was hard again and the skin of his fingers and palm had lost their chill. Then he went still. His hand disappeared, and my entire world ignited as he poured a thick layer of wax directly on one of my cold, diamond-hard nipples.

I screamed. There was no other word for it. It was too sharp and shrill to be a yell or a bellow. I screamed like he'd touched my nub with the burning end of a hot cigar, not merely a heavy glob of wax. It burned and burned and burned, and I felt like it was incinerating me.

He began to thrust again. My entire body clenched and shuddered, and he had to work harder to move his dick in and out of my ass, forcing me loose again. The cycle started all over on the other side, and my screams got even louder, shriller, mingled with incoherent babbles that could have been absolutely anything, from desperate pleas for him to stop to prayers for divine intervention.

He plowed into me, ruthless, unyielding, no matter how hard I clamped around him, no matter how powerfully I shuddered. It took so long for that wax to cool; surely my skin would be blistered.

He gripped my dick and jerked me again. "Come for me, bitch.

Come now, or I swear to fucking God I'll pour the rest of the wax right on your fucking cock."

I wailed, and for a terrified eternity it didn't seem like I *could* come. There had been too much hurt, too much cold, too many times when I'd been aroused and then pulled back. I was tired, fucking exhausted, my nerves jagged, and how was I supposed to come like that when I felt like the last of my energy was being spent keeping myself open to him?

I strained and struggled while he stroked my cock, sliding the skin back and forth with frightening strength and speed.

Then his hand was gone, and I sobbed again, knowing what was coming, trying to reach for my cock to finish myself off so he wouldn't do it. But he slapped my hand away, and something searing touched my dick.

I shrieked and erupted, coming in agonizing bursts, my body locking up with each spasm as it surged through me from my balls outward. I couldn't even feel the cum that splattered onto my chest over the layer of wax.

I came back to find myself whimpering and moaning. Robin's wet hand peeled the blindfold off my eyes and his lips were on mine, kissing me even though I was unresponsive, too overloaded to return it.

"It's okay. Shh. I've got you."

"My dick!" I gasped when that first stunned moment had passed. I was too horrified to be angry, though I wanted the accusation to carry more weight than my helpless, boneless state would allow. "You poured wax on my *dick*."

"Shh, no, I didn't." He kissed me again. "I promise, I didn't. It was ice. Just ice. Your mind tricked you into thinking it was wax."

My eyes fluttered open, and for a moment even the flickering light of the candles seemed too glaring. Blinking in disbelief, I realized he was telling the truth. There was no heat on my cock from still-cooling wax, only a residual chilly numbness and a sensitivity so keen that even the weight of his body resting on mine was agony.

It took every last bit of fortitude I had not to whimper. I trembled beneath him as he pressed gentle kisses all over my face.

"It's okay. I've got you. Shh. You're okay."

I was okay. He'd run me through the wringer, fucking my mind as thoroughly as my body. My skin was too big, too alive, every nerve aflame. My hips and knees were aching from being spread and wrapped around him . . .

My hips and knees. I did a quick mental inventory and realized nothing was damaged.

It felt like it had been hours, eons, since I thought about my hemophilia. Not since he brought out the knife. After that, I'd stopped thinking about anything at all. All I'd done was *feel*.

God, had I felt. Pain and panic and pleasure—but not worry. Never worry.

My shaking grew stronger at the thought, though I had no idea why.

Robin drew back and put his fingertips under my chin, compelling me to meet his eyes. "Okay?"

"Sure," I said readily, eagerly, nodding like a bobblehead.

Then I burst into tears.

CHAPTER TWELVE

Robin

Geoff was flying, and he wasn't coming down anytime soon. Which thrilled me. I'd delivered exactly what he needed, if his teary babbling was any indication. I loved listening to it, loved knowing I'd given him the experience he'd been yearning for probably since he hit sexual maturity.

I basked in it, held him while he lay there, half-insensible. His tears had subsided, but he was still having a hard time making his body and brain connect again. I made him drink several times from the bottle of water I'd placed beside the bed, and he guzzled it as though its cool moisture was the most delicious thing he'd ever tasted.

I was buzzed myself, drained and yet high from launching him into subspace and taking care of him in the aftermath. God, I'd missed this feeling. I'd known topping him was going to be a hell of a ride, but holy *fuck* we had some amazing chemistry in a scene. The connection I'd felt with him all evening, the way our energy had fed off one another, was just *intense.*

So different from that last year with Kyle, when all our scenes had ended with me feeling like I couldn't give him what he needed. That, or with anger because I *wouldn't* give him what he demanded.

When Geoff finally settled again, a dreamy smile on his face, I picked up the knife. Instantly, his gaze sharpened, and he gave me a questioning look.

"I'd suggest you keep very, very still," I said gently, and with complete confidence. I was getting tired, but I needed to keep him in that place where he knew, no matter what I did, he was safe in my hands.

"Oh, God, no," Geoff whispered, quivering.

"Shh." I brushed a kiss over his lips. "Just let it go. It's all on me now."

The knife had been a really big gamble. We hadn't negotiated something that edgy, and normally I wouldn't have introduced it without a discussion first. But I'd spent all day trying to figure out ways of giving him the sense of being forced that he wanted, without resorting to manhandling him into compliance in ways that might be injurious. The knife was what I'd settled on.

There was psychological currency in using something that would specifically speak to the part of him that had such a . . . *complicated* . . . relationship with the concept of bleeding.

Which was what I wanted to investigate now that he was returning from orbit.

"How do you feel, knowing I've got a knife against your skin?" I asked mildly as I laid the flat of the knife flush against his skin and began to carefully pry the hardened globs of wax up. Once the edges were loosened, they often came up easily, courtesy of the oil. Thankfully, he had no chest hair to speak of.

I saw him come to the gradual realization that he was still safe, even with that knife scrape-scrape-scraping at his skin. The fretful expression that had crept in was replaced slowly by bliss, and he sank back into the mattress like all his bones had melted.

"I asked you a question, Geoff." I didn't want him checking out entirely again.

His pale lashes fluttered as he licked his lips and frowned. I was sure he was going to ask me to repeat the inquiry, but finally he murmured, "Strange. Afraid. Contradictory."

I peeled a long stream off his abs, which twitched as the wax caught the fine, tiny hairs close to his navel. "Want to elaborate for me?"

"I know—" He swallowed and started again. "I know you won't cut me. And I know if you do, it'll be something minor. I'm infused, so it won't be a problem. But—"

"But your lizard brain is still telling you you're in danger of bleeding, and for you, the idea of bleeding has all sorts of baggage attached?"

He nodded slowly, licking his lips again.

"But that video you sent me. That sub bled. You want that."

His lips curved. "People want to jump off bridges with just a bouncy cord keeping them from going splat. Doesn't mean it doesn't scare the piss out of them. Oh!"

I was below his navel now, where the hair was getting a bit denser. His startled exclamation was followed by a hiss, and something evil inside me loved that sound. I yanked the next blob of wax harder, grinning at him, and he whimpered and moaned, and his eyes started to look less focused again.

His skin twitched reflexively when the blade touched his groin next. He tensed, bracing himself for the next pull.

The nick was accidental, a minuscule zig when I should have zagged.

I wasn't going to let him know that. I'd be damned if I let alarm and fear ruin this for him. I saw the nick register, saw his eyes fly open, but I didn't react. I gathered up a bead of his blood on my fingertip and held it up for him to see.

"And now you've bled for me." I kept my voice level, confident. He'd said he was infused and that minor cuts were no big deal, so that's how I was going to handle it.

The expression that he rewarded me with was sublime. He stared at that crimson drop, transfixed, and it was like he'd never seen it before. In this context, as something he didn't need to worry about, it was new.

I brought my finger to his lips, and his tongue snaked out to flick the bead away. He closed his eyes, and his hips bucked. His cock filled quickly, and he gave me a look of raw need. What was it about him that made me powerless not to respond?

I closed the knife with a *snap* and tossed it aside. Then I rolled him over, and my fingers were in his ass again, parting him. I hadn't come yet, though I wasn't sure he had realized that until now. I was still hard, sheathed in the condom, but I'd stopped fucking him so he could recover from that first orgasm.

He was going to feel fucking *incredible* around my dick. My nuts were pulled up so tight, so very close to climax, that just about anything could have pushed me over. He shifted restlessly, trying to urge me to do more, and that was no good. I wrapped my hand around his throat again.

"Don't even think you call the shots here." I nipped his earlobe firmly enough to be sure I'd leave a bruise. He moaned softly. I sawed my fingers in and out, fucking him harder, faster. "*I've* got the knife. *I've* got the hand on your throat." I tightened my grasp minutely to emphasize that point. "I've got my fingers shoved up your ass, and if you even think of fighting, I will make you *very* sorry. This is my show. I've got the control, and you're going to do *exactly* what you're told."

He still wasn't a sub. I knew that. But he needed to know I had it under control, and I needed to give him that. He went passive beneath me, heavy and still, as if weights were dragging his limbs down, making him helpless and compliant. As if he'd been drugged.

"Yes," he whispered, shivering.

"Yes, what?"

"Yes . . . sir."

Fuck, that was nice. I hummed softly. "Good. Get up on your knees and spread your ass open for me."

I drew my fingers out, and Geoff moved slowly, as if in a trance. He got his knees under him, pressed the side of his face into the pillow, and reached back, pulling his ass cheeks apart for me.

"Fucking whore." He jumped as I spat directly on his asshole with a sharp, explosive sound. Muscle and wrinkled skin twitched at the impact, the spittle running down his taint and balls. I rubbed the head of my cock up and down, smearing it across his skin. "You want it, don't you? Want me to stick my dick in you and fuck your brains out. Don't you?"

"Yes, sir." His voice was tight, the back of his neck a deep red. When I reached beneath him, a bead of pre-cum dripped from his cock onto the towels.

"I think I'm going to enjoy that," I said cheerfully, and pressed against his hole.

I didn't rush, not even a little. Millimeter by painstaking millimeter, I breached him, mustering every shred of control I had to drag this out, when what I really wanted was to lay into him. I leaned forward and curled my hand around the front of his throat, and he *melted*, going slack before me. God, that was amazing. A moment later, I was buried balls-deep.

"*Fuck*, you feel good," I grated.

Geoff damn near mewled. It was an effort to pick up my monologue again, to give him that edge of humiliation that would keep him out of his head and far from worrying about what was happening to his body. I could barely concentrate, spitting a stream-of-consciousness trickle of epithets and raunchy promises. They erupted from my lips each time I pushed deeper, harder.

"Jesus . . . For a whore you're the tightest piece of ass I've ever . . . Fuck. Gonna go balls-deep . . . gonna pound the *fuck* outta you."

"Yes." He rocked to try to hurry me along. I wrenched back control, restraining him by tightening the hand around his throat again. "*Please*. Please . . ." he begged.

That pleading was too much. He was beyond dignity, beyond pride. He'd say anything he had to say to get me to give him what he needed, and *fuck* that was a heady feeling. I rolled my hips against him, our moans rising in unison, and gradually picked up the pace.

"Fuck . . . Oh, fuck, you *bitch* . . ." I grunted, slapping his ass with my pelvis. Beads of sweat dripped off my brow to splatter onto his back and buttocks.

"Oh God . . . Harder. Come on. Please," he groaned, once again trying to rush me. Then his knee moved, a small shift in position that distributed his weight differently.

I went still, reaching past him to grab the knife.

Geoff froze.

"Who's in charge here?" I demanded coldly.

He whimpered. "You—you are, sir!"

I laid the point of the knife between his shoulder blades, not *quite* firmly enough to prick, but enough to make him clench in fear that it might.

"*Don't* fucking forget it again."

I used the dull edge of the knife to trace random lines down his shoulders and spine, ignoring the tightening grip of his ass around my cock, watching for other cues from his body.

Another shift, and I knew it wasn't impatience or greed but discomfort, seeking a different position. I felt his attention and energy being pulled away from me toward the problems with his joints like a sour note spoiling the heady symphony of emotion and sensation. The longer it persisted, the harder it would be for *any* of this to feel good for him.

I stopped moving, not dropping out of character entirely, but backing off enough to give him room to communicate freely. "Your knees are bothering you?"

I watched the resistance grip him and bleed away. I could have fist-pumped and shouted in celebration when, instead of denying it, he nodded against the pillow.

"Lie on your side," I instructed, sternly enough to let him know that I still had this under my control as I guided him down. He sighed and stretched out with his back to me. That sigh told me a lot about how he felt regarding this concession to his physical limitations, but I wasn't going to let that ruin the scene for us, not after we'd come so far. I slicked more lube on my cock, pressed against his back, and shoved into him roughly. When his moan had faded, I lightly grasped his throat once more and growled, "From now on, if you've got a problem and you don't tell me right away, there will be consequences that will make sitting in a restaurant with a plug up your ass feel like a walk in the park. Got me?"

"Yes!" he gasped, clutching a handful of bedding.

"You didn't think I was done with you, did you?" I taunted. I thrust my top arm between his thighs, lifting the upper one, spreading him open while supporting the weight of his leg so he didn't have to.

"N-no!" Anything else he might have said was lost in the hard pace I set, hammering into him. I could tell by his yelps each time I nailed his prostate. I could feel him hanging on the edge.

"Your ass is still mine." I scraped his shoulder with my teeth. Not a bite, no, but a threat. Menacing. I *could* bruise him or make him bleed. There wasn't a damn thing he could do to stop me.

But I also wanted him to know that I wouldn't.

I think the message got through, because his groans and shouts became more desperate. My dick was so hard and tight it ached, driving into his clenching ass. His cock dripped, the fluid drying into tacky trails down his foreskin.

"What a slut." I slammed into him over and over. "Threaten you with a knife, damn near choke you, and you're still dying for it, aren't you?"

"Yes!"

I rammed him hard enough to jolt his whole body.

"Yes, *what*?" I snarled in his ear. "Am I going to have to teach you some manners?"

"Yes, *sir*." He sobbed, bordering on incoherent. He really was on the edge, but it didn't look like he could come without being touched. Just a little bit to put him over the top. He hadn't done it himself, though. Was he waiting for permission? Had it even occurred to him to finish himself off without it? "Please! Oh Jesus, please!"

"Jack yourself off. Do it now." Another driving thrust. And another. "Show me what a whore you are, that you'll come for the man fucking you, whether you want it or not."

Practically sobbing with frustrated need, he unwrapped his fingers from where they'd twisted in the sheets, and located his rigid dick. I was right; a few strokes was all it took before he gave a ragged shout, hot cum spurting through the ring of his fist to splash onto the bed. It felt like lava was building up at the base of my spine, ready to surge along my nerves the moment I let go.

And I did. Lightning erupted behind my eyelids. My grip on his neck and thigh tightened, and I shuddered behind him, groaning.

When I could think again, Geoff was limp against me. With my sweaty brow resting on his back, my breath exploded against his skin in sharp huffs.

Awareness began creeping tangibly back into his body. I brushed a kiss on his shoulder, holding him. As I pressed close, Geoff's tension began to bleed away.

"You okay?"

"Yeah," he whispered. "I think so."

He shivered.

"Stay right there." He shook harder when I moved my body away from his. Wanting to get him warm and comfortable as soon as I could, I made quick work of getting rid of the towels and pulling the covers up over him. Then I held the bottle of water to his lips. "Here."

"Sorry." He gulped it down as I curled myself around him from behind. After a minute, his shivering subsided and his voice grew steadier. "I don't know—"

"It's okay." I kissed his shoulder again. "Did I take it too far?"

"I don't think so." He closed his eyes and sighed, his expression blissful. "I just wasn't expecting . . . It was intense. But I liked it."

"Good." Of their own volition, my fingers traced the curve of his shoulder and trailed down the length of his arm, like they couldn't get enough contact with his skin. "Enough to want to do it again?"

"Right now?" He smirked over his shoulder.

"Tempting, but I don't think I could manage yet." I kissed the side of his neck. "If you're interested, though, I'd like to keep going while you're here. There's a lot more ground we could cover."

He laughed, a soft, self-conscious sound. I tucked my face against the back of his shoulder and took an emotional inventory of myself. Most of my interactions with him so far had been driven by instinct and impulse, by the signals I was reading from him. I needed to figure out what I was asking for, here. How deep was too deep to get involved, considering he'd be gone in a few days?

Right now we were both high. Probably not the best time to make any decisions. Geoff's body was heavy with lassitude, but there was also tension in him, as though he was feeling echoes of my own doubts.

I squeezed him, trying to tell him it was all right. I knew exactly why he felt so adrift, and I didn't want him to batter himself with his insecurities about how to behave or what came next. I didn't want to see him retreat, and then in a day or a week go back to trolling for an unsafe facsimile of what we'd done.

"It's okay," I murmured, but I couldn't stop his withdrawal as he sat up.

"Sure."

"Rest." I settled for rubbing his back. "It's okay to be exhausted after that."

He pushed himself up. I rose to help in case he was unsteady on his feet. Considering his medical issues, I didn't want him taking a spill on my watch.

He moved gingerly and frowned as if confused.

"All right?" I asked, hoping I was striking the right balance between solicitude and stepping on that pride of his.

"Everything just feels . . . strange. I get why my skin's sensitive, but why would my muscles— They don't really ache, but I don't want to move much right now?" He ended on a raised note, like he was asking a question rather than making a statement.

"Release of tension. Adrenaline. It's all right. As long as you're not in pain or distress?"

I watched him do his own inventory. "No. I'm okay."

I considered it something of a victory that he leaned heavily on me as he shuffled to the bathroom. We brushed our teeth together. He took a moment to stare at the fading pink blotches all over his pale skin. He evicted me while he took a piss, but by then he seemed steadier. I remained right outside the door, just in case.

"I feel drugged," he said muzzily when he emerged, wrapping himself around me. I blinked and had to check my surprise. I'd been worried that he was going to react badly once he finally felt more stable, but instead he just . . . went with it.

I hugged him back, engulfing him as best I was able, and kissed his temple. God, I'd missed this part of being in the scene. I'd missed taking a guy to a place where macho posturing and pride had no relevance, where he wasn't ashamed to require comfort and support.

Maybe Geoff, more than most men I'd met, needed that.

I chuckled. "You pretty much are. I should have realized; you haven't really researched this at all, have you?" He shook his head as I slid an arm around his waist and escorted him back to his room. "Shit. I should have stopped to explain it a bit more."

His voice was an indistinct slur. "Didn't want to stop."

I tucked the covers around him again after he crawled back into bed, and located the spare blanket to lay over him from the bottom drawer of the dresser. I slipped under the bedding to draw him against my chest. He was still shivering.

"Tomorrow, do some research," I urged, breathing into his rumpled hair. "Especially about the effects of pain endorphins. That adrenaline rush from the fear play probably isn't helping, either."

"'Kay."

I pulled away to reach for the water bottle, and by the time I rolled back over, his breathing was already evening out. I didn't have the heart to wake him and push more water on him.

Instead, I settled in beside him and smiled, then let myself drift away.

CHAPTER THIRTEEN

Geoff

The next two days were a lot more mundane. Robin had meetings with his mortgage broker and realtor, and teleconferences with people back in New York, so somehow it ended up that the wealthy playboy I'd landed for my vacation fling was too busy for days of marathon sex. That was okay. It gave me time to do my prophy and hang with Jace.

My next-to-last day of vacation, the weather was gorgeous, so Robin took me out on his boat, navigating from the marina on Kalamazoo Lake along the short remainder of the Kalamazoo River to where it drained into Lake Michigan.

It was an afternoon full of lazy conversation, perfect except that Robin somehow seemed to divert any discussion about him back onto me. I don't think he did it intentionally. He just had a habit of steering things that way. I finally had to say something.

"Let's change things up and try to have a conversation that isn't about me. Let's talk about you for a while."

He laughed at that, ducking his head self-consciously. "Was I grilling you? Sorry. Old habits die hard, I suppose. I used to sort of do that for a living. Get people to talk about themselves, I mean."

"Let me guess. You were a cop and that's where all this interrogation comes from."

"No!" His smile widened for a moment, then faded as his eyes grew wistful. "I used to counsel homeless LGBT youths at a shelter. Street kids."

"Ah." A lightbulb came on. "So that's what you meant when you said you'd had experience with people acting tough."

He shrugged. "Yeah. It's a story that comes with a lot of things that were said in confidence. I can't get into it much."

That I understood. "How did you go from that to wanting to open a gallery?"

The wistfulness in his eyes redoubled, veering toward melancholy. "Um, it started when the shelter was hit hard during Hurricane Sandy. Some of the reconstruction money went missing, and it turned out my boyfriend, Kyle, was the one embezzling. I had no idea and was cleared of any wrongdoing in the investigation, but there were a lot of politics and guilt-by-association from the donors. It was better for the program for me to leave."

A dozen questions crowded my brain.

He held up a hand, forestalling them. "Can we not talk about all that? It's still a sore spot, and there are legal resolutions pending. My lawyer probably wouldn't want me discussing it with anyone."

I frowned, stung by his evasiveness. I could understand the legal stuff needing to be kept under wraps, but it seemed unfair that he could prod into all my most painful shit and declare his off-limits. What about this trust he said we were building between us?

Licking my lips, I nodded. "Yeah. Sure. Okay." I could make a big deal of it, or I could let it go. With my boundary issues, the latter was probably the better option. "So you decided to open a gallery?"

He leaned back against the sofa in the outdoor lounge. "My parents did well selling art, so I figured I could be most helpful to the center by making a lot of money and donating as much of it as I could."

"And your parents?" I was picking through potential conversation fodder, trying to find something that wouldn't force him to talk about the circumstances under which he'd left New York. "Aside from running them ragged when you were young, how do you get along with them?"

"They're great. They didn't bat an eye when I came out in high school, and they've always been supportive. You don't need to tell me

I live a charmed life. I don't mean to brag, but it's true. Some of my friends haven't been so lucky."

"In what way?"

His mouth tightened, like he was going to shut me down again. Then he blew out a long breath and answered instead. "When I came out at fifteen, I did so as part of a pact with my first boyfriend. We were going to tell our families together so we wouldn't have to hide. We went to my parents first, and that couldn't have gone better. Then we went to his family."

"They didn't handle it so well?"

"No." He pulled his knees to his chest. "Never in my pampered, innocent little life could I have imagined parents calling their child the things they called Isaac. His dad stormed out. Then his mom took over, trying to convince him he really didn't mean it. Why was he playing such a *cruel joke*, and was he sure he wasn't just *confused*? And I could see he was about to give in and agree, but his dad came downstairs with an armful of his clothes and threw him out, right there on the spot."

"Oh shit." I reached for him without thinking about it, almost drawing him to me before I decided the intimacy of that was still too much. I settled on squeezing his shoulder.

"He stayed with us for a while, but he never really healed. Having his family discard him like that broke something inside him. He began drinking, partying. We broke up when I was sixteen, when I told him I didn't feel I was ready to have sex with him. Truth was, I just didn't feel comfortable being around him anymore."

He set his chin on his knees, his words coming faster as the rest of the tale poured out.

"My mom put her foot down and told Isaac if he was going to continue to live with us, he'd abide by the same rules I did, and for a while it seemed he'd cleaned up his act. Then I learned he'd been prostituting himself around school, giving blowjobs to closeted jocks under the bleachers, that sort of thing." He sighed, shaking his head. "I don't know why I'm having a hard time talking about this. I've told the story before to kids I've worked with, to show them how I can relate to what they've dealt with."

"It's different here, though, isn't it?"

"Yeah, I guess it is." He gnawed his lip for a second, then continued. "He tried to blackmail a teacher who may or may not have fucked him, and the guy lost his job. Then Isaac got caught in an online prostitution sting while making dates with johns in chat rooms. While my mom was down at the courthouse, bailing him out and delivering his laptop so they could find out who his clients were —because, of course, he was still a minor—my dad searched Isaac's room and found drug paraphernalia. He'd started doing meth."

"Christ," I whispered, dragging my hand down my jaw.

"So, when they got him home, my mom and dad told Isaac his choices were to move out or go to rehab in the city. He chose rehab, but he walked out and disappeared less than a week into the program. He called me a few times over the next couple years, usually asking me to transfer some money so he could come home to us, which I did, but he never showed up." He shrugged, a self-conscious *What can you do?* gesture. "When I went to Columbia University, I tried to search for him, but I could never find him. After I left home for college, we never heard from him again."

"I'm sorry." I curled my hand around his biceps, and after a moment he mustered a smile. I shifted gears, going for a more neutral subject. "What did you study when you were at school?"

"Business management and social work." He snorted.

"That's a strange combination."

"No, no, see? I had it all figured out. When I came into my trust fund, I was going to open a shelter for kids like Isaac. I was going to *save them all.*"

I frowned. The bitter edge in his voice didn't seem to match the easygoing guy I knew. "That's where you were counseling?" I ventured.

"Yeah."

"And you were forced to leave? All that work, when it meant so much to you?"

He stared out across the water with a melancholy in his eyes that I felt an inexplicable urge to wipe away. "It didn't work out. That's life, I guess."

When we were far enough from land that the houses were pale blurs against the backdrop of the dunes, he made me strip and took his time slathering me head to foot in sunblock. I spent the better part of the afternoon wrapped only in a blanket to ward off the chilly wind. Robin fondled me at will, just enough to keep me constantly on edge.

"So you're ready when I decide I want to have you." He let the boat drift as he groped my ass with frank crudity.

I groped back, squeezing his backside with both hands through the soft fabric of his pants. "And what if *I* decide I want to have you?"

He dimpled at me before he laughed, ducking his head and blushing. "Will you believe it has nothing to do with ego or power trips when I say I don't bottom?"

"I'm pretty sure everything has to do with ego where you're concerned, but do tell."

He chuckled again, accepting the hit with a shrug of acquiescence. "I've tried. Many times. And I've spoken to people and read all the advice that said it's an acquired taste, but I never grew to enjoy it. I don't like the sensations. Whatever it is that makes the prostate so amazing for other guys is just blah for me. The feeling of being penetrated makes my skin crawl, which of course makes it hard to relax, and *then* it starts to hurt. Eventually I accepted it was never going to work for me."

"Ah." I nodded slowly, turning that over in my mind. My taunt had been more academic than anything, a nonchalant poke at the power dynamics of this fling to see if they were reversible. I had no trouble with bottoming exclusively, but I wasn't sure I wanted to be passive all the time. All the time, of course, being our remaining day and a half.

He flashed me another grin and rubbed his linen-clad erection against my hip. "Which is not to say I wouldn't be perfectly willing to consider any other ways you think you might want to have me."

"Oh, really?" I let my fingers slide down the ridge pressing against the fly of his trousers. "Maybe you should drop the anchor, then."

I pushed him onto one of the padded benches. The heavy, weatherproof curtains, or whatever they were, sealed us off from the wind. Straddling his thighs, I fucked myself on him at my own pace. His hands helped raise and lower my weight to ease the stress on my joints. When I heard him groan, felt him shudder and pulse, I urged him off the bench to his knees and fucked his mouth until I was spent.

WE WERE AWAKENED MIDMORNING the next day, my last one at the Dunes, by the persistent ringing of his cell phone. It took me a moment to recognize it because it wasn't Robin's usual ringtone, which I'd heard several times by then.

Robin, however, shot out of bed like a bullet, and bolted across my hotel room to grab it from the pocket of the trousers he'd discarded the night before.

"Yeah?" His voice was still groggy with sleep and scratchy from me forcing my cock down his throat.

I couldn't hear the other side of the conversation, and Robin's side consisted largely of unhelpful "uh-huhs." But it ended with, "I'll be there this afternoon or early evening, depending on how soon I can get a flight."

After he disconnected, he sat there on his haunches, nude. He hung his head and exhaled slowly, then glanced over at me.

"Going someplace?" I asked, trying not to be disappointed.

"Yeah, I need to go to New York to take care of some stuff." The heavy droop of his shoulders suggested it wasn't going to be pleasant business.

"Of course." I forced down an irrational surge of irritation. I had no grounds to be disappointed, much less annoyed. This was a vacation fling, and absolutely nothing more. The fact that he was the first steady fuck I'd had since an incredibly difficult attempt at a relationship back in art school didn't alter that, no matter how high I was on amazing sex. Besides, I was leaving tomorrow morning anyway.

So seriously, self, get real.

I rolled out of bed, trying to locate my own scattered clothing in the mess, and squashing any flouncy impulses under a merciless heel. I could damn well find something else to do today if I wanted entertainment. Fuck, if I was still horny—and, really, the past few days ought to have taken care of that problem quite handily—I could even find *someone* else to do.

"Go ahead and help yourself to the shower. I'll make coffee."

"Not yet." Robin surged to his feet and in a few strides had me backed against the wall. "I'm sorry." He nuzzled the line of my jaw.

Time to pretend ignorance. "Why should you be?"

That question seemed to startle him. He blinked at me, then took a step back, his demeanor cooling. "Because I'd been looking forward to having one last day to play with you. But hey, if you're not bothered, guess I shouldn't be either. I'll go take that shower now."

Fuck. Was he *offended* that I wasn't acting disappointed? What the fuck was that about? *He* was the one taking off for some vague *business*.

A fact for which he'd apologized and I'd been a bitch. Goddamn it.

After I put on the miniature pot of coffee, I grabbed Robin's cell phone and made sure he had not only my number, but also my email address and even the address of Jace's apartment in Chicago. Just in case. I wouldn't try to make more of this than it was intended to be, but if he was ever up for a repeat performance, I'd make certain that could be arranged. Then, drawing a deep breath, I laid my hand on the knob of the bathroom door and let myself inside.

Robin went still when I drew back the shower curtain and slipped in behind him. Looking at me over his shoulder, he squeezed the last of the suds from his hair. I ran my hands over his wide, muscled shoulders, disrupting the rivulets that streamed down his skin. He shuddered, turning to face me.

"Sorry." I leaned in for a hard, hungry kiss. I didn't bother for subtlety but went straight for his cock. It was rising satisfactorily under its own steam, but I was more than happy to help it along. Then I smiled, and tried to mean it. "One for the road?"

He didn't *quite* slam me against the tile wall, though it was a near thing. His fingers bit into the flesh of my biceps hard enough that I knew I'd have bruises even though I'd infused before our boat ride, and his lips mashed and ground hard against mine. His tongue plunged into my mouth like a battering ram, and our slick skins slid against each other. His cock prodded my groin, rocking along the length of mine.

"Fuck me." I caught his bottom lip between my teeth, biting hard enough to make him wince. I'd be damned if I was the only one who'd leave with bruises.

He groaned, pushing harder against me. "I need to— Oh, *Christ* . . ."

I wrapped my hand around his cock again, jerking it firmly.

"I don't care. Just fuck me." I wriggled to make space to turn and face the tile, offering him my back.

"I don't—" He moaned as I ground my ass against his cock. "Oh, fuck it."

The herbal scent of Jace's conditioner hit my nostrils the second before Robin smeared a glob of it over my hole. Then he was pushing into my ass, thick and blunt, and I was tight and unready. For the first time this whole week, he hadn't made any effort to stretch me, so it truly burned, and it was *delicious*.

"*Fuck*," I hissed, arching my spine to open to him as much as I could. "Fuck, yeah."

"Too much?" His breath mingled with the steam and sweat to dampen my neck. His hips butted against mine.

"No." I shook my head wildly. I was too far gone for explanations, to try to make him understand that I wanted the ache, wanted to feel it after he was gone and I went back to my life. A reminder—something I would carry for a day or two until I had to let go of the memory.

And ache it did, because he didn't hold back. There was no hint of caution in his grasp, in the rough pounding of his hips as they slapped wetly against my ass, in the way he hauled me back, bent me over, and hammered into me without mercy.

Fuck. Oh, *fuck, yes*.

My groans filled the tiled enclosure as I grabbed my dick and began jacking it. Our cries became more desperate, and I had an instant of coherent thought that Jace and whoever he might be with in his room were no doubt getting quite the concert. Then it was swept away when Robin pushed into me so hard he slammed me up flat against the tile, buried deep and pulsing.

"Jesus!" His spasms seemed to go on and on, one after the other. I clenched tight around him, trying to draw them out longer, wanting to hold him in that moment as long as I could.

Then he went heavy and boneless against my back, his shaking hands soothing up and down my wet skin. I turned my head, and he claimed my mouth in a breathless kiss as he drew me away from the wall. His hand snaked around my hip, closing over mine where I grasped my rigid cock. He guided my hand up and down, controlling the strokes. His dick, still lodged half-hard in my aching ass, rocked in and out again.

I went slack, leaning on him, letting him support my weight.

"That's it, baby," he muttered fervently against my ear. "Give it up to me. One last time. Let me see you come."

Desperate, I gasped and groaned and strained, and finally stiffened and cried out, spurting through the ring of our joined fingers.

We were subdued as we dressed. I helped Robin pack up the gear he'd brought with him, the toys and candles and such. I escorted him to the door, murmuring polite nonsense about how I'd enjoyed the week and to take care, et cetera, et cetera. It was miserably awkward, but I honestly didn't have the first clue how to handle this sort of situation with anything resembling grace.

"I had a good time too," he said, looking no more comfortable than I was. We stared at each other.

I wanted to send him off with a jaunty smile and a kiss and a "thanks for the fun ride," but I wasn't feeling it. In fact, I was feeling downright glum. It blew out of the water my certainty that this had been a casual vacation fling. But if I tried to kiss him right then, it would have been too intimate. Too needy. Though, frankly, I wasn't sure how much of that neediness was coming from me. There had been something raw and wounded in Robin's eyes since his phone call, and part of me wanted to offer him comfort, which wasn't helping my resolve.

I drew back instead, folding my arms and retreating into my own personal space.

"You have my number," I said with no apparent concern. "If you ever end up in Chicago, give me a call."

Robin's gaze slid away as he nodded, and damn it, where was all his fucking smooth confidence now? Finally he hitched the strap of his duffel higher on his shoulder and muttered, "See you, Geoff," and disappeared.

An hour later, an androgynous stranger shuffled out of Jace's room. They mumbled a passing salutation to me, and Jace saw them out with a polite farewell and a casual peck at the door. No awkwardness whatsoever.

Why hadn't I been able to pull that off with Robin?

Jace made a beeline for the coffeepot, then flopped down beside me on the sofa, nearly causing me to spill my own coffee.

"Problems?" He lifted an eyebrow, sipping his coffee.

"Did I recognize them as one of the drag queens from the club that first night?"

He grinned broadly, looking *very* self-satisfied.

I let my head flop against the back of the sofa. I could practically feel Jace's inquisitive stare.

"Don't mind me." I waved him off. "Postcoital depression."

"Ah. They say it's worse the better the sex is."

I groaned. "Then God help me."

He chuckled and fell silent, slurping periodically.

"So, it's our last night here," he ventured at last. "Want to hit the club again tonight? Or did you have plans with Robin?"

"Nah, he's off to New York. He has *business*." I waved my hand vaguely. I kept my eyes closed and considered the proposal. Something in me resisted the idea of trying to have a good time, and it *really* resisted the idea of trying to go back to what I'd been doing before.

That part of me wanted to hang out in my room and indulge my moody bent. Which was, of course, the best possible argument for going. I'd be damned if I would go into mourning because a few days of sex (okay, good . . . okay, *spectacular, phenomenal, mind-blowing* sex) had come to an end.

"Sure." I finally lifted my head and straightened up. "Hitting the club sounds great. Wrap it up with a party."

"Excellent." Jace flashed his ready grin. "I think I'm going to go get some more sleep."

"That . . . sounds like a solid plan." I set my coffee cup aside and rubbed my bleary eyes. "Hard to go dancing if you're so fucked out, you're walking into walls."

Unfortunately, my bed smelled like Robin, which made it difficult to do anything other than think about all that had happened since that first night at the club. After a half hour or so, I gave up and climbed into Jace's bed instead. Sure, it smelled like the perfume his companion had worn, but it was still better. Jace curled up behind me, flopped an arm across me, and said nothing.

He understood how lonely I was. Of course I was going to mourn the end of this week. In the last six days I'd had more intimate contact with another person than I'd had for the whole of my adult life.

At the least, I could look back on this vacation as a learning experience, one that showed me my horizons were far broader than I'd thought they'd be. I could be bolder, seek out the things I wanted more actively. Really, I should thank Robin for helping me figure that out. I'd spent most of my twenties isolated, but I didn't have to stay that way.

Smiling, I closed my eyes and let myself drift off to sleep with a newfound determination that when we got back to Chicago, it would be different.

CHAPTER FOURTEEN

Robin

I shook Char Stryker's hand in the doorway to her office, but I couldn't seem to muster any happiness at the fact that the charges were finally, *officially* dropped and the whole ordeal was over.

"Look, Brady," Char murmured to me, leaning in close to keep the discussion confidential. She had her lawyer hat on still, which was fine, because the *Hey, good work, let's go celebrate with a beer* sense of exultation I'd been expecting was totally absent. "Just because Kyle recanted doesn't mean everything is clear sailing. You know that, right?"

I frowned at her. "No, I don't know that. What the fuck is that supposed to mean?"

Char looked grave. "It's all still on record that Kyle made the accusations, that you were investigated and charged. Yeah, it's on record also that he changed his story and the charges were dismissed, but if you ever have legal trouble again and they pull that file, they'll try to use it against you, no matter how inadmissible it's supposed to be. It could easily be made to look like you're a repeat offender who skated on charges that should have stuck, if only the complaining witness hadn't backed out. You're going to want to keep your nose very, very clean, or you could find yourself railroaded."

I took a moment to study the woman who'd spent a lot of time mentoring me when I first got into the scene. Char hid some very Old Guard kinks under that designer suit, making her the perfect defense attorney for kinksters trying to contest charges born of prejudice or ignorance. Or, in my case, malice and selfishness. It wasn't only the fee I was paying her that made her worth listening to.

"What trouble do you think I could get into now?"

She shrugged expressively. "All I'm saying is, choose your play partners *very* carefully. Negotiate your scenes to a T and make sure you have everything in writing. A play contract might not stand up in court, but it goes a long way toward establishing consent. Okay?"

After the days I'd just spent with Geoff, her words couldn't have been more of an indictment if she'd tried. Christ, had I been *looking* to get myself into trouble again? What the fuck?

Subdued, I thanked Char and stepped into the elevator, intent on getting back to my hotel and packing my stuff. I should never have attended the Buns & Baskets party. I should have stuck to my intention to stay out of the scene for good.

Never mind that those days I'd spent with Geoff had been some of the hottest, most fulfilling scenes I'd ever done, made even more so by the palpable sense of wonder he'd experienced at finally getting to taste the sort of play he'd been dreaming about. I had the skill to give him what he needed, and it had been incredible. And damn it, if I knew I was better off not playing, why did I keep obsessing over calling Geoff as soon as I got home?

I left the elevator and crossed the lobby to the street, so lost in debating with myself that I almost walked smack into the slender, pale man who stepped deliberately in my path.

"Robin—" Kyle reached out a hand as I stumbled to a halt. He looked gaunter than when I'd seen him last, shivering in a microfiber windbreaker with frayed cuffs. If the waxy skin, bloodshot eyes, and twitchy energy were any indication, he was using again. If he'd ever really stopped. "I hoped I'd catch you here."

The muscles in my jaw tightened so fast it hurt. "What, have you been staking out Char's building, waiting for me to show up?"

He hung his head. "Once I found out the charges were going to be dismissed, I knew you'd have to come back. I needed to see you. Robin, I'm sorry—"

"Oh, fuck you," I sneered, turning on my heel and dodging foot traffic to put him behind me as literally as I was trying to do figuratively. I could feel him there, though, trotting to catch up.

"Robin, please!" he called out, and the anger that had begun seething inside me at the sight of him erupted.

I whirled on him. "What the *fuck* do you want from me?"

"I don't know!" Tears glittered in his eyes. "Everything is all fucked up, and I thought if I could see you, make you understand—"

"I *understand* just fine. You got caught, and you tried to save your own ass by throwing me under the bus."

He opened his mouth to try to deny that, then snapped it shut again. We both knew I was dead on. His complaint against me had been an effort to make my testimony against him look retaliatory.

"But you got caught in a lie, so you backed down. So what are you after now? Need money for a better attorney? Need a character witness at your sentencing?"

"No. No!" Kyle's face crumpled. He scrubbed his cheeks, erasing the tear tracks. "I just need you. I need you to forgive me, to *be* here when this is all over, so we can work through this."

My eyes popped open, and my jaw dropped. "Are you *fucking kidding me?*" I dragged a hand through my hair, my fingers catching on tangles. I'd let it grow these past months in Michigan. "You tried to ruin my life! I never did a damned thing to you that you didn't *beg* me for. *You* kept pushing the limits, not me. You falsely accuse me of assault, and now you want to *work through it?* Fuck you."

I turned away in disgust, but before I got a couple steps, he grabbed my arm. Passersby bumped against us, because of course he couldn't be bothered to notice we were blocking the sidewalk. I spun back around, barely stopping myself from clocking him.

I jabbed my index finger into his chest instead. "Hopefully, you're going to jail for embezzlement. If they tack on some time for filing a false complaint, I'm okay with that. Maybe you'll use the downtime to get your shit together. But when you get out, there is only one thing I need from you: *don't* come looking for me. There's nothing for us to work through. Get clean, don't get clean, I don't care. Just stay the fuck away from me."

I stormed off before that broken look on his face could take the edge off my anger. Kyle deserved every bit of my rage, no matter how badly I wanted to empathize with him. The instinct within me to help people—to fix them and make them better and solve their problems—was making grabby hands in his direction. I couldn't let myself be sucked in by him again.

My mind skipped back to Geoff. The encounter with Kyle reaffirmed that getting involved with anyone this soon was a bad idea. And yet I couldn't stop thinking about how close he was, geographically speaking, from where I was settling down. It would be easy to work something out with Geoff, without becoming embroiled in the kind of needy, codependent relationship things had devolved into with Kyle. With Geoff, I could indulge my taste for the subtle, intense psychological play I enjoyed, because while Geoff might think he wanted the physical brutality Kyle had pushed for, he knew he could never demand it. This could be the opposite of what I'd had with Kyle.

But Char was right. We needed to negotiate things better, have a contract in place, work on establishing limits and building trust.

I knew just where to begin.

CHAPTER FIFTEEN

Geoff

"So, did you meet any interesting men?" Ling asked as I sat with my sketch pad, trying to translate a design that had been hovering elusively in my mind ever since we returned to Chicago.

"Did you?" I shot back at the phone lying on the table. I had her on speakerphone so I wouldn't have to locate my headset. I didn't want to be drawing while holding the phone between my shoulder and ear.

"Yes, and a couple women too. Would you like details?" There was a slight smirk in her voice. While I'd been in Saugatuck, she'd gone with a few friends to Cabo.

"Don't you dare."

"Seriously. Did you have a good time?"

"Yeah, I really did." Despite the fact that a frankly annoying melancholy had beset me since the end of my vacation. It came too close to mooning about, and I didn't moon. Instead, I tried not to think of the fact that I was envisioning what this design would look like inked into Robin's freckled skin. I *also* tried not to think of how he would sound and feel and move under my hands as I etched it into his flesh, if for no other reason than I didn't want to deal with a hard-on while talking to my sister.

"So what are your plans now that you're back in Chicago?"

I sighed, refining an elegantly curved tendril twining up the ribs to be a little bolder. "I suppose I'll start looking for a space to open my own studio. And, of course, an apartment. I can't crash with Jace indefinitely."

That was going to be a challenge. I needed to find a studio space in a high-end part of town, stylish but not too conservative, where my nonthreatening, clean-cut appearance would be more of an asset than a detraction. I'd have to cash in on my Hollywood credentials and package myself as a tattoo artist of class, refinement, sophistication. A cut above.

It was all bullshit, naturally. There are graffiti and street artists with more talent and expression than many "fine" artists whose work ends up displayed in museums, and body art is no different. My designs were different from those of artists who never went to art school, but I wouldn't dare call them better. But perception was everything, right? I'd make my studio a haven for pampered upper-middle-class rich kids who found the seedier parts of town too intimidating.

Problem was, real estate in the higher-end parts of town came at a premium.

On paper, of course, I could have paid for it out of pocket, but the insurance money was sacrosanct. Not only because of my uncertain future, but because of everything my entire family, including Ling, had sacrificed to be sure my needs were met. I had tied up most of it in judicious investments, overseen by the financial adviser my parents had started working with back when they'd begun putting every spare penny into the life insurance policies. Which was good, considering what the last couple of years had done to the stock market. Otherwise I didn't touch it, and certainly not to start a business venture that might very well fail.

So right now, except for the money I'd managed to sock away while working for Rogier, I was effectively penniless, despite having an eight-figure portfolio.

With that bank balance, I could easily have gotten a small business loan to lease the space and purchase the equipment I needed, but my medical condition made me a questionable proposition as far as loans went. The chance that bleeds could leave me unable to work for weeks or months, or make me so arthritis-ridden that I wouldn't be able to walk, were significant.

"Well?" Ling prompted, dragging me back to the conversation. "Do you have any leads? On either?"

"Not yet." I blew out a breath and laid down my pencil. "It's going to be tricky finding a space. I'd be better off working in someone else's studio, but I'm not sure I want to risk being in another artist's shadow again."

"It'll happen," Ling said with absolute certainty.

I chuckled at her confidence. "Yeah, but 'Will it happen before my savings run out?' is the question."

"So work as a contractor in someone else's studio for a while, to keep from dipping into your savings while you get everything in order." Her voice was so nonchalant, I could easily picture her shrug. "Or better yet, set up shop in someone else's studio, build up a huge client list, and then threaten to walk with it if they don't make you an equal partner and give you top billing."

I blinked at the phone. "That is *devious*."

"It could work."

"You're far more bloodthirsty than I am."

"If your name isn't the first one on the awning by the time I'm done with my doctorate, I'm going to head to Chicago and make my bloodthirsty ass your manager."

I laughed and traced my finger down the side of my sketch pad. "Hey, say the word and ten percent of my take is yours. Now go study or something. I want to finish this design. I'll text you tomorrow."

"Okay." She hung up, and I reached for my phone to set it to silent so I could work uninterrupted, then hesitated, staring at it for a moment. It had been three days since we'd left the Dunes, and Robin hadn't made any attempt to contact me. I didn't know why I'd thought he might. It was a truly idiotic notion, and yet something in me had held out hope that it might happen.

I set the phone down with the ringtone still on its normal volume.

That Robin had gotten inside my head, delivering things I'd never known I wanted, hadn't helped. But I had *some* perspective, at least. I wasn't in love. Yet. Though something intense had happened there, hadn't it? Something more than just sex. A connection had been formed. He'd done things to my body, yeah, but he'd also gotten under my skin. And it had seemed like he felt the same. Or had I misread things?

My cell rang as I gazed down at my design, trying to decide how the pattern would shift as it moved from the back and shoulders down onto the ass, thighs, and arms. There was something distinctly oceanic about its lines, I thought, fumbling for my phone. Which really, considering the inspiration, was to be expected. Maybe I should go full-out oceanscape with it, in shades of blue that would make Robin's eyes snap.

Jace's face flashed on the screen. I tried not to be disappointed. "Yeah, dude. What's up?"

"I'm going to the bathhouse to lift weights. Wanna join me?"

A corner of my mouth tipped up. "You realize you're the only guy in Chicago who lifts weights in that place for any purpose other than to pick someone up?"

"Hey, until I can build up a bigger client base and sell more paintings, this is the closest to a gym membership I can afford."

I laughed at that. Jace had arrived in Chicago with barely a dime to his name. Eight or twelve-hour rentals for the cubicles that passed for rooms at bathhouses were cheaper than any motel and safer than any shelter. He used the bathhouse's patrons to spread the word about his graphic design start-up. One of his first contracts had been with the new owners of the bathhouse.

"Thanks, but I think I'll pass tonight."

"You sure? We haven't worked out together since before we went to Michigan."

I understood his unspoken question. *Are you sure you're getting enough exercise to keep your joints healthy?* Jace understood that moderate weight training helped strengthen my joints, decreasing the chance of spontaneous bleeds. I'd never be a bodybuilder, but I was usually reasonably diligent about putting in enough workout time to keep myself healthy.

"Yeah. I'll go lifting with you in a day or two. You enjoy yourself." I couldn't explain why I was reluctant to go out tonight, but the idea didn't appeal to me at all.

"All right. Don't wait for me to eat dinner or anything. I've got a new painting I've been sketching ideas for, and I have the studio space to myself tonight for as late as I want it."

"Okay. I'll see you in the morning if I'm asleep before you get home. Have fun."

I hung up and stared at my sketch awhile longer, but my concentration had been broken and I couldn't get back into it. Tucking the pad away, I grabbed my laptop and opened it to check my email and perhaps browse for a station at a decent body-art studio.

My pulse tripped and stumbled when I saw the most recent email —sent less than an hour ago, in fact—was from Robin. The subject line read, *In case you were concerned*, and I clicked to open it, my breath coming faster.

I thought I would send this along on the chance you might have any concerns about that last morning before I left. Take care.
—Robin

There was an attachment. When I clicked it open, I saw it was a scan of lab results for a full panel of STI tests, dated the day before. All the results were negative.

I sat there blinking at it for a long moment, wondering why he'd felt compelled to send it. What did it mean?

I'd made it clear that morning in the shower that I wasn't willing to wait long enough for him to retrieve a condom. It might have been a stupid risk, but I'd decided to take it nonetheless. And while I wasn't proud of the decision—somewhere in my mind, my mother wailed, and that omnipresent voice of caution had demanded to know how I could risk such a thing—I had refused to allow myself to fret over it. The fact that using condoms had been the undisputed default for the five days we were together suggested Robin had good, consistent habits in that regard.

Some part of me never fully let go of worry. But I hadn't been worried about that last morning with Robin. Foolish, but true. I'd accepted that it had happened and that I'd get tested in a couple of months, just in case. I usually did it a couple of times a year anyway, even if I hadn't gotten laid. It was a holdover from the eighties and early nineties when no one had really trusted the blood supply yet.

Had Robin taken the time to be tested and send his results to me out of concern for *my* peace of mind? Or was he worrying about it for his own sake?

Closing the laptop with a snap, I grabbed my phone and dialed Jace back.

"Hey. You know what? I think I'll join you after all."

"Sounds good. I'll swing by and pick you up on the way."

So I got my workout whether I'd been in the mood for it or not. Afterward, while Jace decided to indulge in a soak in the hot tub, I went downstairs to the booth set up by one of the city's AIDS-awareness organizations. They offered rapid-results testing all day, every day. Less than thirty minutes later, I tucked the paper they'd given me into my gym bag and hitched a ride home with Jace.

I waffled for hours before finally scanning the paper and replying to Robin's email.

Robin,
Thank you for the email. In case you were concerned, I'm sending my own along. Keep in touch.
—Geoff

There, I thought as I closed the laptop. I plodded dutifully through my flossing routine, then stared up at the ceiling of Jace's spare bedroom in the darkness. That put the ball firmly back in Robin's court. Whether he'd return it was anyone's guess.

I wanted to see him again. It was less than a three-hour drive from Chicago to Saugatuck. Or hell, the trip might be even shorter if he came on his boat. How fast did those things go, anyway?

I managed to lie there sleeplessly for nearly an hour before giving in and grabbing my phone off the bedside table, checking my email. And there at the top of my inbox was a new message from him.

Thank you. That's handy to know. We should discuss this further. Send me a text tonight or tomorrow and tell me when it would be a good time to talk uninterrupted.

My heart hammering, I immediately thumb-typed another reply.

Jace is out of the apartment until late tonight. No idea what his schedule is tomorrow.

My chest felt hollow and my entire body thrummed with that sweet, breathless surge of adrenaline and arousal. It was all I could do to keep from fist-pumping in triumph. The rush of my blood in my ears marked the heartbeats as a few anxious minutes passed.

And then my phone rang.

CHAPTER SIXTEEN

Robin

"I don't usually do that" were the first words out of my mouth when Geoff answered. "Forgo rubbers, I mean."

"I didn't think you did," he said. The background noise of the airport was so chaotic that I could barely hear him when he spoke, but he sounded pretty laid-back about it. "I hope it goes without saying that I don't, either."

I could believe that. Given how closely he'd dodged the bullet in his childhood and his own brother's death, I imagined it was something he took seriously most of the time. "I want to see you again. I feel bad that we didn't get to enjoy that last day you were in town."

"I'm sure that could be arranged."

"Good."

I floundered a moment, trying to find the calm, centered, rational place from which I could be an experienced dom walking a neophyte sub into the sort of arrangement I was hoping for. I needed to talk to him about all the things Char had mentioned. No more winging it the way we had while he was on vacation. We needed to negotiate, and he needed to understand what my boundaries were, because that was where I'd gotten into trouble before.

"So, how was New York?" Geoff asked before I could find a way to segue to the subject I wanted to pursue.

"Aggravating," I groused. Thankfully Geoff let that go. "How was your trip back to Chicago?"

"Oh, you know, it was a drive."

"And what are your plans now that you're back there?"

He laughed, and then a flight at a nearby gate was announced and I had to ask him to repeat himself.

"You and my sister have both asked me that today," he said again.

"Important question, I take it?" At which point he launched into an explanation of his plan to search for a space for his studio.

I tried to envision Geoff at work—all that earnest, nerdy concentration focused on making art of the sort I'd seen in his sketches. It was a very pleasant mental image. "Once you're open for business, I'll have to come and have you ink me."

He gave a thoughtful hum that sounded like he was trying too hard to be noncommittal. "Have you been contemplating that for a while?"

"I've thought of it off and on, but seeing Jace's tats, knowing you designed them, showed me what I've been missing. Now I've gone from a passing curiosity to giving it serious consideration."

"In that case, we might be able to work something out." He sounded pleased, which really wasn't much of a surprise. I'd worked around enough artists to know they all liked their genius stroked now and then.

It seemed as good a time as any to begin feeling him out for the kind of play he wanted to indulge.

"So tell me—" I glanced around the seating area and pitched my voice low, turning away from the people gathered there. "Our experience aside, when you usually hook up, do you swallow?"

"No. Never."

"I thought not. You get a facial, don't you? You make them leave their spunk all over your face so you can feel like you've been marked."

"Oh *Christ*." I heard a rustle, like he was shifting, squirming. "Yes."

"I know the papers only tell so much. You only have my word that I don't usually bareback. And I only have your word that you're careful as well."

"I trusted you enough to let you hold a knife to my face. I think accepting your word on the subject of rubbers is at least a step down from that."

"True, but here's the thing: I want to do it again. Fill you up. Leave my load in you and on you. Make sure you're dripping with reminders of who had you. Every time."

I was going to wind up in the john, jacking off, if I wasn't careful.

"I, um . . ." He sighed. "I'm not sure how to answer that."

"Answer it the same way you answered me that afternoon we were texting about what you wanted. If we're going to do this, you need to know you're safe with me. That you don't have to worry about being safe or what risks to take, because I'm looking out for you. That's where the freedom is." I paused to let that sink in. "So answer me the way you would if you didn't have to be afraid."

"Then I want that too."

I closed my eyes and released a long, slow breath. That was what I'd been hoping for, but it wouldn't have surprised me if he'd gone the other way.

"If we see each other again, if we make a habit of it, will you accept my word that I won't do anything to put you at risk? I'm willing to accept yours, trust being the essential element it is, if we're going to continue to do some of the things we've done."

"Yeah. I'll take your word." His voice sounded unsteady. "You'll use protection with anyone but me?"

"There won't be anyone but you."

Geoff's breath caught. "Come again?"

"Relax. I'm not saying I want to start playing house," I hastened to assure him. "But exclusivity is a thing with me. I don't share, and I don't expect whoever I'm with to share me. It might only be for a week, or however long it goes on, but when I'm with someone, that's the way I work. Now, if this is a problem, let me know. We can just leave it at we had a good time while you were here on vacation, and maybe someday we'll hook up again. But if we're thinking of playing together regularly—which it seems like we are—or at least I am, that's my expectation, and it swings both ways."

"I see." Had I thrown him? Maybe. Hell, probably. Most guys our age acted like "monogamy" was a dirty word. But Geoff didn't strike me as a scene queen. More the type to hook up anonymously for convenience when the itch got too strong to ignore. If we were playing together, though, I intended to see he was well-scratched enough that it wouldn't be an issue.

But my proposal took us out of the realm of hookup and into an undefined *something else*. It was a lot to fling at him on the fly like this.

"What are the boundaries?" he asked rather than giving me the promise I was seeking. "It really goes both ways? You weren't cruising the woods behind the Dunes that night to catalog the nocturnal wildlife."

"It absolutely goes both ways. You'll recall I offered exclusivity on my part first and foremost."

"I, um, I can handle that."

"Good." I dropped my voice again. "I don't just want to fuck you. I want to *play* with you. I want to make you scream again. With pain and with fear. I want to take you right to the edge of what you can handle."

The sharp catch of his breath was audible even in the noisy airport.

"Jesus," he moaned, his voice full of yearning. "And what do you think that might entail?"

"We'll figure it out as we go. Slowly. We need to have some long, serious talks about boundaries and your physical—" I knew the word "limitations" would go over like a pregnant pole-vaulter "—considerations. We'll draw up a contract, make sure everything we expect and require is in writing, to protect us both."

"Okay," he said slowly, pausing as though to take that all in. "Why make barebacking the issue? We could do all that with a condom."

"Because biting and bruising are something we'll have to approach with caution, but I'm dying to leave my mark on you. So that's how I'll mark you. And in case you're wondering, that's not something I've ever asked for or offered to anyone else, even in committed relationships."

"All right." His long, slow breath gusted, scratching against the speaker of the phone. "Yes. To all of it."

"Good." I released my own pent-up breath. Over the PA, the airline clerk announced that my flight would begin boarding soon. Suddenly the idea of being this close to him and moving on was unacceptable. "We'll have to discuss this in more detail soon. I took a few risks with you some people would really frown upon. Frankly, things could have gone very, very badly if you'd had a severe phobia of knives. Or fire."

"Oh. I never even thought of that." Of course he hadn't. He'd been expecting beatings and other things that might be an unacceptable risk with his hemophilia. He had a bit of tunnel vision there, as if he couldn't perceive risks that didn't relate to his condition.

"For now, though, I really would like to see you again."

Geoff chuckled. "You mentioned that."

"Did I mention I sent those test results before I got on a plane, and now I'm sitting at O'Hare on layover, waiting for a flight back to Grand Rapids?"

Silence. Followed by a slow, careful exhalation. "How'd you end up there?"

I smiled. "Pretty much anything going into Grand Rapids stops at Chicago or Detroit first. But if there's a reason to stay in Chicago, I don't have to make my connection tonight."

Another weighty silence, and then he swallowed audibly. "Yeah. There's a reason."

"I thought there might be, seeing how you gave me your address. Jace won't mind if I show up on your doorstep?"

"No. He won't mind."

"I'll catch a cab. Be there within an hour. Get yourself ready for me. You know what I expect."

I hung up before he had a chance to do more than acknowledge his instruction. I wanted to see how well he remembered the drill—clean inside and out, stretched, and lubed.

I wasted no time getting out of the airport. What would take Geoff the most time was infusing, and I was hoping to get there before he was done. In Michigan, he'd always managed to do it while I was in meetings or on calls, but if we were going to play regularly, that was a process I had to be intimately familiar with. More importantly, it was necessary for him to get over his insistence on keeping me out of it. No part of the process of ensuring his well-being was going to be off-limits to me. I wouldn't allow it.

Unfortunately, I got there just as he was cleaning up, which was irritating, especially coupled with the obvious relief on his face that suggested he was glad I hadn't arrived sooner. I filed it away as number one on the list of top-priority negotiation points we needed to deal with.

Then lust took over, and all that got shuffled to the back of my mind.

We barely exchanged greetings before we were stumbling toward his bedroom, trying not to trip over our half-shed clothing. We didn't bother to turn on the lights. As impromptu as this was, I wasn't going to set up any sort of scene, but it was glorious that he was hungry enough for me that *caution* wasn't even a word in our vocabulary. He was freshly infused, which he'd explained meant he clotted as well as a non-hemophiliac for a day or so. I didn't need to be all that careful. I could push him down on the bed and pin him there roughly. He offered some resistance, fighting against my weight, and I lifted my head to look at him in the darkness.

"Is all this squirming you're doing a sign that I should let up, or does it mean 'hold me down harder'?"

His eyes glittered up at me, catching the light filtering through the blinds. He licked his lips and rasped, "Harder. Make me feel like I can't get away."

"That's what I thought," I growled, and tightened my grip on his wrists. I pushed my tongue into his mouth and tongue-fucked it ruthlessly, grinding my cock against his hip.

"That's it. Fight me," I snarled against his mouth. I swallowed his gasps, not giving an inch as he tried to wriggle away again. Despite his superior height, I outweighed him by a good sixty pounds, and he didn't really want to be free. He just wanted to feel more held.

And to be honest, the tussle suited my mood, even if it was rougher than I'd planned to be before we had a chance to negotiate. I was still raw from running into Kyle and having to lay to rest all the bullshit he'd put me through.

I wedged my hips between Geoff's thighs, hooked his legs up over my shoulders, and drove into him, grateful he was already prepped, as I'd told him to be. There wasn't quite enough lube, and the struggling had made him tense. The rough friction guaranteed he'd be sore in the morning.

But Geoff wasn't objecting, so I didn't care. I wanted him to ache, wanted him to feel the burn of tight muscles resisting and finally giving way simply because I left him no other alternative. They spasmed and clenched around my dick as my hips butted up against his ass. He rolled his head in a state of confused near-delirium, which fed the raw thing inside me.

He pushed at my shoulders weakly, until I pinned them beside his head again. I reined myself in enough to pause, though.

"All right?" I gritted, my breath slashing in and out between clenched teeth. I scanned his features, which were barely discernible in the darkened room.

He nodded, wetting his lips. "Yeah." There was more than a little whimper riding the edge of his voice, and I shuddered above him as he relaxed by slow increments. It was the last chance I gave him to tell me to take it easy. Once I began to move, I made sure he didn't have the breath to do anything more than groan.

"Christ!" I panted in his ear, my hips pistoning, his moans rising and falling with each shove of my cock past his prostate. And through it all, his hands remained pinned beside his head. All he could do was use the leverage of his calves on my shoulders to push against my thrusts and help drive me deeper.

"Thought about . . . fucking you . . . for days," I rasped, harsh explosions of breath punctuating every few words. "Want you. Wanna hurt you. Wanna make you scream."

"Yes. God, *please*, yes." He begged beautifully, without shame, all that prickly pride evaporated in the delirium of his passion.

Since I'd departed Saugatuck, all I'd wanted was *more* of him, more of what we'd just started to scratch the surface of, more of all that I'd sworn off before I left New York. It was reckless and stupid to go there when we still had so much to figure out, but at that moment I didn't care. I wanted to handle him with all the roughness he was pleading for.

Releasing one of his wrists, I grabbed his jaw, thumb and fingers pressing on the hinge. "Open."

He didn't have much of a choice with my fingers digging in. His mouth dropped open, and I crashed down on it, my weight folding him in half as I forced my tongue deep inside.

I ended the kiss as abruptly as I'd begun it, rearing back and ramming into him hard enough to make him shout. "Someday soon when I fuck you, it's gonna be your throat I drive my cock into. Gonna fuck your face until you can't breathe."

"Yes!" He nodded avidly each time my hips collided with his ass. His dick was tight and rigid between us, dripping pre-cum on his stomach with every thrust, like he could have come from fucking and words alone. All it would take was a stroke, I was sure. He reached for himself, but I batted his hand away.

"You wanna come?" I hissed in his face. "That what you want?"

"Yes, please. Oh Christ, please . . ."

"I'm not done with you yet." I glared down at him fiercely. "I'm not gonna stop just because you come. Don't give a shit if you like it or not."

"*Please*." The look Geoff gave me was desperate, beyond caring about anything other than easing the pressure building in his nuts. "Please. Need to . . . Need it."

"Then do it." I seized his cock and jacked him with quick, rough strokes, my hand twisting around the swollen head, wrenching a scream from him. His face contorted, his entire body tensing as if he was having difficulty coming, as if he was so far gone that he *couldn't*. And then he pulsed and began to spurt. His body clenched with each surge, but my weight kept him pinned beneath me, kept him open and at my mercy.

I thrust my fingers into his mouth, dripping with his own spunk, force-feeding it to him so roughly he nearly gagged. Then I jerked out of him and flipped him over as though he weighed nothing. I hauled his hips up with one hand while I pushed his face into the pillows with the other. They muffled his yell when I rammed into his ass again.

He went wild. He tried to buck me off, to scramble away, but I held him down and used him despite his struggles.

"I warned you," I ground out. "Now you take it. Take it for me. Take it until I'm done with you."

He took it. Not without resistance, but he endured until his shoulders relaxed. When he turned his head, I could see a Zen-like expression of contentment, his mind visibly disconnected from his body's ordeal. It was beautiful, that sublime ecstasy, and it made my nuts tighten and draw up, heat and electricity flaring at my tailbone and working its way up my spine as I surged past the point of no return.

Twitching and shuddering, I collapsed against his back. A secret thrill shook me, knowing I'd bred him, *left my mark* with the slippery seed I'd pumped into him.

Geoff grumbled when I finally pulled out and flopped over to lie panting next to him. Despite my exhaustion, I smiled to hear it. Beside me, he stretched each limb in a way that felt furtive, like he didn't want me to know he was taking inventory of his physical state.

That wasn't going to fly with me.

"Tell me," I growled, running a hand down his torso as he rolled onto his back and lifted his legs.

He sighed. "Just checking for an iliopsoas bleed. That's the biggest concern with anything that impacts the pelvis. Fucking, spanking, et cetera. They can be bad news and cause nerve damage. Thing is, most information about hemophilia and sex assumes the guy is straight, and so there's information about how thrusting can cause bleeds. Not much about bottoming."

"There's not even information for women?" I asked, thinking back over my research.

Geoff smiled. "My sister loves to tease me about how that's one of the benefits of having redundant X chromosomes. Get a bum one, the other takes up the slack. She says it evens up the cosmic imbalance ever so slightly, that genetic disorders are one of the few areas in which guys get the short end of the evolutionary stick." He shrugged. "But seriously, most of the information about women with bleeding or clotting disorders and sex deals with periods and childbirth."

"Ah. Not so helpful then."

He snorted. "Not really. Anyway, one of the causes of a psoas bleed is getting hit on the ass, so . . ."

I nodded slowly. This was my chance to show him he could be honest with me about his physical condition and it wasn't going to scare me or put me off. I imagined that would be a lesson we'd have to go over a lot before it finally sank in.

"Okay. You're the one who knows your body best. So tell me honestly: is it better if I don't fuck you like that again, or is it an acceptable risk?"

The corner of his mouth lifted in a wry smile. "You think anyone would advise straight bleeders not to fuck their wives because there's a risk? Yeah, you were slamming against my ass a bit. I'll do what they advise other guys to do—keep an eye on things, treat it aggressively if there is an issue. But I don't think there's any reason to say we can't do that at this point."

"Good," I rumbled, rolling toward him to scrape my teeth down his throat without biting. "Because that felt good."

"Yeah, it did." He hummed. "That's what I've always wanted fucking to be. What I've always held back from. Or what guys who knew shied away from."

"I won't," I promised him. "Not unless we've assessed the risk together and decide not to go there. If that happens, we'll find alternatives that still give you what you need, okay?"

"Okay." His smile was shaky, his eyes a little too glossy in the sketchy half-light. But he sank into my kiss, his body relaxing by inches until he finally tucked his face into the crook of my neck and sighed.

CHAPTER SEVENTEEN

Geoff

S ilence descended, and I couldn't decide if that was awkward or not. Despite the rigorous fuck, neither of us was falling asleep. But then I wasn't in any hurry to make conversation that might lead to uncomfortable stuff, either, and I was cozy there tucked against him.

"So, what emergency took you to New York?" I finally ventured.

Robin's fingers, which had been brushing my shoulder, stilled long enough to let me know that this was another New York–related subject he was reluctant to get into.

"Legal stuff," he answered, an edge to his voice. "A lot of it relating to the shelter, transferring the lease of the property and the accounts to the new administrators, among other things."

And that required him to drop everything and take off at a moment's notice?

"You didn't have any warning?" I lifted my head to look at him.

Robin shrugged, his eyes evading mine. "Some of it was time sensitive."

"Ohh-kay." I could sense I wasn't getting the whole answer from him, and that sort of pissed me off, considering he was adamant about full disclosure of all my shit.

Now the silence was definitely awkward, and Robin looked

annoyed. He blew his breath out in a puff. "A lot of it had to do with my ex. Kyle."

"The one who was embezzling?"

He nodded. "It was more than that." I could hear the tension in his voice, feel it in his body next to mine. "I cooperated with the investigation when it became apparent that funds were missing. I was the one who spotted some of the stuff linking Kyle to the discrepancies. So he—"

Robin pulled away from me and sat up on the edge of the bed, gripping the rim of the mattress. "He wasn't just my boyfriend. He was my sub. And he tried to make my testimony about the embezzlement look suspect by accusing me of abuse. He used marks left over from our last scene as his 'evidence.'"

I froze in the process of sitting up to reach for him. He'd been accused of domestic violence? Shit. Was I getting involved with an abuser?

Robin peered at me over his shoulder. "I swear to you, I never laid a hand on Kyle without his wholehearted, enthusiastic consent," he said, turning to face me fully. "Yes, I left bruises and welts on him, but he expected— Hell, he *demanded* them. He was always pushing me for harder play, edge play, things that crossed a line I wasn't comfortable crossing. The scene where I left those marks on him happened at a friend's play party; I had witnesses that he had consented and had even begged for more. Luckily, the police and prosecutor who investigated the charge were both LGBT-friendly and knew a little about kink, or it could have gotten bad. Eventually Kyle recanted and the charges were dropped."

Trust. Robin had been hammering away at the importance of it since we'd met. But this was . . . Jesus. Of course, no one wanted to be involved with a batterer, but for me, even a comparatively mild assault could be catastrophic. Was I endangering my life?

His pale eyes radiated fear. And . . . resignation?

"I know that must sound scary. Who in their right mind would want to start seeing someone who's been accused of abuse, no matter how they try to explain it? I'm not sure I would chance it, especially if I were in your situation. But hiding it would look worse, so . . ." He trailed off on a sigh. "Better to let you know now if we're getting into something long-term."

I bowed my head, flashing over our relatively short acquaintance, looking for anything that could be a warning sign of an inclination toward domestic violence. But how did you even look for such a thing?

Trust. He was entrusting me with this confession, wasn't he? And it wasn't the first time he'd extended his trust since calling me earlier. He'd asked for my trust, and he was giving me his in return.

I met his eyes. "Thank you for telling me."

The tension drained out of him in a rush, leaving him slumped and somehow smaller, sitting there on my bed, bare and vulnerable. A golden Norse god shrunk to a mere human. I laid a hand along his chin to bring him in for a kiss. It was maybe a more tender gesture than anything we'd shared so far. Was I giving away that I'd started to develop feelings for him? Did I particularly care if I was?

If I inadvertently clued him in, Robin didn't seem put off by it. I ended up beneath him again, in an entirely different way. Wrapped around each other, sharing kisses for the sheer enjoyment of kissing, no intention of taking it further than our sated bodies cared to.

Eventually we paused to catch our breaths and get his weight off me. I stretched out, plastered against the side of his body, my head on his furred chest.

"It still amazes me that you went from spending your life helping homeless LGBT kids to opening an art gallery in a Lake Michigan tourist town," I mused. "I mean, I know you explained about the donors and the politics, and of course, now I understand about Kyle, but—"

"Yeah, well, that was only part of the story. I left for several reasons." He sighed and shifted to lie on his side facing me, curling his arm under his pillow. His eyes flicked to the dark ceiling for a long moment, then back to me. "One of the biggest is that I couldn't cut it."

I lifted my eyebrows and lay there silently, not prompting. He let his fingers walk up my arm to my shoulder, stroking lightly before he finally continued.

"It takes a special type of person to do that work, especially the counseling. Someone with a fortitude that it turns out I don't have. I don't know. Maybe it's because I started out intending to help kids I saw heading the same direction Isaac went in, so I felt a personal connection to them all, or— I don't know. Could be I'm just a spoiled rich boy who can't understand when things don't work the way I think they should." He briefly tightened the hand that had been caressing my shoulder and then released, as though he was afraid he might grip me too hard.

"Whatever it was, I couldn't get enough emotional distance and perspective to deal with their pain and keep my own sanity. I internalized it too much. Every tragic story, every failure to help a kid who decided to run off rather than be helped."

Something in my chest shifted, beginning to ache, though I couldn't say if it was *for* him or merely in sympathy with him.

"Even before Hurricane Sandy and the embezzlement mess, I was drinking more than I should have. I was a problem drinker heading for alcoholism. I'd lost my emotional bearings. Things kept hitting me too hard, so every minor crisis blew up into a catastrophe in my mind." He blew out a long sigh. "I was on the verge of a breakdown. Then the rest of it happened, and I realized I wasn't doing anyone any good that way. I couldn't help the kids, and I definitely couldn't help myself. The best thing I could do for everyone was to step back and leave it to people who were better able to do the work." His fingers squeezed mine. "I went to Michigan to start over because I couldn't even be around New York without trying to be involved. Honestly, it's just best for everyone if I stick to writing checks."

"I'm sorry." I drew his hand to my face and pressed a kiss to it. "For you to care as much as you do, that alone is a big deal. More than other people even bother with. I don't think it's a failure that it turned out to be work you weren't suited to."

"No." He tucked our joined hands under his face, pillowing his cheek on them. That twisting ache in my chest grew tighter. "The failure came in that I didn't let go early enough. I held on too long, and almost destroyed everything we had been working to build."

I frowned. It sounded like he blamed himself for the embezzlement as well, even though that was clearly all on his ex. He didn't offer any clarifying details to go with that statement.

I heard water running in the next room and realized Jace had finally come home. The silence once again stretched out into something that threatened to become uncomfortable. The only thing that saved it was the intimacy of his face tucked against the back of my hand.

"When did you reschedule your flight for?" I asked, for lack of anything better to discuss.

"Tomorrow evening. I have to be back in Saugatuck the day after tomorrow. "But . . . There's no reason I can't return. Regularly."

His pale eyes held mine. I swallowed, clueless as to how I was going to navigate this thing but unable to resist its allure. "There's no reason I can't make the drive up to Michigan either."

"Good." Robin withdrew his hand from mine and planted it on my shoulder, rolling me onto my stomach with a single pull. His mouth found the junction of my neck and shoulder as he draped himself over my back. He didn't bite—he never had, not since I told him not to—but his teeth scraped my neck, and in a way it was like the blade of the knife that had caressed my face. Skirting the edge. Hinting at danger enough to charge my nerves, making me feel electrified.

Alive.

I writhed beneath his weight, humping the bed as my dick swelled. I could feel his firming up, first against my hip and then along the crack of my ass, which was already slick with his semen. I loved that thought for the same reasons I loved the scrape of his teeth.

His fingers laced with mine and stretched my arms above my head, wrapping them around the slats of the headboard. He ground against me hard enough to make me whimper after the way he'd already pounded me into the mattress.

"Are you sore?" His voice was a menacing purr behind my ear.

"Yes," I gasped, even as I shoved my ass against his cock.

He drew back, his hand moving between us, lining him up until he pressed tauntingly against my tender hole.

"Good," he growled, and pushed inside.

"Sore" didn't begin to describe my state the next morning. Really, it was closer to noon, judging by the light creeping in around the blinds. Robin had taken me at my word that I wanted to hurt. In the process, I realized that my fantasies had barely scratched the surface of the reality.

I was frustrated by the lack of paraphernalia this unplanned encounter entailed, because he couldn't hurt me by brute force. I'd set limits on pinching and biting and things that would strain my joints or impact my deep muscles, and even at his most brutal, Robin abided by them. It never got to the point where I needed my safeword.

He woke me up by making good on the threat he'd issued the night before—forcing his cock down my throat. If I hadn't so recently infused, I wouldn't have dared do it. We're warned that mouth and throat bleeds can cause swelling that could block the airway. But when I came abruptly to consciousness with Robin dragging me so that my head hung upside-down off the side of the bed, I didn't try to stop him. He stuffed a pair of underwear—his or mine, I wasn't sure—in my hand and told me to drop it if I needed to stop. Then he commanded me to open my mouth, because he intended to use my other hole this time.

My throat was elongated, a straight line from my mouth down my esophagus. I was open. Vulnerable. At his mercy.

"Think you'll be okay like this for a few minutes?" he asked. While his tone was relaxed, the look he gave me was sharp enough that lying wouldn't have been a good idea.

"Yeah, I think it's fine right now."

Robin simply nodded, which made me really glad I hadn't tried to downplay anything. *Trust.*

He fucked my mouth in shallow thrusts until I got used to the position and the angle. Then he rammed himself down my throat, cutting off my air and making me gag. I flailed involuntarily, my body struggling for life-sustaining breath even as my mind exulted that I was checking off another fantasy on my mental wish list.

He drew back to let me cough and splutter, drool wetting my face, and then shoved in deep again. His taint pressed against my nose, his balls swinging against my eyes. He laid his hand on the front of my throat, and said, his voice harsh and choked, "Fucking hell. I can see my dick moving in your throat."

I would have given him a needy groan if I'd had the breath for it.

He fucked my throat fast and hard, with the same heedless roughness he'd used to ream my ass three times during the night. By the time he went still and shuddered, his spunk gushing down my esophagus in thick spurts, I could add saliva and tears to the list of fluids soiling me. At that point I was nearly delirious. Lack of breath and a strange Zen made my struggles and suffering irrelevant. I was hard and didn't even realize it until Robin eased me back up onto the bed. He curled around and over me, jacking me off while he spread kisses on my begrimed face. The orgasm that rushed up from my nuts was gentle, a sweet lassitude spreading through me as I came all over my stomach.

When I finally caught my breath, he left the bed, pulling the covers over me with no regard for the mess. "Stay there. I'll be right back."

Dazed and lethargic, I nodded and let myself drift. I was vaguely aware of water running in the bathroom next door, and the sound of voices outside the bedroom as Jace greeted Robin. The word "coffee" was spoken with all due reverence and longing. Then Robin was back, sitting on the bed and washing me with a wet cloth, starting with my face and belly and ending with my aching ass.

"How you doing?" he asked, setting the cloth aside and pressing a kiss between my shoulder blades as I lay half-melted into the mattress. "Hungry? Thirsty?"

"Yeah. Tired." I blinked at him sleepily, feeling so incredibly good that I wanted to crawl inside him and stay there, basking in him and this feeling for as long as possible.

He smiled, his teeth white and straight and perfect and his eyes warm despite that cool, pale blue. It occurred to me that maybe I should try to rein in the sex-drunk bliss before I got downright moony, but I couldn't be bothered. Especially not when he was giving me that indulgent look and touching me with such care.

"I don't blame you. Jace is making eggs and coffee. Let's get some breakfast in you. Then you can get some more sleep."

"What about you?" My voice was a harsh rasp, my throat sore. I managed to regain enough muscle control to lift my head off the pillow. "You were up most of the night too."

"I can sleep later. Jace is going to show me some of his work at the studio. But I'll be back for at least a couple hours before I have to go to the airport. You rest while we're gone." There was a doting softness about his smile that made me think I wasn't the only one feeling moony. "Once I get home, we can work out a schedule for when would be the best time to visit."

"'Kay."

He leaned over, and I rolled to my back to meet his kiss. I lingered in it, grateful for the peace that made it feel unimportant to question how this had turned into . . . whatever it was. Maybe by the time I came down from the high, I would acclimate and not freak out or feel insecure about it.

After a moment, he drew back. His eyes searched mine, and it seemed like he wanted to say something. But he smiled again and helped me out of bed.

I DID sleep while Robin showered and gathered his stuff near the door. Just before he and Jace left, though, I woke to a feeling I'd been dreading since I met him.

The bleed was in my left wrist, a tickling, prickling, bubbly feeling that would eventually blossom into agony. I didn't think we'd done anything to cause it, but sometimes there wasn't a reason; it just happened. It was already painful: white-hot flares radiated from the joint with every movement.

I went into the kitchen for water to wash my Percocet down, and for a bag of frozen peas to use as a cold pack. Robin paused by the door. "Can't sleep?"

I shrugged and blinked sleepily, pretending I wasn't wide-awake and pissed off with the universe for giving me a bleed *right now*.

"Thirsty," I said, trying for a drowsy smile. I closed the freezer door and opened the refrigerator as if I were too out of it to know what I was doing. I turned my back to dig in the fridge for a bottle of water, trying not to look like I was only using one hand.

He'd be leaving in a few hours. If I could play it low-key, he'd never need to know I was having a bleed, never need to question himself and whether he'd done something to cause this. He'd never get that cautious look in his eye that people got when they suddenly began thinking of me as breakable.

"Okay." His smile was as dotty as before. "Be back in a bit."

When the door closed, I downed two Percocet and wrapped my wrist before mixing my factor and sitting down at the table to infuse again.

By the time Robin and Jace got back, I'd returned the peas to the freezer to let them chill again. The pills had muted the pain, but it was bad enough that I'd had to take something stronger. I was on my way to well and truly stoned. Bleeds always made me irritable, and this one even more so. Of all the fucking rotten timing. It couldn't have waited four hours? I was half-drugged and half-furious and one hundred percent irrational.

Fuck. I was probably too loaded to keep it on the DL. Robin would see and know. He'd start to question whether he really could play with me the way I wanted to play. Those glorious few hours between the time he'd arrived at our door and the time he'd left with Jace would be the last time I'd experience the sort of dangerous pleasure I craved from him.

Jace looked at the pill bottles on the coffee table. I hadn't put them away because I was worried about staggering into something and causing another injury. I could see him weighing his options, trying to decide how best to offer assistance while respecting my right to choose what to tell Robin. He also knew that bleeds made me cranky as fuck and that I would want to be left the hell alone.

Sucking on his cheek, he murmured something and went to his room.

"Hey." Robin greeted me with a kiss and a smile, and I returned them, reaching for him with my good arm and trying to force my fury at my stupid fucking disorder aside.

"Hey." I was high, and I'm sure my smile must have been lopsided. Or maybe I swayed. Something gave it away. Robin looked at the pill bottles and back at me.

"Something wrong?"

"Don't worry about it," I said tersely.

He frowned at the bottles again, his jaw flexing. His eyes passed over me, assessing, but I had my wrist tucked where he couldn't see how swollen it was.

"Where's the injury?" he asked softly.

"It's not an *injury*, it's a *bleed*. Seriously, don't worry about it." I curled my good hand around the back of his neck and drew him closer, angling for a kiss. Frankly, I wasn't much in the mood for sex with my wrist throbbing, but I'd ignore the fucker and try to show him a good time until he left. "I can handle it."

"Handle what, exactly?" Robin let me pull him close, but he held back from the kiss, his expression shuttered.

Blame the drugs, but I wasn't exactly thinking clearly or making the best decisions. "It's no big deal."

"I'm not making a big deal out of it. I'm not freaked, but I need to know." He squatted in front of me. "Tell me."

"Will you *stop*?" I snapped, the irritability taking over. I wasn't a nice person to begin with when I was in pain, my wounded pride made it worse, and the meds obliterated the filters that kept me from spilling that shit all over people. That wasn't an excuse, but it was what it was. "It's not your business!"

"It *is* my business," he insisted, and I could see him getting tense, hear the edge in his voice. "If you can't let me in on this, then there is no point to us even talking about spending more time together. I need to know what your body and health are doing or I can't take care of you—"

I flung out the arm with the injured wrist, regretting it when the jolting movement sent hot flares of pain up my nerves. "No one is asking you to fucking take care of me!"

He drew back as though stung. "Yeah, you fucking well are if you want me to do the things you claim to want. This is my hard limit, Geoff. No exceptions. Either you level with me about this shit or we're *done*."

Growling in frustration, I thrust my sleeve up to my biceps and bared my arm for him. "Fine. It's this wrist. It's not necessarily anything we did. Sometimes this shit just happens. Happy?"

Robin's carefully neutral expression pissed me off worse, but I let him take my arm gently. He didn't touch my wrist, but even touching the arm sent molten zings of torture into the joint.

"When did it start?" he asked softly. When I didn't answer, he looked up and took my chin, lifting it until I met his eyes. "Geoff? This started before I left, didn't it? You were lying to me about why you got up."

I jerked my head away and glowered at the wall.

He carefully turned my arm to look at the underside. There,

along the antecubital vein, hematomas both fresh and fading discolored the visibly scarred skin. They were nothing he hadn't seen before in Saugatuck, but now it seemed like he was seeing something else.

There was a reason some of my hemo acquaintances tagged their Instagram pics #notajunkie.

"I know these are just from infusing," he murmured, a strange note in his voice. His face seemed like it'd lost a little more color. "Right?"

Of course, knowing *why* he was asking and not being insulted by it were two different things.

"What, you going to accuse me of shooting up?" I sneered, wanting to yank my arm away but unwilling to suffer the pain the motion would inflict. "You wouldn't be the first to jump to conclusions."

He muttered something that sounded like, "That would be just my luck," but then he shook his head. "I saw your med stash. I believed you when you explained it. But I have to say—" He drew a deep breath, swallowing hard as his fingers swept past my track marks without touching. "Right now, seeing *this*, the way you're acting, it's poking some sore spots that haven't had nearly enough time to heal."

His expression as he stared at my arm was enough to make me get a grip and dial back the asshole a bit, despite the pain. He looked . . . raw. Like he was seeing something that wasn't there.

Eventually he set my arm down very carefully and pulled back, springing to his feet as if he'd discovered his ass was on fire. "I've got to go."

"What? I thought you wouldn't have to leave for a couple hours. If you're running away because of *this*—" I gestured with my good arm, my temper flaring again.

"I'm not," he said quickly, then squeezed his eyes shut and hung his head. "Or I am, but not for the reasons you think. Geoff, I can cope with your condition. I know I can do that. I can give you what you're looking for, but—" His jaw flexed, and I watched him pull himself together. "I'm not sure I *should*. I don't trust—"

"Me?" I narrowed my eyes at him.

"*Me*." He looked so bleak and conflicted that I had to tighten my grip on my anger and outraged pride. He'd *asked* me to expose this for him, the bleeds and the pain and all the parts that made me feel like I couldn't have a normal life. He'd *insisted* on it, and now he was bolting? "Look, this is baggage. So I'm going to go, and we'll . . . think about this. Once your wrist is healed and we've had a chance to let it settle . . . we'll see."

"'We'll see'?" I managed to pour enough derision into those two words that even I cringed, but that was about the weakest excuse for a brush-off I'd ever heard, and I'd heard plenty. "Fine. Go."

He retreated toward the door, and I stared after him, absolutely furious and completely bewildered. All that arrogance of his, all the confidence he'd exuded since that first night in the club, they were nowhere to be seen. I was too doped up to make sense of it, how he could be acting this hurt and lost when *he* was the one fucking turning his back on *me*.

He hesitated by the door as though he would say something more, but I cut him off. "Just get out." I shoved myself off the sofa to grab another bag of peas from the freezer. The cool air hit my over-heated face like a wave of frost, and I shut my eyes, letting it soothe me until I heard the click of the front door closing.

I didn't believe he'd really left, though, until I returned to the living room and found him gone. I stared at the door for a disbelieving moment. Then I picked up the prescription bottles and hurled them against it. Working one-handed, I hadn't closed the Percocet the entire way. It popped open, raining pills across the room.

"*Fuck!*"

CHAPTER EIGHTEEN

Geoff

I'm sorry I was an asshole. I don't handle things well when I have a bleed.
It was the fifteenth or so text that I'd composed and would probably delete without sending. They tended to vacillate between apologies for my behavior (I really did crank the asshole-itude up to eleven when I had a bleed) and indignation that he'd walked out and hadn't bothered to contact me.

I stared at it, my thumb hovering over the screen.

"You're not going to get any points for playing the martyr." Jace gave me a level look over his easel. I was putzing around his studio, unable to bear the silence of the apartment any longer. "So Robin has issues. Hallelujah. The dude was too perfect. He needed some fucking issues. It sucks, but it can be dealt with. You're welcome to come with me when I drive the paintings up to him."

It had been almost two months since Robin ran out of the apartment, and this was the most Jace had said on the subject. I knew he'd been in contact with Robin about the purchase of some work for the gallery, but I also knew he wasn't about to step into the middle of my fucking mess. That was one of the best things about his friendship: he was a great sounding board, but he never veered off into being a busybody. Playing mediator wasn't his responsibility.

I shrugged, trying to see something through the clouded glass of the window. "I'm not sure he wants me there. I mean, he's the one who decided he couldn't deal with . . . whatever."

"Seems like you're entitled to some answers, but you need to ask the right questions first. Which maybe you neglected to do before."

"Excuse me?"

"Come on, man." Jace glanced at me wryly. "You were totally convinced that any problems between you and Robin were going to come from your end. That it would be about your medical issues, one way or the other. You never bothered to find out if he might have stuff that would need to be dealt with."

"That's a lot of words to say I made it all about me."

"Call it like I see it, dude."

I sighed and drummed my fingers on the windowsill. We'd been friends long enough that Jace understood most of the self-esteem issues I had. My mother's neuroses hadn't helped any. I'd lost count of the number of times I started to feel like I was a part of things until she stepped in and reminded me I was different, weaker, less able to do what other people took for granted.

The hell of it was, she was both right and wrong. Yeah, being a hemo kid came with challenges, but most of the moms learned how to find a balance and let us have a sense of normalcy. My mom had rejected any well-meaning input as meddling. She'd been too afraid to loosen her grip. And I'd allowed it long past the point where I should have told her to back off and let me live my life.

Which I'd never really done. Not until the trip to Saugatuck.

But the fact remained: as much as I hated them, as much as I was learning to manage a sense of normalcy despite them, I did have limitations. My presence in Jace's studio that afternoon was a perfect case in point.

I should have been at work. I'd finally leased a station in a body-art studio with the intention of building up a clientele and establishing a reputation. But my third day on the job, one of the other artists had left a box where it didn't belong. I tripped over it and fell against a chair, starting a muscle bleed in my thigh that had put me in the hospital, and left me unable to work for over two weeks. I wasn't sure when I'd be capable of standing and moving freely for long enough to resume working. I'd finally sent Jace to pack up my equipment and tell them to lease the space to someone else.

I would have to apply for disability benefits if bleeds kept me from working. Working for Rogier had paid well, even if it had sucked, but my savings from LA were quickly dwindling.

"Disability." That one ranked right up there with "delicate" on my list of most-hated words. Especially now, after that brief time when I'd felt what it was like not to be seen that way.

I wished I was one of the men who could wear the bleeder badge with pride. I tried to do my part, to rally for the cause, for education and health-care reform and research to make our lives better. I wanted to be one of those guys who could take the fucking rotten hand we'd been dealt by our genetics and turn it into something positive. But I wasn't.

I hated it. I hated that I'd spent the first quarter century of my life feeling that my mother's anxiety was my fault. I hated that I'd tried so long, that I'd even felt it necessary, to compensate for my brother's death. I hated that I had the joints of a man twice my age. I hated that every time I sat down to dose myself with factor, it felt like *surrender*.

I wasn't in denial about my condition. I just despised it.

But Jace was right. I'd been so convinced that any impediment to what was happening between Robin and I would come from me that I'd never thought to find out if he had issues of his own. Not until he'd bolted.

Maybe it wouldn't have mattered if he'd remained just a casual fuck. But something had changed, especially that last morning at the Dunes and again when he showed up in Chicago. I wasn't ready to put a label on it. It could be hormones run wild, the thrill of something new and unaccustomed and incredibly, *incredibly* intense.

It could be. But I wasn't betting on it.

So now I needed to figure out how to deal with the fact that other people had issues too.

Jace continued painting behind me as I went over this well-worn ground. Not pushing. Not judging. Just there, waiting for me to make up my fucking mind. Finally he murmured, "Probably easier to leave it be. If you go after him, you've got to accept that your hemophilia isn't the problem for him. I get it. That's got to be hella weird for you. I mean, how can anyone else be okay with who and what you are if *you're* not?"

I turned and lifted an eyebrow at him, snorting. For a guy with such a carefree, laissez-faire approach to life, he was astonishingly profound at times.

He never so much as glanced up from the easel.

I looked away again. "I'll think about it."

JACE DIDN'T SAY anything about his meeting with Robin after he delivered the paintings to the soon-to-be-opened gallery, and I didn't ask.

I wasn't having any luck finding another space to lease in any studio I'd want my name attached to. A persistent thought nagged at me: namely, maybe a large city wasn't the right place to establish myself. Maybe a beachfront town would be better. Tattoo shops always did well along boardwalks and such.

Of course, Saugatuck wouldn't have the level of foot traffic as, say, Venice Beach, and they were far more buttoned-up than a city would be. The county was entirely conservative, and the locals too, despite it being a popular gay and lesbian resort town. Which would be perfect; there, my clean-cut appearance would be an asset. Reassuring to rich townies and vacationers looking to do something adventurous but not too scary. And if I could get a space where the tourist traffic was relatively heavy, the displays of my designs would do all the advertising I needed. I'd only seen one body-art studio while we were there, and they were outside of town. While they looked like they did good work, they weren't on my level.

Finding a space I could afford would be a challenge. The issues with getting a loan were still with me, no matter where I went, and after the incident with the misplaced box, it was obvious I needed my own studio. Someplace I could organize to keep things safer for me. I had to be my own boss, because there would be times when I couldn't work for days or even weeks on end.

Regardless of whether I ever made myself speak to Robin again, moving to Saugatuck would be a sound business strategy. If it gave me an opportunity to pursue things with him, that would be wonderful. If not, it would give me a chance to meet other men of a more down-to-earth sort than the big-city scene queens I was used to.

I'd be lying if I said I wasn't *really* rooting for option A.

"GEOFF. Use the fucking life insurance money." Ling's annoyance was obvious. I was Skyping with her while I sketched a design. It was another inspired by Robin, as I imagined what might look good on him or suit his personality and interests. This one was less oceanic and more sanguinary. A dressage whip, like in the video I'd shared with him, crossed the back on a diagonal from right hip to left shoulder, and a single red drop hung from the end of the lash. At the waist on the right, a longer single-tail bullwhip sat coiled, and on the right shoulder, a pair of leather cuffs dangled as if from a hook overhead. The entirety was set against a rippled backdrop that, with careful shading, would look like purple velvet drapes.

It wasn't even remotely discreet, and I doubted it would ever become reality, but it was where my imagination took me.

"That money is for an emergency." I gave Ling a stubborn look.

"That money is for your future, to see that you are able to take care of yourself. What better way to do that than to start your own business and make it grow?"

"Starting a new business is a risky venture. What if it doesn't work? I'll have wasted the money, and everything that you and Mom and Dad sacrificed over the years so they could afford those insurance policies will be for nothing."

Ling's growl rattled the laptop speakers. "Jesus! Weren't you just telling me you thought it was time you took some fucking chances?"

Verbal aggression was so unlike Ling that I nearly dropped my pencil. I stared at her in astonishment.

"Geoff—" She sighed, leaning her elbows on whatever table or desk she had her computer set up on. "All our lives, you've always been so careful and dutiful. Especially when it came to Mom. The way you took care of her, sacrificed things you wanted to avoid upsetting her . . ."

I glanced away, blinking. Remembering her without anger *hurt*. Despite how unhealthy our relationship had been, I missed her. "She was just so emotionally fragile. She needed it."

"She wasn't *fragile*, she was neurotic," Ling said bluntly. "She used your desire not to upset her against you. She manipulated you into not doing things she didn't want you to do. Everyone tried to tell her to back off: me, Dad, the counselors at the Hemophilia Treatment Center, the other hemo moms. She ignored us. Everyone could see it happening except you, and you wouldn't hear anything about it. You didn't owe her that. You weren't responsible for David's death, and you're certainly not responsible for the fact that you have a genetic disorder. It's not your fault, and now she's gone anyway. You don't have to keep trying to placate her."

I breathed a bitter laugh. "You wouldn't accuse me of doing that if you knew how reckless I've been recently."

She slapped her hand on the table beside her computer, and my speakers crackled with the loud bang. "Good! It's about damn time!" Even on the blurry webcam, I could see her eyes blazing. "It's long overdue. I'm not saying you have to go crazy, but some calculated risks now and then aren't a bad thing."

I wasn't about to tell her how many of those risks involved sex. "Seems an awfully big chance to take for a thrill."

Ling shrugged. "People do all sorts of crazy shit for thrills. Skydive. Cliff dive. Climb sheer rock faces without ropes. Swim Lake Michigan in the dead of winter. Drive Interstate 76 during rush hour. I'm pretty sure whatever you've been getting up to isn't half as harebrained as most of that."

I felt my eyebrow creeping up. "People drive I-76 during rush hour for thrills?"

"I can't think of any other earthly reason to take it on." She gave a negligent toss of her head. "So think about it. You've got the opportunity and means to establish yourself doing something you love, something at which you're amazing. As the sole remaining person to whom you feel obligated, I absolve you of the fact that the money you'll be using came at the expense of the digital cable, high-speed internet, designer jeans, fashionable footwear, personal car, and iPhone I could have had when I was sixteen. Now go forth and live."

When she put it that way, who was I to refuse? As August inched toward September, I packed up everything I owned and uprooted my life for the second time in less than six months.

CHAPTER NINETEEN

Robin

B y the time mid-September rolled around and Geoff hadn't contacted me—and I had been too chickenshit to contact him—I figured any chance of us working things out was gone. Which was a good thing, right? Considering how everything had gone that last time we'd seen each other in Chicago, I needed to give up this whole idea of us being together.

I'd kept myself busy. My gallery opened in August, in plenty of time to get some traffic before the slow season. In the hope of drumming up business from the locals, I scheduled my first show. I featured several of Jace's paintings, so it should have come as no surprise to me that Geoff would attend.

Hell, who was I kidding? I'd made the decision to spotlight Jace with at least a little forlorn hope that fate would throw Geoff and me together.

He looked good, despite the fact that he was leaning heavily on a cane and grimacing. Immediately I cursed myself for not providing seating—typically, gallery shows didn't, in part to encourage people to move around and see all the work on display—and ran upstairs to the office to bring down a chair.

"Here," I said, setting it next to him where he stood propping up a wall. He turned, narrowing his eyes as he glanced from me to the chair and back again. "Don't give me that look. I'm not going to make a fuss, but it's obvious you're in pain. Even if I had no idea you'd be here, I still should have considered that not everyone can mill around on their feet all night. That was remiss of me."

Slowly his shoulders inched down, and then sagged as he sighed. "You're right. I really need to get off the leg. This bleed's taking a long time to heal, and I don't need to end up in the hospital again. Thanks."

He sank into the chair, and I couldn't help but ask, "How long has it been?"

"I injured it at the end of July." He grimaced again and met my gaze defiantly.

I kept my tone light and casual. "Wow."

"Yeah, well . . ." He rolled his eyes, and his lips quirked in a self-deprecating grin. "It was on its way to healing when I aggravated it by moving, so I only have myself to blame."

"Moving? So you finally got your own place?"

His tone hedged. "Sort of."

To press for more information or not? I was still trying to decide when someone touched my arm to draw my attention, and asked about one of the pieces. Shit. I was working.

"I'll be right there," I assured the potential buyer, and turned back to Geoff. "Look, do you think you can stick around until the show is over? Or can I call you if you need to go?"

He nodded, his voice light as he said, "I'll stick around. Go make Jace some money."

I DON'T THINK I was all that attentive to my would-be clientele after that. My attention was constantly drawn to Geoff—if he was still sitting, if he looked like he was in pain, if he looked like he was going to renege on his promise and slip away. Finally people began to filter out, and he was still there, discreetly downing a pill with the sparkling water Jace had brought him. They had a quiet word as I saw the last of my guests out, and then Jace, too, left. Geoff and I were alone.

I glanced around at all the detritus to be picked up and decided it could wait until the morning.

"I have an office upstairs if you want to talk there, or—"

"I can make it down to the marina if we go slow," he offered, getting me off the hook for deciding how much would be pushing my luck. If he wanted to come back to my boat, things weren't a total loss.

"That'll work. I have a house now, but it's being renovated, so I'm still sleeping on the boat. Let me lock up and we can go."

The weather was growing cooler, and the night breeze coming off the lake was stiff and getting close to chilly. The haze of clouds approaching across the water suggested the possibility of rain. Geoff hadn't brought a jacket, tempting me to drape mine over his shoulders, but it didn't feel like I had the right to indulge in that sort of solicitude.

I let Geoff set the pace for the few blocks from the touristy shopping district that was "downtown" Saugatuck to the marina. He was definitely putting a lot of weight on his cane. I tried not to pry but couldn't help asking, "You said you'd been hospitalized?"

He nodded, frowning. "For several days. Major bleed in my quadriceps. That happens to be a very hard muscle not to use unless you're totally bedridden. I was in a wheelchair for over a week after that. I had to get a hotel room because Jace's apartment isn't wheelchair accessible. Crutches for several weeks after that, and now the cane."

He let me take his arm to help keep him steady on the ramp from the dock to the boat deck. Then he sank onto one of the benches in the lounge, rather than trying to head belowdecks.

"So, um . . ." I hemmed, for once at a loss for words. Geoff, thankfully, didn't have that problem.

"So. *You're* a dick," he announced, leveling a finger at me. "All that bullshit about communication and trust and how I needed to talk to you about shit, and the first time *you* need to talk something out, you pull a stunt like that? That was an asshole move."

I accepted the tirade. "I know. I'm sorry."

"And yeah, I shouldn't have misled you about the bleed when it started, and I owe you an apology for that, but still—"

"It's not about that." I sighed, settling onto the bench opposite him. "At least, not directly."

"Then what was it about? And you better damn well make this good."

"*I didn't see it.* That you were hiding the bleed before Jace and I walked out the door. I didn't notice. For us to have the kind of relationship we were discussing, I need to be able to recognize when you're in trouble, even when you don't."

I rubbed my forehead, suddenly feeling the long hours I'd worked the last few days getting ready for the show. I was really too tired to be having this conversation, but now was the time it was happening. "Do you really want me having the responsibility to take care of you if I can't even see when something isn't right?"

"*What?*" He gave me an incredulous look. "You bolted because you're not a fucking mind reader? Just because you can't somehow magically intuit when I'm hiding a bleed from you, you're a shitty dom? Jesus, Robin."

A very valid point, but still *missing* the point, because he didn't know where all this had started. "It's not the first time I've overlooked signs of a problem that I should have picked up on. Maybe someone with that sort of track record doesn't have any business being responsible for someone else's well-being."

Geoff's eyes narrowed. "This isn't about me, is it? This is about your ex. Er, Kevin."

"Kyle."

"*Whatever.*" Geoff's glower clearly said I'd better start talking.

"He was using." I slumped, both ashamed of myself and too weary to care. "That's why he embezzled. He'd started using again, and he was into his dealer for thousands of dollars."

"Again?"

"He was a counselor we'd hired in part to show the kids that things really could get better. A success story." I couldn't even manage a derisive smile. "He'd been a street kid, thrown out by his parents when he was thirteen, turned out by a pimp, hooked on drugs, but eventually he got himself off the streets and cleaned up."

God, it still hurt. Not the betrayal, but my own sense of *failure*. Unable to stand Geoff's eyes on me, I shot to my feet and crossed to the railing to look out over the dark lake.

"I didn't see it. In retrospect there were about a hundred times I should have, but I always managed to rationalize it to myself. He was under stress at work. He'd heard from his family for the first time in twenty years, and it hadn't gone well. There were plenty of excuses." I scoffed. "I went everywhere for explanations except to the most obvious place."

My eyes started burning. I shook my head hard until the feeling went away. "I was his dom. I was supposed to recognize when something wasn't right. And I totally missed it."

A soft *thud* and shuffle of Geoff's cane, and then he was there at my shoulder, his voice soft. "He didn't want you to see. You missed it because he hid it from you. And you missed my bleed—in the whole thirty seconds you saw me before you were out the door—because *I* hid it from you. I'm *really damned good* at doing that." He snorted softly. "You may be perceptive bordering on psychic, but is it possible your expectations of yourself are a bit too high? Just saying."

I chuckled without much humor. "I never claimed my reaction that day was rational. I was already raw from running into Kyle when I was in New York. I didn't think to question when you went from drowsy and wanting to go back to sleep to wide-awake and supposedly unable to sleep. And then? Seeing you high on painkillers? It all just sort of— I couldn't cope with it, so I bolted. I'm sorry."

"You ran into him?"

Was that a bit of jealousy I heard in Geoff's tone?

"Well, more accurately, he staked out my lawyer's office, knowing I'd be coming back to handle some of the paperwork, and waylaid me. He thought he could get my forgiveness for almost ruining my life. Really, that's the other reason I took off."

"What do you mean?"

I swallowed, gripping the rail tighter. "I know you said your wrist bleed that day wasn't necessarily caused by anything we did—"

"It *wasn't*."

"Okay, but the fact is, when I walked through your door, the way I behaved with you, especially that first time—that wasn't about you and me. I wasn't paying much attention to what I was doing with you that night because I was still pissed off about running into him." I inhaled deeply and blew it out slowly. "If I *had* hurt you, it would have been because I was taking my anger at him out on you."

"I don't recall complaining." Geoff sounded bewildered.

I spun to face him. He was so close, but now wasn't the time to touch him. Which only frustrated me more, because now that we were on the water, he was practically shivering. And I could have used the comfort of physical contact.

I reached behind me to grab the railing again, just to give my hands something else to do.

"But I *know* better. You don't do scenes—especially scenes involving impact play—when you're upset, for exactly that reason. It's pretty much one of the first rules of domming." I closed my eyes, exhaling hard again. "I'm not in control of myself. I haven't been for months, since all that shit with Kyle happened. I'm swinging like a weather vane, one minute certain I need to just swear off playing altogether, and the next thinking maybe I can do it better this time, avoid all the mistakes I made before. But I'm just adding on new ones."

"Maybe." I opened my eyes to peer at him, and he shrugged. "Maybe you are making mistakes. Last I checked, you're human, so you don't get a pass on those, right? You suck it up, learn from it, and move the hell on."

Fuck. He wasn't getting it. Hell, I wasn't sure *I* was getting it. I just knew that right now, I couldn't pick up where we'd left off. I dropped my gaze to the deck. "If I screw up with someone else, I'm not likely to kill them."

A beat of silence. Then another. Then—

"Oh, *fuck you*," Geoff hissed. "You're going to go there *now*?" He stomped away in his uneven gait. When I looked up, he was pacing furiously, or as close to pacing as he could get with the cane. "After what we've done, after everything I confided in you, after all your assurances that you wouldn't let my hemophilia put you off, you're *going to fucking go there*?" The swing of his arms was as explosive as his shout. "*My medical condition is not. About. You!*"

I shook my head, trying to stop the tirade. "That's not what I—"

"The hell it's not!" He stopped pacing to glare at me, his shoulders rising and falling rapidly with his breath. I'd seen him bitter and resentful and mistrusting before, but I'd had no idea he was capable of this sort of anger. "I put my life on hold for two decades because my mother made my disorder and everything we did to handle it about *her* fears and *her* grief and *her* guilt. You can fuck right off if you think I'll do it for you!"

My jaw tightened. "Now who's making the discussion about someone who isn't even here?"

Okay, not the most helpful thing I could have said, and definitely not in that confrontational tone. Damn it, I knew better than this.

"Oh, believe me, if I could say it to her, I fucking would!" Abruptly the fight went out of him, and he sagged, planting his weight on both hands where they gripped his cane. "Holy fuck," he rasped after a moment. "Ling was right."

My own anger drained away like it had never existed. Keeping my movements careful, I walked to the bench and sat down.

"What was Ling right about?" I asked. I ignored the sheen in his eyes as he looked up at me, though everything about his defeated posture was making me ache with the need to comfort him. I kept my own posture open, inviting. Eventually he took me up on my offer and shuffled over to sit across from me.

"I never let myself be angry with her," he finally said. "I've been taking it out on everyone else for years whenever they showed even the slightest hint of concern, but I always protected her. Defended her." He turned his face to the sky, letting his head fall back. "And now she's gone, and I'm never going to have a chance to put all this where it belongs."

"It seemed to me, based on the discussions we had a few months ago, that you never really gave yourself a chance to mourn her." I offered the observation gently. "It's understandable that this would come out sooner or later. Do you think you might have been afraid of experiencing that anger, that maybe that's why you shut yourself off from grieving for her?"

He brought his chin down and gave me a piercing look. "You're wearing your social worker hat with me now?"

I shrugged, smiling slightly. "It's kind of like muscle memory. Eventually you just do it without thinking about it."

"Can we not? Please?" He scrubbed his hand wearily down his face.

"Sure." Taking a chance, I crossed to sit beside him, laying a hand on his knee. "Can I get to the point I was making so badly before you got pissed off?"

He dropped his hand and nodded. "Yeah. Okay. Go ahead."

I took a deep breath. "Please believe me that if your hemophilia were the only issue we were facing, this wouldn't be a problem. I could do everything I promised you I would and more, and I wouldn't have a second of doubt about it. Okay? Can you believe that?"

His mouth tightened, and the muscles in his jaw flexed a couple of times. But he drew a shaky breath and nodded. "I'll try."

"All right." I hesitated a moment, searching for the right words. "The problem is that we're dealing with *two* issues here. The other one, the bigger one, is my doubt *about myself*. I didn't even realize when I made you all those promises that I was full of shit, portraying myself as being so cocky and self-assured. I'm not assured of *anything* about myself right now. Nothing at all."

He looked at me, and I let him stare. Gave him every bit of honesty and openness I could put into my eyes and expression. Eventually, he nodded again. "Go on."

"It's called risk-aware consensual kink, right? So let's be totally frank about the risks. If I were to make a mistake with another person—assuming we weren't doing edge play—I might hurt them. Piss them off enough to safeword or make them refuse to do a scene with me again. But if I fuck it up with you, I could put you in the hospital, or even kill you." I watched the play of emotions on his face as he started to glower, then stopped himself and nodded a third time, reluctantly. "So, yes, your hemophilia is a stumbling block, but only because I don't trust myself to play with you at present."

He dropped his eyes, folding his hands in his lap and staring at them. Eventually he sighed. "Okay. I believe you." The sharp knot of his Adam's apple bobbed at the front of his thin neck. "So I guess that's it, then? For us?"

Now it was my turn to swallow hard. "I don't know. Is it?" I asked carefully, a hollow feeling in my gut. "Is the kink all we're here for?"

His head came up sharply. "No." The haste and emphasis with which he fired that off was gratifying. "At least I'm not," he added, more subdued, uncertainty creeping into his eyes.

"Me neither," I said softly, but with feeling. His eyes sought mine, his expression somber, but then he nodded.

"Okay." A slow smile curled the corner of his mouth, and my own face stretched around a wide grin.

"That isn't to say I wouldn't like to play with you again," I added, my voice dropping to the husky growl that made his pupils dilate just . . . like . . . *that*. "But someday later on. After we know each other more. After I can read you better and we're both doing a better job of communicating things."

He licked his lips and rasped, "And in the meantime?"

"In the meantime . . ." I inched closer, sliding the hand I'd had on his knee up his thigh. "How much can you do with that bum leg of yours?"

"Not much." His mouth twisted ruefully. "Certainly nothing vigorous. I've put too much strain on it tonight."

"That's okay," I murmured, slipping to my knees on the deck before him. I reached for his belt buckle. "I've got plenty of nonvigorous activities in mind."

CHAPTER TWENTY

Geoff

R obin had barely finished swallowing before he urged me, still panting and boneless, down the stairs to his berth, keeping a grip on me to make sure I didn't stumble. There he undressed me and then himself, and laid me on my back to straddle my head and allow me to return the favor.

What followed was a night that made me rethink everything I believed I knew about "careful" sex. I don't know what made it different, but I never felt shortchanged or like I was being handled with kid gloves, even with all the cautious maneuvering we had to do because of my leg.

Maybe I was outgrowing my paranoia about being seen as weak or fragile. But I'd put my money on Robin being the element that made the difference.

Somewhere in the wee small hours before dawn, Robin asked, "When do you go back to Chicago?"

"I don't," I murmured, toying with the light hair furring his chest.

"Unh?"

I lifted my head, snickering at the sleepy grunt that somehow still managed to carry an inquiry. "I said I got my own place. I never said where. I just closed on a space about two blocks from your gallery for my *artisan* tattoo and piercing studio."

I gave the pretentious name the wry twist and eye roll it deserved. I was a damned good body artist, yes, but I had enormous respect for others in my trade (with the exception of that jackass poser, Rogier). The affectation of the branding I was planning to do with the studio was entirely for the benefit of a snooty—and hopefully very well-paying—upper-middle-class clientele.

Robin gawked at me. "Holy shit. Really?"

I shrugged, my face heating up. "I figured, regardless of how things worked out with you and me, I'd be able to distinguish myself better in a small town than in the city. Studios in vacation towns can do quite well. Something about being out of their usual element makes people impulsive, ready to try something new or take risks they normally wouldn't."

"Where are you staying?"

"There's a studio apartment above the shop, or at least that's what the space will be when renovations are done. But while my leg is out, I'm staying at a motel where I can have a ground-floor room. No stairs to climb." I hesitated, then made myself speak. "I need to go back early. Until my leg is healed, I need to infuse every day."

"I'll drive you whenever you have to go," he offered calmly, with the perfect balance of solicitude and respect for my independence. "If you'd prefer, I can pull the car up closer to the marina, so you won't have to walk as far."

"Thank you." I realized my heart was racing and put my head down quickly, trying to slow my breathing.

"Can I make a request?" he asked carefully.

Oh God. Dread settled in my gut, and all my efforts to slow my heart rate went out the window. "What?" I put a lot of effort into not snapping.

Wow. This hard adrenaline response was seriously unexpected. Was that what the anger and lashing out had been about? Keeping myself from experiencing this sort of generalized anxiety?

"I know you said you weren't comfortable with it before, and if that's still the case, I won't push yet, but sometime I would really like to see you infuse."

I pulled away from him and closed my eyes and made myself count until I could speak without snarling. "It's not exactly a spectator sport," I got out between gritted teeth.

"I know that," he said shortly, and that made me stop and open my eyes. When I started to hit the asshole place, Ling usually gave me censuring looks. Jace let it roll off him, or sometimes quipped about it until I realized that I was being a dick. No one pushed back like Robin did. "This isn't idle curiosity."

"Then why?"

He tilted his head. "Because someday—I very sincerely hope— we're going to play together again. What if you get a bleed while we're playing?"

"Then I'll handle it."

"Okay. But here's the thing: You get sort of shaky and unsteady when you're coming out of that headspace. Being abruptly yanked out of it tends to make that reaction even worse. A lot of subs and masochists can find it very disorienting to go from flying to a sudden stop with no period of easing out of things. Do you *really* want to be trying to stick a needle in your vein when you're in that state?"

I blew out my breath in a rush. "Okay, that's a really good point," I reluctantly admitted. His shrug spoke volumes. "I'm sorry."

"I get it, I do," he said. "I'll wait for you to be ready, but I'm going to insist that I be proficient at doing it for you before we start playing again. Hard limit."

I gave him a long look, but he wasn't flinching. Instead, he rolled me under him and settled his weight over me, nestling his exhausted dick next to mine.

"Besides," he purred, lacing our fingers together and using the grip to pin my hands down on the pillow. He dipped his head and slowly licked the scarred and bruised skin over my antecubital vein with a broad, flat swipe of his tongue. My breath caught in a gasp, my entire body flushing hot, and holy shit, maybe my dick wasn't so exhausted after all. How the fuck was that even erotic? "There's something phallic about a needle, don't you think? You'd watch me sliding it into you, knowing there's no part of you I can't penetrate. Nothing off-limits. There's no reason it can't be part of our play if we want it to be."

My eyes searched his, my breath coming faster, my heart pound-ing. I had one of those moments of revelation that kept happening when I was with him, where everything I thought and felt about myself and my hemophilia was reframed, reconceptualized.

Suddenly my prophy, which I'd always resented and done with reluctance, was something I thought I might . . . really want to do?

"Okay," I rasped, tugging against his grip on my hands. "Let's go. Now, before I overthink it and forget why I might want to do it."

He studied me, then nodded decisively. "Okay. Let's go."

BY THE TIME we got to my motel room, the sexy had worn off and been replaced by nerves. I didn't really know why.

I made him practice on himself first, going through several butterfly needles in the process. My veins were in bad enough shape without him doing multiple sticks. Then we had to deal with the false start as he went through the vein, and the shock when he pulled too far back and the needle came all the way out, resulting in a spurt of blood because he hadn't released the tourniquet yet. When it finally seemed he'd gotten the hang of it, I prepared my factor and gave him another new needle.

It had been two decades since I'd let anyone infuse me if I wasn't in the hospital. Once I learned how as a kid, I'd refused to let my mom do it anymore. I understood now that her nerves had made me tense, which made everything more unpleasant.

Now, I had some tension, but it wasn't because of any nerves on Robin's part. He went about cinching the tourniquet and swabbing the alcohol wipe on the crook of my elbow with the same calm confidence he seemed to approach most things. He was too intent on doing it right to eroticize it, but even so, my whole awareness of what was happening had shifted. *I* was eroticizing it: the slide of the needle into my flesh, the small stab of pain upon entry that quickly faded. The courteous check-in: was I okay to proceed?

Yes, definitely. Pleasure might not have followed immediately after, but now the process was intense rather than the tedious and annoying chore it had always been.

And *safe*. How ridiculous was that? To be able to trust someone with doing this for me?

When he withdrew the needle and dropped it in the sharps box, I noticed a sheen on his forehead. He'd been more nervous than he'd let on. But his pale-blue eyes were hot and fierce with triumph.

He quickly shrugged out of his clothes and skinned me of mine, pressing me back onto the motel bed. He kissed me until I hooked my uninjured leg around the back of his thigh and ground against him. He gripped our cocks in his large hand and jerked us off in tandem, pinning me with his stare as much as his body. I held out as long as I could, holding his gaze until orgasm slammed my eyelids shut and pulled my whole body taut, then released, leaving me limp and depleted as our cum slid down the hollows of my pelvis onto the sheets.

No, I definitely wasn't with him just for the kink. In fact, feeling the gusts of his breath against my throat and his weight on top of me, I thought I could be perfectly content even if we never went there again. As long as we could stay just like this.

"Is that your equipment?" Robin asked after we'd napped and showered and gotten off again.

I nodded at the carefully packed boxes in the corner. "Yeah. Having a few renovations made on the space before I open up shop. Might be another month or so, which is good because it will hopefully mean my leg is healed before I have to start working."

"Will you show me?"

"Sure." Limping on my cane—I really had done too much walking the previous night—I drew the chair from the pathetic excuse for a desk over to the boxes and sat to open them. I gave him a tour of the tools of my trade: my liner and shader machines, the needles and grips, a full spectrum of pigments, some preordered and some I'd mixed myself.

Then, feeling more self-conscious than I usually felt about my work, I gestured to the sketch pad on the bedside table. "I, um, did a few designs with you in mind over the summer."

I didn't move from my chair, and he didn't bring the pad over to me. Instead, he flipped through it as he sat on the edge of the bed, and I could tell he recognized which designs were meant for him. The nautical and kinky tableaux that were intended to cover the whole back, and a number of smaller arm, shoulder, and chest designs as well. He studied them like a man with an eye for aesthetics

—which of course he would have to be in his line of work—nodding slowly.

"This one," he said finally, tapping a finger on the one with the purple velvet drapes backdrop.

"Okay." I took the sketch pad from him, looking it over to see if there were any changes I wanted to make before we finalized it.

"What do you need to make it happen?" Robin asked.

"Once I have my shop set up, nothing."

"What about before?"

I blinked. "What, you mean here? Today?"

He nodded. "Sure, why not?"

"You don't want time to think about it?" I looked around the motel room with a critical eye. "This place is probably a sanitation nightmare."

"What about my boat?"

"The rocking could be a problem." I shook my head, frowning. "My studio space is a disaster right now. The wires are hanging out of the walls while they bring the electrical up to code. Okay. Here it is: I need a whole bunch of bleach-based cleaner, aerosol disinfectant, some clear plastic sheeting to lay over the bed and carpet, bulk quantities of sterile gauze—we can get that at the beauty supply store —and we'll need to set up my magnifying glass on its stand and my lamps, because the lighting in here is for shit."

"Will do." He reached for his jeans, grinning. "I'll be back soon."

DOING the whole design in one session was out of the question, of course. A massive piece like that would take hours. It would have been too exhausting for both of us—especially for him, since he'd be dealing with the pain—to do more than an hour or two at a time.

While he was gone, I worked on replicating the outline of the design on transfer paper. Like Jace's red-rock design, the folds of the velvet drapes and some of the implements of pain and pleasure would be shaded to give the illusion of three dimensions. But today would be about getting down the lines that defined the entire picture.

We disinfected every possible surface and laid layers of plastic down for good measure before I let any of my equipment touch any part of the room. Then Robin helped me assemble all my gear. I had two high-intensity lamps that I shined on his back like spotlights. I put the pedal of the machine under the foot of my uninjured leg. I took a couple of nonnarcotic pain relievers to make sure I had no distractions, and gave him a couple as well, since it would take the edge off the sting when I was working on particularly sensitive places.

Then I turned on my machine and got to work.

I'd had my black-gloved hands on the skins of hundreds of people, including Jace, working this way. In most respects, working on Robin wasn't any different, and yet it was far from business as usual. Even for Jace, it had never felt this personal, this meaningful. This was the needle *I* wielded, penetrating *his* skin. When I sponged away blood and ink with the gauze, it wasn't just blood—it was his blood.

The air was filled with the buzzing of the machine and his purposely steady breaths. Despite his best efforts, occasionally that steady rhythm would stutter or fracture on a gasp. His skin was warm through the nitrile gloves, twitching and rippling and smoothing beneath my hands.

During one of the regular intermissions I called to allow him a break from the consistent discomfort, and me to work out any tension or muscle kinks the work had given me, I couldn't stop myself from kissing the back of his neck, tasting the salt of his sweat there.

When we went to bed that night, the black lines that scrolled across his back from shoulders to waist were edged in a deep pink that would fade soon. He was too drained from coping with the pain and too unwilling to move for sex, but it didn't matter. He slept on his stomach and didn't press against me and use me as his grown-up teddy bear like he normally did, and that was okay too. I fell asleep feeling satisfied that we had cleared several hurdles, confident for the first time in years that I was where I needed to be and going where I needed to go. I was pursuing this whatever-it-was that had chanced upon me unlooked-for, to whatever conclusion it would come to.

CHAPTER TWENTY-ONE

Robin

The weeks that followed were sublime and also a hard dose of the reality that was Geoff's life, as I watched him struggle to heal his leg injury and set up his body-art studio.

The healing was a long, slow process full of setbacks, forcing him to go slower than he really wanted to. Until I watched him work through it, I hadn't truly grasped how badly an injury most people wouldn't think twice about could fuck him up. Tripping over a stupid box and bruising his thigh had put him in the hospital and left him with months of recovery time. What would have happened if he'd hit his head?

The building he'd leased for his studio was taking longer to get set up than he would have liked. He was in my office, working on his laptop, as I closed the gallery for the day, which meant I was just coming upstairs and caught his grimace.

"Everything okay?"

"Yeah." He shut the laptop decisively. "I'm just worrying about the gamble I took opening the studio. I knew I'd be running in the red for a while, opening in the off-season. I figured it would give me time to put together a portfolio of local work on top of my experience out in LA. But if things don't pick up enough in the summer, it could get ugly really quickly."

"How ugly?"

His voice was heavy with disgust. "My factor costs about forty thousand dollars a month."

I choked on my own spit. "A *month?*"

"Twenty-seven hundred per dose times fifteen doses a month if I do my prophy every other day. Right now it's more, since I'm infusing every day. Then there are the hospitalizations and frequent doctors' visits." He smiled ruefully. "When I was a kid, my dad had to change jobs every few years because we kept maxing out what our insurance would allow us to spend. Hopefully President Obama will actually manage to reform health care and that won't be an issue much longer. But for now, if the studio doesn't start turning a profit come summer, I'm going to have operating costs on top of medical expenses, and it won't be good."

"Opening the studio was quite a leap of faith," I observed, sitting on the arm of the sofa to stroke his hair back from his face.

"Ling kicked me in the ass until I went for it." His eyes took on the fond, tender expression he got every time he spoke of his sister. "She was right; I needed to take the chance. But I still have a panic attack every time I check the balances on my accounts and see the money my parents left me dwindling faster than it should." He blew out a gusty breath, grabbing his backpack and shoving the laptop in. "It'll work out. It has to."

Luckily, I knew how to relieve his tension, though the dominant inside me was prodding me to do something more effective to get him out of his head. It was getting harder to ignore the inner voice that pointed me at a sub in need like a compass to true north. Geoff never complained, which surprised me. He'd been so keen to play when we first met. I thought he'd be chomping at the bit to get back into it, but he was treating my request to keep things vanilla for a while with absolute respect. If he felt he was missing out, I never knew it.

Which, ironically, made me question myself more. Was he getting frustrated and I wasn't picking up on it? One of my goals was to learn to read his unspoken signals, but the apparent absence of those signals could mean I just wasn't catching them.

I was doing his infusions most mornings, and Geoff allowed it without argument. I was becoming more comfortable with the process and more skilled at hitting the vein on the first try. Sometimes he was very clinical about it, offering me instruction and critique. Other times he was silent, intent on watching what I was doing, and I knew he was replaying what I'd said to him about the symbolism of this act.

That, too, was making my inner dominant restless. And giving him *ideas*.

I KEPT him at bay as long as I could. It wasn't hard for a while; even in the off-season, I was busy with my gallery, and Geoff was still working on healing and getting his studio set up. But we made time for dates, whether I took him out for the evening or we had a quiet and simple dinner on my boat. He stayed with me more often than not, unless his leg was bothering him particularly badly, in which case I could usually be found in his motel room.

Sometimes there was sex; sometimes there was pain medication, television, and an early bedtime. It didn't really matter. I was getting to know the man behind the restless masochist who had first caught my eye. A man with a quick, dry wit that could easily lapse into scorching, scathing derision when he was provoked. A man who was so deeply loyal and sensitive to the moods and emotional currents around him that he'd spent a lifetime shouldering other people's baggage, to his own detriment. A man who was deeply devoted to the people he had left in his life: his sister and Jace and increasingly, I liked to think, me.

There was also more work to do on the tattoo taking shape over the entirety of my back. Geoff was keeping the sessions spaced out— every couple of weeks, for no longer than two hours.

Our third session took place in his studio, which was nearly ready to open. It was light and bright enough to appear reassuringly clean and sterile, but decorated well enough to feel comfortable. Rather than pinning up a hodgepodge of snapshots, he blew up and framed his best designs, and consulted me on the best way to display them. His portfolios were clean and well-kept, the photos mounted neatly on the pages. He kept the space warm in deference to the seminude state of many of his clients, with an optional privacy screen that would protect clients' modesty while allowing him to greet anyone coming through the door.

I hadn't anticipated how much the process could hurt, particularly when he worked over my ribs and spine. But Geoff's hands were skilled and sure, brisk without being brusque. His demeanor was sympathetic, reassuring. It was surprising, really, that someone with Geoff's low threshold for irritation could be so calm while he was working. Almost like dealing with an entirely different man.

Or at least like dealing with a facet I hadn't bothered to get to know before. When he was etching his design into my skin—inch by burning, stinging inch—there was a joy and expressiveness in his eyes I hadn't seen at any other time. He *loved* what he did. He was driven to it the way only those people with a passion for their art truly are. He wasn't like Jace, whose expression could come in photographs, on paper or canvas, on a blank wall or in the aesthetic of a room. Jace was driven to beautiful things, but it didn't matter much what he was making. For Geoff, it had to be this, had to be beauty comprised of pain and flesh and blood.

Maybe that made a certain amount of sense after all.

When he paused to give us a break, he stretched. His shirtsleeves were rolled up, baring the length of his left arm between his black glove and his elbow. The cluster of bruises along the bend there caught my eye. On the table past his arm lay the full-size drawing of the design he was inking into my skin. I closed my eyes as an image took shape in my mind. I could see so clearly the things I wanted to do with him.

Which prompted my oft-stifled internal dominant to take control of my mouth, bypassing my good intentions.

"I want to try a scene again," I announced. Which might not have been the best idea with the euphoria of pain endorphins coursing through my veins, but it was too late to take it back now.

"Really?" That note of hope and excitement in his voice made it worth going along with whatever my id was getting me into.

"Yeah. Something that won't require much by way of movement or stressful positions." I was already mentally composing a list of the supplies we'd need.

Geoff's eyebrows quirked, and he gave me a faintly exasperated smile. "Is this going to be another surprise?"

I hadn't meant it to be, but now that he mentioned it . . . "Yeah. I think it will be. Plan to spend next Friday night on my boat with me. I'll have everything ready."

He nodded, accepting my evasiveness with apparent good grace. When it came time to resume working on my tattoo, the machine buzzed and his hand came to rest on my back, but the needles never touched my skin.

"Fuck," he said with an incredulous laugh. "Now you've got me all distracted. I'm not sure I should be working like this."

The machine stopped humming, and I turned, smirking at him. "Like what?" I slid a hand into his lap, gripping the tight denim covering his crotch. "Ohh, like that. I see."

"Asshole." He snorted, still smiling. "I didn't just mean the hard-on. I mean my attention is going to wander with me trying to figure out what you have planned. My concentration is blown to shit."

"Well, maybe we should do something about that," I murmured, stroking more firmly.

He groaned and pressed against my hand for a moment, then laughed again and pushed me away. "Turn around and let me at least clean up and finish tending to that ink, even if we're done for today."

As the week crawled by, I started refining a generic BDSM contract for our purposes, and Geoff began testing his leg to see if he could phase out the cane. His determination gave me pause, and by midweek I couldn't keep from asking what was up. "Are you trying to prove to me you're fit to do a scene?"

Geoff gave me a flat look. "Unless you're planning something more athletic than the sex we normally have—which it didn't sound like you were—what would be the point?"

I shrugged, feeling like I might be on the wrong end of things. "You just often seem to think you have something to prove. And if that's why you're pushing yourself, then clearly we're not doing as well communicating as I thought we were."

He paused in the process of organizing the racks that held all his pigments. From my view of his profile, I could see his jaw flexing, but he didn't fire off a quick retort the way he might have once done. Instead he took a few even breaths before he spoke.

"Okay, that's a fair enough concern. But it's misplaced." He gestured at the work area of his studio, where everything was halfway set up. "If I want to open next week like I planned, I have a lot of work to do. I also need to know I'm going to be able to work without my leg giving me a problem. I'm not pushing myself. I'm making sure it's healing as well as it seems to be." He met my eyes without the slightest bit of evasion. "That okay with you?"

I nodded, slumping against the wall. "Yeah. I just needed—"

"I know what you needed. Look, I get it. I don't have a great track record of being honest with other people about what my body is doing, and you don't have a lot of spare trust to throw around right now." He grimaced and went back to sorting the bottles of ink. "But if this is going to work, sooner or later you've got to accept that I'm trying to make sure you know everything that's going on. I won't put you in the position of not knowing if I've got an injury again."

"You're right. I'm sorry." I pushed off the wall and squatted to open a box. "It's probably going to take a while, and that's my issue, not yours."

Geoff tossed off a shrug. "We've got time."

"We do. Still, I think this is stuff we need to make sure is included in our contract before we play again." I paused in emptying the box to look at him directly. "You're a lot calmer about this than I would have thought, considering I poked you right in a sensitive spot."

"Yeah." His hands stilled on the bottles of pigment, and he turned a puzzled frown toward me. "I am. I think getting laid regularly is mellowing me out."

He said it offhandedly, but there was something about the confusion on his face that drew me across the room to take him by the hips and tug him close, kissing him slowly before I answered, "Probably doesn't hurt."

He pulled me down by the pressure of his fingers on the back of my neck, kissing me harder. There was a lot of need in that kiss, in the way his fingertips dug in, and I realized "getting laid regularly" was code for everything that was growing between us. I didn't think we were ready to put it into words, except to say that it wasn't just our compatible sexual interests that kept us coming back to each other. He was too new to having a relationship, much less one with emotions attached, and I was still too badly burned.

But it was definitely happening, and I didn't think there was a damn thing either of us could have done to stop it.

CHAPTER TWENTY-TWO

Geoff

I arrived on Robin's boat on Friday evening at exactly the time he'd instructed, determined not to start us off on the wrong foot by being deliberately provocative. I wasn't much of a sub, and by the terms of the contract we'd both signed the day before, it was clear he didn't expect me to be, but it was in both our interests for me to hand the reins totally over to him.

Which was why he'd informed me that the first thing we'd do in every scene was have him infuse me, so I could adjust my prophy schedule accordingly.

I was getting used to him doing it for me now, and he was quite good at it. Still, that one provision more than any other was going to be the one that rankled.

"It's a good starting point," he explained when I asked him why. "A ritual, signaling that we're beginning. From that point on, I'm the one responsible for taking care of you until we're done."

It made sense, but it was harder than I thought, laying my well-being in someone else's hands like that, trusting him with it. I hadn't considered that angle in all my little fetishes and fantasies. It was about a lot more than the kinks we indulged, and he took that *more* very seriously.

Under my arm, I carried my sketch pad, which I didn't go

anywhere without these days. Robin had specifically asked me to bring it tonight—a curious request but not an objectionable one. I bumped down the short, steep flight of stairs to the galley without my cane. It had only taken the better part of three months, but my leg was holding up fine. I was confident now that it wasn't going to give me any problems when I opened next week. In fact, I planned to spend the rest of the weekend moving from the motel into the small apartment above my studio.

Robin greeted me with dinner and a kiss. His galley was small, but very well stocked, and Robin knew how to make the most of it. He was a good cook and enjoyed doing it, so I was happy to let him plan the meals when we were together.

"Put your stuff by the bed and take your clothes off while I set the table," he instructed, going back to the stove. He tossed out the order as though it was nothing major.

"B-before dinner? You want me nude while we *eat*?"

He turned toward me, his eyebrow coming up slowly. "Was I in any way unclear?"

"No. No. Sorry." Disconcerted, I carried my backpack to the low berth and stripped. I wasn't sure why that command threw me off-balance, but it definitely focused my attention on the fact that tonight wasn't going to be the usual dinner and sex.

I stupidly had to fight to keep from covering myself when I went back to the galley and sat down at the table. It wasn't until Robin asked me if the food was all right that I saw I was fiddling with it more than eating.

"Yeah." I stared down at my plate, realizing I'd been completely distracted, trying to guess what was coming. God only knew how many polite, noncommittal noises I'd made, responding to questions I couldn't even remember. I shook my head rapidly to focus myself. "Sorry. My mind really isn't on food tonight."

He gave me a cocky grin that had my dick rising to meet the underside of the table. "Good. Eat anyway. I don't want to have to stop because your blood sugar is crashing."

I smiled wryly, more sure of myself when I could hide behind witticisms. "Well, that's some damn good motivation."

Somehow I got the food down, and then tried to concentrate on clearing the table the way he told me to, instead of hovering while he prepared my factor.

"Close your eyes and let it go," he murmured as he swabbed my arm with an alcohol pad. "It's all in my hands now—all your responsibility and all your worries. Just let it go. I've got it."

Strangely, that part wasn't difficult. Once he started speaking to me in that tone, gentle but in command, my brain packed it in for the night. I released the burden of looking out for my own safety. It was so incredibly *easy* to do with him.

The bed was covered in a sheet I last saw while I was vacationing with Jace in June. Then, Robin had used it to protect my hotel room bed from wax. There were no candles in evidence now, though. Once he had me lying down, he slipped a sleep mask over my eyes, blocking out all sight. I'd been blindfolded by him enough to know that sensory deprivation was one of his favorite ways of giving me that edge of uncertainty and danger. Of course, I could have ripped it off at any time; he never tied me up. But I didn't. I lay there feeling helpless and vulnerable and very, very exposed.

Which was a strangely contradictory state of mind to the heat that rushed through my veins when he engulfed my cock in his mouth and began to suck.

"Oh God!" I gasped, my back arching until he pinned my hips down with both hands and set about driving me out of my fucking mind. When I wanted harder and faster, he backed off. When I was lulled into relaxation at the slow, gentle pleasure, he picked up the pace and force so suddenly, my senses couldn't keep up. And when he had me on the quivering brink of coming, he stopped.

"No!" I pleaded, squirming to get all that nerve-singing pleasure back. But Robin grabbed the base of my cock and squeezed until I was well and truly off the brink.

"Who's running the show tonight?" he demanded.

"You," I sighed, stifling an unmanly urge to whimper.

"Good boy. Roll over. Position your arms and head so you're comfortable and breathing easily. You're going to be there awhile."

In the darkness of the blindfold, I did as I was instructed, hugging one of the pillows under my cheek.

I twitched when I heard the sound of a spray bottle. A cool mist touched my back. The sharp, astringent scent of alcohol followed, evaporating quickly on my skin and leaving it chilled.

I bit my tongue on the urge to ask what he was doing. His hands felt strange when he stroked them lightly over the fleshy parts of my back. Was he wearing gloves?

"Just breathe and try not to tense up," he said calmly. I heard a wrapper rustle, and then he gripped a small bit of my skin gently between his fingers. I felt . . . a pinch?

No, a *poke*. A pin or needle of some kind, though not the short, lower-gauge butterfly needles I used for infusing. This was longer, narrower, going through the skin on both sides rather than into a vein.

It was painless. Almost. More like heat and a lingering sense of something being there that shouldn't be.

"Have you ever used needles for anything other than work or medical necessity?" Robin asked conversationally, sticking a second needle firmly through my flesh less than an inch away from the first.

"No?" I'm not sure why I answered like I was asking a question, except that my brain and nerve endings were trying to make sense of what was happening and not getting very far. I couldn't have told him my own name with any surety at that moment.

"These are one-point-five-inch, twenty-seven-gauge hypodermics. They're individually wrapped. I thought we'd start with a higher gauge and see how severe the bleeding and bruising are before we decide if we want to try a lower gauge another time."

Several more needles went through my skin as he spoke in even, reassuring tones.

"Don't be surprised if the endorphin rush hits you hard and fast. Something about play piercing does that to people, even though there's not all that much pain, comparatively. But if you feel dizzy or faint, let me know right away."

The next needle went through the thinner flesh covering my ribs, and it hurt more. I gasped, my senses still trying to comprehend all that was going on. A hot bead of something rolled down my side, quickly cooling. Blood. I was bleeding.

Having delivered his explanation, Robin fell silent, leaving me in the darkness with only my own rapid breathing, the crinkle of needle wrappers, and the faintly tantric, meditative thrum of some sort of spa music coming over the boat's stereo.

I had pierced hundreds of people before, but I'd never been pierced. Never thought I'd want to be. But this was something different altogether, wasn't it?

Unless the skin was particularly thin or sensitive, I barely felt the prick of the needle going in. Coming through the other side was more intense. Some felt like they bled more than others, but most of my attention was on the strange not-quite-pain of the needles already puncturing my flesh, resting threaded through my skin. When I twitched or shifted or did anything to move them, heat blossomed in a near-agonizing eruption of sensation.

So don't move, you dolt, I told myself, and promptly began to giggle.

Which made it tip over into actual pain. Which made me giggle more.

It wasn't that fucking funny. What the fuck?

"I sound like I'm high," I gasped when I'd caught my breath.

"Damn right you are," Robin said, his voice mildly amused.

"This is crazy." I was half-euphoric and halfway to that floaty, transcendent place where nothing could touch me. Robin gently nudged the hubs of the needles, setting off a cascade effect of pain and squirming and more pain *because* I was squirming. The pricking of the needles going in was lost in that constant, rising ache of the ones that were already in. I had no idea if Robin was sticking them in willy-nilly or if he had a pattern he was following. Time ceased to have any meaning. We might have been there minutes or hours. Occasionally he would stop adding new needles to play with the ones already inserted, reigniting the whole chain reaction. I didn't know—couldn't begin to know—how to process it.

"Just ride it," Robin urged in response to my random babbling. "I'm almost done here. I'll take them out. They might have begun to heal already, which means pulling them out might hurt a bit more."

"Okay," I said breathlessly. I might have zoned out or dozed off while he removed the needles. Occasionally I heard the quiet *click* of them dropping into a sharps container, or felt beads of blood roll down my skin, but I wasn't aware of much else.

The high wore off a little during the process, and I was back in my head by the time he rolled me over and spritzed alcohol over my chest and abdomen.

"I'm not sure I can—" I gasped sharply, cut off when the first needle went into the flesh of my pec just below my clavicle. "Oh shit."

"You can." His voice was still low and calm, reassuring and not in the least bit jarring. "Relax. Take a few breaths. Let the tension go and sink back into it."

And I did. Impossible as it seemed, I did. I floated right out of my head as he worked the needles into my skin in a pattern only he was aware of. First one pec and then the other, then down my abdomen and back up, until he had reached the hard nub of my nipple.

Which he took between his fingers, startling a cry from me that set the whole thing to blazing. "No! Oh God, please, no."

"You sure?" he crooned, not pinching, but holding my nipple in the same light grasp as he had every other tent of skin.

"I can't," I whispered.

"You could. And you *would* if I told you to. Wouldn't you?"

"I can't," I said again, helplessly. I wasn't tied down in any way, and yet I couldn't have moved even if I'd wanted to. I couldn't refute his claim, but I was too frightened to concede the point. It left me overwhelmed and at a complete loss.

"Someday you will," he said with absolute confidence, but he let go of my nipple. I thought perhaps he was done, until I felt him jostling and tugging on the hubs of the needles—not withdrawing them, but doing something that increased the pressure on them.

"Thread," he explained. "Gonna lace you up like a shoe." And then I could feel it. He'd loop it around the hub of one side of a row, and then around the other side, so that a movement in one direction tugged in the opposite direction. Suddenly there was no escaping the escalation of pain, no matter how still I tried to be. Especially when he stopped lacing them together and started toying with them.

And as he played, he spoke to me, muttering low, growly threats and promises.

"Maybe I'll fuck you while they're in. That'll feel real good. Your ass will be so fucking *tight* with all that pain riding you. I'll have to ream you open like you're still a virgin just to get it up in there." His hand stroked my dick, which was only half-hard at that point, bringing it up to full arousal. I moaned, a glorious wave of bliss washing over me as I thought of the way those needles would feel, jolted by every hard slam of his body into mine.

He leaned close to my ear, menacing. "Oh, you like that thought? I must be doing something wrong, then. I said it would feel good. I didn't say it would feel good *for you*."

My entire body bowed, the motion pulling on every damned needle, awakening a tidal wave of pain that surged through me. A paroxysm of fear and arousal so keen, it stopped me short of coming. It knocked me completely out of my head, divorced me from any awareness of myself. The world consisted of nothing more than Robin's voice and the burn and tug and sting of those needles.

"Please!" I whispered, trembling, desperate. I didn't know if I was asking for him to stop or keep going or both.

I couldn't bear it.

I wanted it never to end.

What the pain of the needles couldn't accomplish alone, the terror inspired by his threats handled easily. Each writhing movement I made pulled on the needles, and yet I was powerless to keep still, hard in his hand and begging for something I couldn't name. And so he kept pushing.

After a swipe of lube shoved roughly into my ass with two fingers, he was inside me, groaning his pleasure while I whimpered my pain. He used me; there was no other word for it. Every crude thrust and derisive sneer dismissed the possibility of concern for whether I enjoyed what he was doing. It kept me flying, aware of but untroubled by the ordeal my body was going through. It was so damned *good*. I'd spent so much of my life intimately familiar with agony, but this . . . this was sublime.

"Sounds like you're enjoying yourself more than you should be." I was too far gone to be gratified by his labored panting and the harsh rasp of his voice speaking of his struggle to keep control. "Maybe we need more needles, but I'm running out of skin to use."

His hand seized my dick, pumping firmly, rolling the foreskin up tight over the head.

"Well, huh. Here's some we haven't stuck any needles in yet."

I think I might have screamed. I know I begged, and this time there was no doubt that I was asking Robin to stop. Sobbing, I pleaded for mercy, and still my safeword never so much as occurred to me. I didn't fight him, didn't even try to push him away. I didn't want it, and scratching at the edge of my awareness was some niggling thought there wasn't really any reason to be afraid, but I couldn't remember why. I knew if it came down to that, I would let him do it to me. I'd let him do anything at all.

He released me. I felt him shift and heard the wrapper of another needle tearing. Cool alcohol spritzed my dick, and then he resumed rolling my foreskin up and down. "That's it, baby. Yell for me. Beg me not to stick this needle through the skin of your cock."

"*Please-please-nononono-ohGodplease . . .*" My voice came in a reedy, breathless torrent, the sort of cry you silently make in your nightmares when you're trying to scream and nothing but a whisper emerges. He sat there, rocking his dick in and out of my clenching asshole while I begged and begged.

"What, don't want me to?"

"*Nono-please-no-don't!*"

"That's very touching, but you seem to be forgetting something." Robin's voice dropped to a wicked purr, his breath brushing my ear. "What you want doesn't matter."

I felt a pinch on my foreskin, and I shrieked and flew apart.

WHEN I CAME BACK to myself, the blindfold was gone and Robin was murmuring softly to me. My ass was aching and empty, wet with his cum, and I could feel the weird rasp of latex gloves and the tug of the needles being drawn out, one after the other, clicking as he dropped them into the sharps container.

Tiny, hot trickles of blood streamed down my ribs, cooling as they rolled along my skin. My face was already wet with sweat and tears I hadn't even realized I'd shed.

"There's a little more bleeding and bruising than you usually see with needle play," Robin murmured calmly. "But I expected that."

"My dick—" I couldn't seem to raise my voice above a whisper. My screamer seemed to be broken. I reached down to seize my cock, finding it still mostly hard. I hadn't come yet, I realized with some astonishment, and as far as I could tell, the skin was unpunctured.

I looked askance at Robin, who simply shrugged and continued with his task, removing each needle with slow calm.

Another mind-fuck. I should have known, after the stunt with the wax. But then, he'd made good on his threat to drip hot wax on my dick the second time we did wax play, so I knew when he made a threat like that, he was perfectly willing and able to carry it out. If I'd been too complacent, I had no doubt he would have truly stuck that needle through my foreskin.

My traitorous cock hardened more at the thought, and the insatiable part of my mind whispered promises of *next time*.

I let myself drift away again on the tug and sting of the needles coming out, the heat-then-cool of blood streaming and drying on my skin. I was alive to it all in a way I'd never been before, each sound and sensation enormous, seemingly too big for my senses to contain.

"Look, baby." Robin touched my jaw, compelling my eyes to open. I could see rusty streaks of blood smeared along the side of his gloved hand. "Look at yourself."

I lifted my head to gaze down the length of my torso, moaning softly to see my skin lined with tiny crimson rivulets. The white and red played against one another in a shocking contrast that was painterly.

Something about the swirls of pinpricks and tiny bruises caught my eye.

"Wait, is that—" I glanced over, and sure enough, there was my sketch pad, open to a page with a simple, quasi-tribal pattern that very closely mirrored the marks on my skin. "You used my design," I said, my eyes tingling.

My body was finally the piece of art I'd wanted it to be. My art had been injected into my skin. Even the streaks of my blood, with which I had such an ambivalent, adversarial relationship, made me beautiful.

Robin ran his fingertip through the russet trails, creating swirls and variations, shades of pink between the light and dark. He formed all his fingers into claws and raked them down the length of my chest, scraping through the whorls. My back arched, my body thrusting toward him, and he seized the opportunity to swallow my cock to the root. I came, screaming, pulsing down his throat, with his fingertips smearing my blood down my skin.

I lay floating as he cleaned me up and swabbed alcohol on the tiny punctures. I felt like I'd climbed the Matterhorn, triumphant and blissed out of my mind.

We could do this. Robin *truly* was willing to do this with me, regardless of the concerns my hemophilia might raise. And I was capable of doing it. Yeah, maybe we'd have to refine the approach. We'd never be able to do the whips-and-chains thing most people would think of. I'd never be able to take the brutal beatings I loved to watch in porn. Ours would need to be precision play—a scalpel approach, rather than a hatchet. But we could get what we needed out of this.

He could make me feel like I was anything but delicate.

He could make me fly.

Afterward, I curled up in his bed because the neediness that happened after we played was upon me again. It didn't throw me the way it had in the summer. Robin stroked my hair and skin like he was petting me, until I lay half-asleep and completely unconcerned about anything.

"I was thinking of seeing if you might sleep all wrapped up and mummified tonight." He slid his body along mine from behind, spooning against my back as he kissed my temple. "But I think you've had enough for today."

My voice was a sleepy slur. "You may be right."

He breathed a soft laugh that ruffled my hair and warmed the back of my neck. "Have you looked at yourself since the bleeding stopped?"

I shook my head and opened my eyes to glance down. Blotchy, uneven hematomas were beginning to form in relatively parallel rows across my chest and down my arms and both sides of my torso. Even so, the design was still discernible. If I couldn't be bruised from a beating, it was an acceptable alternative. I smiled and closed my eyes again. "I like it. Thank you."

"You're welcome. Next summer, I want to take you out on the water and do it up on deck, out in the sunlight, and have you wear them for hours while we cruise up and down the shoreline."

That sounded downright idyllic . . . in a very kinky way, of course. "I'd like that."

Sometimes in the aftermath like this, he mused quite a bit. I didn't mind it.

"You know, it's strange. Circumstances being what they are, we're doing this all backward. We've jumped right to things other people might consider edge play. They take months, years working up to it. The stuff most people would cut their teeth on are the things we have to take slowly and carefully." His body moved away, and he dragged his lips down the bumps of my spine. "Week after next, we'll play at my house."

"Your house?" My head came up, surprise piercing my lassitude. Since I'd moved to Saugatuck, he'd only let me see the outside of his house. The inside, he said, was still being worked on.

"Mmm, yes. No more maneuvering down here where it's so cramped. Or hauling all our gear to your place, which isn't much larger."

"I'm eager to find out what the big secret is." I lay back down, relishing the ache as each movement pulled on the dozens of sensitive little punctures in my skin. "I mean, I'm assuming you've been making some sort of playroom or dungeon . . ."

He snorted, rolling me onto my front as his lips reached the dip in my waist. "I think you can take that as a given. Let's just say I've been arranging it with our particular situation in mind. I'm eager to try out some of my ideas."

"Sounds fun." I quickly forgot any other rejoinder I might have made when his thumbs slipped between my ass cheeks and pried them apart, his moist breath wafting down my cleft. His tongue darted out to flick against my hole, and if he objected to the taste of lube or his own semen, he gave no indication. I was exquisitely tender after the rough fucking he'd given me earlier, and even those light caresses made me catch my breath and writhe.

He had me begging before he slid his body over mine and drove into me again, grabbing my hands and pinning them to the bed to keep me pliant beneath him. Even stretched out like that, I tried to lift my ass, let him plunge a bit deeper.

I loved the feeling of him draped over me, pumping away at me. I don't know how it was possible to feel sheltered while at the same time being victoriously aware that he didn't consider me weak or fragile, that he wasn't holding back with me. But that was how it felt.

More and more, I was coming to crave that feeling, the sense that he engulfed and surrounded me. And not just on an evening like this, when I was still coming down off the endorphin high.

I loved the feeling of him going still above me, pulsing inside me, his weight getting heavier as he relaxed in the aftermath.

But, in a twist I could never have anticipated, I realized this sex wasn't any better than it had been any other time these last four weeks since we'd started seeing each other again. As rewarding as everything we'd done tonight had been, it didn't trump the simple, thorough pleasure of him making love to me.

CHAPTER TWENTY-THREE

Robin

I f I had needed any more evidence that I'd been bullshitting myself the previous spring and summer with my ideas of giving up the leather scene entirely, the playroom in my house would have been it.

I'd started the renovations after I bolted from Geoff in Chicago, and I'd continued them even after I lost the balls to contact him and try to fix things. If he hadn't shown up with Jace at my gallery, the playroom would have gathered dust indefinitely.

Now, though . . . now I had a definite purpose in mind for it. We were still going to take the kink slow; I didn't plan on us scening or even having particularly rough sex more than once or twice a week. But here in my house, we could really begin to experiment and explore things we couldn't have on the boat or in Geoff's small apartment.

Weekends were particularly important times for both our businesses, even in the off-season. Once he opened his studio, Geoff and I didn't see each other much from Friday onward. But Mondays we both were closed, and that was going to be a very important day for us, no matter what direction we took our relationship in. So Sunday evening, after we'd closed up for the day, I picked him up at his shop and took him to my house.

It was a gorgeous, updated historic home on top of a hill over-looking downtown Saugatuck and Kalamazoo Lake. Being a trust-fund brat had its perks, and I wasn't ashamed to enjoy them. I'd kept the decor simple, comfortable but utilitarian, because whether it was Geoff or not, I hoped someday to have a partner and family in this house who would put their own stamp on it. The playroom was the one room I'd applied my own sense of aesthetics to.

I gave Geoff a quick tour. The large bedroom downstairs with the attached bath was clearly meant to be the master suite, but I'd chosen one of the smaller bedrooms upstairs to be mine instead. In the corner, I had a dorm-sized refrigerator stocked with water, electrolyte-laden sports drinks, and high-protein snacks. Everything I'd need to take care of my sub after a scene. I watched Geoff take a quick inventory of what I'd stored there before stowing his factor. As he straightened, I rested my hands on his shoulders, kissing the back of his neck.

"Want to see the playroom?"

He nodded, his bluish-gray eyes wide and eager.

I kissed him again, lightly, on the lips. "Okay, but first we need to talk, and I need to let you know my ground rules. Let's sit down."

Geoff perched on the edge of the bed. I sat farther up toward the headboard, crossing my legs in front of me. After a moment, he turned to face me fully and mirrored the position.

"I don't think either of us has any plans to make our BDSM play a 24/7 type of arrangement, right?" I asked. "Even if someday we decide to move in together, I don't think we want that, do we?"

He gave me a wry smile. "Oh, please. Can you see me letting *anyone* tell me what to do 24/7?"

He made the remark without any of the defensiveness I might have expected from him a few months ago. He *was* mellowing. I didn't flatter myself that it was—as he'd quipped—getting laid regularly that was responsible for it, but *something* had changed. The bitter shell had cracked and started to peel off sometime over the course of the summer and fall.

I chuckled, unable to stop myself from reaching for his hand. "I really can't, but I want to make sure we're on the same page with this. When we play—if we play—there's going to be a beginning and an end to it. And I'd really like to delineate those boundaries as clearly as we can."

"Like starting off with you infusing me," he said with a slow nod.

"That's one way, yes. You're not really a sub, so I'm never going to require much in the way of obedience training with you. But one of the problems we've run into quite a bit is your issues around feeling vulnerable or being in a position you think might give someone the impression you're weak." I ran my finger over his knuckles, feeling the twitch as his hand tried to tense up.

I spoke slowly, choosing my words with care. If he was going to get his back up, this was the point at which it would happen. "When we're doing a scene, I'd like you to get used to me seeing even the things you usually keep private. Get used to the idea of there being no secrets, nothing you can hold back. So when you're here with the intention of playing, I want you nude, like last weekend on my boat. Even if we're just making dinner or watching TV, you won't be dressed."

Geoff licked his lips, frowning, but then he nodded again. "Okay. I can do that. Now?"

"No, we need to finish talking first before we get into that." I waited, studying him to make sure he understood the purpose behind that, then continued, pointing at an open door on the other side of the room. "That's the bathroom. It adjoins both this bedroom and the playroom. When we're playing, the door always stays open, no matter what you're doing in there."

He gave an incredulous laugh. "Wow. You weren't kidding with that whole 'no secrets' bit." I watched him struggle with that. Not surprising. A lot of people—myself included—were raised with a hefty sense of modesty relating to tasks performed in the bathroom.

"Okay, fine," he said finally, setting his jaw. "But you know, I'm getting a lot of you laying down ground rules for me. I assume we'll be amending our contract now that we're playing here, but I have to ask: what's *your* part going to be in making sure we've got all this trust and open communication happening?"

"That's a fair question. I'm the one who bolted rather than talking something through, so I suppose I don't have much of a moral high ground here, do I?" I frowned. "It won't happen again. I was still raw about a lot of stuff that summer. Dashing out like that isn't normally my style. I'm not sure I can do much else to reassure you. I'm typically more of a dominant than a sadist. I'd expect a certain level of unquestioning obedience from most people I've played with. For you, though, I'm willing to give you full leeway to require me to explain myself, especially if you feel I'm doing something that hits your buttons."

I saw his shoulders drop. I think he'd expected me to go full-on authoritarian with him, which only emphasized how important this accommodation was.

After a moment of letting him take that in, I added, "However, I am going to ask that before you question me, you think it through, see if you can figure out for yourself why I might demand something. If possible, give me the benefit of the doubt. I'd like to further request that at some future date, when we feel like the trust and comfort are there, we revisit that policy and see if you find a little unquestioning obedience to be to your taste. Sound fair?"

His mouth opened but then closed again. He thought about it. *Really* thought about it. Then he nodded a third time. "Yeah."

"Anything you want to add to the negotiations?"

Geoff frowned. "This bathroom thing—this isn't because some part of you is afraid I'll be in there shooting up or something, is it?"

I reared back, probably looking like a fish on land with my mouth gaping open. "*What*? Wow. No. *No*, I swear, that wasn't part of my reasoning."

"Okay." He blew out a breath, his eyes still troubled. "Because, you know, I'd be lying if I said there weren't hemophiliacs whose access to all these prescription pain medications turned out to be a problem for them. But so far I haven't developed any dependencies."

"I believe you," I said firmly, trying to regain my equanimity. One of these days I'd stop being completely taken aback by how suspicious he was of the way other people perceived him. But then, maybe someday he'd stop feeling like he had reason to be so suspicious. "Promise me you'll let me know if you've taken anything stronger than Tylenol, even if it means we have to reschedule something we were looking forward to? Because I can't emphasize strongly enough how important it is that we *don't play* if either of us is at all under the influence."

"Promise." He gave me another wry smile. "Odds are if I'm feeling bad enough to hit the heavy stuff, I won't be up to doing much anyway."

That was true. Over the weeks while his quadriceps had been healing, we'd spent several evenings together in front of the TV or in bed before full dark because he'd had to take something for the pain.

I uncrossed my legs and closed the distance between us, kissing him until I had him flat on his back under me. When he was so much goo, I pulled away.

"The bathroom thing is about achieving a state of mind," I said, leaning in to nuzzle his throat. "Within the negotiated boundaries, nothing's off-limits, even the personal, inconsequential stuff. No modesty, no polite little barriers. That's all it is. Okay?"

"Okay," he agreed breathlessly. His cock was hard against mine, and he rocked up against me. "So, are you going to show me this playroom, or are we going to fuck right now?"

I laughed and rolled off him. "I'll show you the playroom. Get naked, then go get cleaned up and ready to play."

THE BATHROOM RULE really was going to be a challenge for him. He closed the door out of sheer habit when he first went in, and I barged in to remind him not to.

"I meant what I said. Never close a door between us." I opened it as far as it would go without slamming it back against the wall. "Doesn't matter if you're bathing or taking a piss, you don't hide anything from me."

It wasn't as though Geoff had any particular hang-ups about me seeing him nude. Skinny-dipping, visiting the sand dunes off the beach where most of the men were bare, soaking in the hot tub. He'd showered with and in front of me many times without any hint of modesty about it. But knowing that the *potential* for privacy had been taken away would make his awareness of its absence far keener.

I showed him briefly where everything was, and then left him to wash up on his own in the spacious tile bath with its glass-enclosed shower and Jacuzzi tub big enough for two. Since I could hear him no matter which of the two rooms I was in, I didn't need to watch him; I just needed him to be aware that I could if I wanted to.

From the playroom, in particular, I could catch glimpses in the wide mirrors over the sinks. Which meant I observed out of the corner of my eye the way he dithered self-consciously before he finally gave in to the restriction and used the enema attachment.

I could see the shift in his frame of mind when he stepped, towel-dry but nude, over the threshold into the playroom.

Blackout curtains darkened the windows, and the room was strangely quiet thanks to the soundproofing. Against one wall leaned a padded St. Andrew's cross, adapted with ladders of eyebolts along the outside of all of its struts, top and bottom. In a nearby corner, a swing built of leather straps hung from the ceiling. The walls were covered in shallow cabinets containing a pervert's cornucopia of sex toys and pain implements. A nest of pillows on a futon-like pad occupied the floor in another corner, waiting for him to collapse upon it if he couldn't manage to stagger the twenty feet to the bedroom.

I stood quietly, awaiting his reaction.

"Why soundproofing?" Of all the things he could have been curious about, I wasn't expecting that. "I mean, no one else lives here, so why?"

I shrugged, realizing that now I felt self-conscious. "Well, I'd like to have a family in this house someday, but I don't want to give up my other interests to do it."

"Ah." I could hear both of us overthinking that; me wondering if he'd be the one, and him wondering if he was the person I had in mind when I said that. And that was really more thinking than I wanted either of us to be doing tonight.

I pulled his attention back to the present rather decisively by shoving him against the padded wall, cupping a hand around the back of his head to keep it from impacting when the rest of his body did. I pried his mouth open, plunging my tongue inside, breathing in the faint chlorine scent of the treated water and the floral accents of the body wash he'd used. Geoff went limp, melting into the wall as I ground my clothed body against his bare one.

Afterward, I rested my forehead against his. "From now until you walk out the door or use your safeword, I'm in charge. You can ask questions, but I'm running the show. Understand?"

He nodded, and I caught his hair, tipping his head back.

"No. There's no room here for any sort of confusion or ambivalence. You answer me aloud, and you speak clearly so I know you know what you're agreeing to."

He opened his eyes to stare back soberly. "Yes. I understand."

"Good. Now go get your factor."

I followed him into the bedroom and prepared his factor silently, taking my time about it for no other reason than I knew it was still something that made him antsy and eager to be finished. I touched him more than I really needed to as I handled his arm and inserted the needle, giving him plenty of contact on his bare skin.

When we were done, I led him back to the playroom and picked up four lengths of heavy black twill that clinked with D-rings every few inches.

"What are those?" Geoff blurted.

I smiled. These were an innovation I was particularly pleased with, and I'd spent a lot of time online trying to find disabled people or people with disabled partners who were in the scene, getting suggestions before I decided upon them.

"Arm and leg binders." I held them aloft. "They'll zip around your arms and calves, giving me points where I can bind you to the cross or swing or wherever. That way I can immobilize you without putting stress on your joints if you struggle. Now come here."

Geoff stepped forward, still eyeballing the binders dubiously.

"Hold out your arms."

I slid the sheaths up his arms and zipped them from wrist to shoulder. They fit like a second skin, allowing no wiggle room.

"Good. Come on." I escorted him to a padded bench, which was narrow like a weight bench. It had a seat with thickly padded knee rests on either side of it, and a sloped, elevated back that ended in a face cradle, adapted from a massage chair like the one he used to work on back tattoos in his studio. Facing forward, he could recline with his legs on either side of the bench, spread open. Or he could kneel and rest his chest against the slope, and he'd be semi-upright with his back exposed.

I knelt and wrapped his calves in black sheaths of the same strong twill. They zipped down the back, tapering from the swell of muscle at the top of his calf down to his ankle, and they had D-rings along the sides.

My goal was to give him a shallow overview of the myriad things we could do in this room. I placed a hand on his hip and nudged him toward the bench. "Can you take kneeling for a few minutes, or do I need to put you in the swing to have access to your ass?"

His breath caught at the casual crudity, which it always did. He loved dirty talk. "I can kneel."

"All right, on the bench here, then, facing the back." I positioned him on the incline, clipping the rings on his sleeves to bolts on the bench. Then I secured his calves to the knee-rests.

"Struggle a bit. I want to see if those binders are going to put pressure on your wrists or ankles."

He jerked and tried to pull away before shaking his head. "I don't know about a prolonged struggle, but right now it's good. The only pressure is on my knees, and that'll be okay for a few minutes."

I nodded in satisfaction. "Okay. There shouldn't be any reason for you to put up a prolonged struggle today, but we'll give it a more exhaustive test later. Be right back."

From the cabinets, I retrieved three things. Geoff's breath hitched at the sight of the first one: a light quirt was something I knew would get his attention. The second was a rather thin butt plug, and the last item looked like the top two-thirds of a butt plug, with the wide flange, narrow neck, and flaring body. The part where it would narrow to a point for insertion was missing. I held it where he could see it and crushed it in my hand to show that it was malleable.

"Have you ever read *Story of O*?" I asked, pulling a bottle of lube out of a drawer and bringing the lot of it over to set on the bench before his eyes.

He shook his head and got a quick, sharp snap of the quirt for it.

"Verbal answers, if you please."

"No!"

"Better." I caressed the lovely red line on his pale skin, then stepped in front of him so he could see what I was doing. I inserted the thin plug through the half plug, demonstrating that the blunted one was hollow. The small plug now provided the rigidity and structure the malleable one lacked. "O's masters insisted she remain open and available to them at all times. Not only could she not wear underwear, she wasn't allowed to cross her legs or close her mouth, even when she was outside their presence. She had to always be accessible. I think that's a rather noble sentiment myself, but I'd take it a step further and ensure that not just your mouth and limbs are open, but also your asshole, available to use whenever I want it. Specula are too clumsy and bulky, however. *This* is called a tunnel plug. Want to guess what it does?"

A rich blush crept up Geoff's back and shoulders. Without making him answer, I backed away, moving behind him. He twitched at the cool smear of lube against his hole, and I chuckled softly. "I can see you're starting to get the idea. From now until we're done, you're going to be open to me. I can see inside you, put anything I want inside you. I can stick toys in there, shine light inside you, even piss in there if I wanted to. When I blow my load in you, you won't be able to hold it in. It'll just pour out down your legs."

Geoff made a querulous sound, letting me know he didn't care for that last bit.

"What, you don't want it to drip back out? Well, you'll have to earn that reward, won't you?" I leaned close to his ear. "If you're good, I'll breed you when we're done, without the plug, so you can take it with you."

He moaned, his hips shifting, humping the bench.

"Yeah, that's what you want, isn't it?" I stilled the writhing of his hips and pressed the cool silicone of the plug against his sphincter, working it inside. Once the tunnel plug was seated, I pulled the smaller one out, leaving a tube that held his ass open to my fingers. It stretched enough that I could even fuck him through it if I wanted to, and he wouldn't be able to feel the friction of me moving in and out.

One benefit was that it would make him feel more used. If he guessed that my other purpose was to keep him from getting chafed or abraded from prolonged anal play—which would, of course, require longer to heal—he didn't seem to mind.

"How does that feel?" I asked, studying that dark, gaping hole.

It took him a while to answer, which told me he was getting to the headspace I wanted him in. "Strange," he said finally, his voice breathy. "Cool air inside is weird."

"Good." I lubed my fingers and slid them into the plug, teasing him with touches inside where the plug ended. "You look so slutty with your hole gaping open and ready to use."

He made another discontented sound. "I can barely feel you touching me."

"Well, now you see why it's important that you be a very good boy and earn your reward. Otherwise when you walk out that door, you'll hardly feel like you've been fucked at all."

I removed my fingers and unzipped, lubing up my cock. The silicone of the plug stretched easily, but it was nothing like fucking the tight, hot grip his ass usually was. Too smooth, too cool. I could tell it was frustrating Geoff; he kept trying to hump back against me, trying to force me to thrust harder and faster. I nailed his prostate a few times, which, judging from his reaction, was even more jolting when he could barely feel everything else.

"Stop," I growled, going still when he tried to hump the bench again.

He groaned. "Please! I want—"

I pulled his head back by his hair. "It doesn't matter what you want. Your wishes are irrelevant unless and until I choose to grant them." I thrust once more, slowly, as though I had all the time in the world and was in absolutely no rush to end this. "Use this time to come to terms with that."

I fucked him steadily, waiting for it to sink home how at my mercy he was, bound to the bench, his pleasure withheld and even the inside of his ass exposed to my whim. I waited for him to go slack, giving up control. The tension drained out of his shoulders and neck as he let his face fall into the padded cradle. He went silent except for the pants and gasps when I nudged his prostate.

Fuck, that was sexy. It only took a few hard thrusts and the startled yelps they evoked before my orgasm gripped me by the balls and made me empty my load inside him. There was an immediate backwash when I pulled out, cum sliding down his taint and balls to drip onto his thighs. Geoff squirmed, trying to press them together as if he could keep the mess inside. The flush on his skin grew darker when I unclipped his restraints and pulled him to his feet, increasing the flow of semen seeping from his open ass.

I smirked. "Now how does that feel?"

"Filthy," he muttered, not meeting my eyes. His cock was hard and angrily red, which told me *filthy* was hitting all his buttons just right.

"How are your knees?" I knelt to massage them gently. Kneeling could be a problem even for people without joint issues.

He hesitated, and when I looked up, it was obvious he wasn't delaying answering, but checking in with his body. "They're okay," he pronounced finally.

"Think you can stand being bound to the cross for a while?"

Irritation flared in his eyes, replacing the dreamy look. "I'm fine," he gritted.

I quickly rose and caught his chin, forcing him to meet my eyes. "I *have* to ask. It's my responsibility. And I expect an honest answer."

I could see the process as he reined in the flash of temper. "My knees ache, but I think it's just from kneeling. I don't think it's a problem."

"Okay." I kissed him, a soft, indulgent brush of lips. His eyes had grown dreamy again by the time I pulled away. "If there's a problem that's related to your physical condition, don't worry about safe-wording. Just tell me what it is, and I'll try to take care of it without breaking the scene if possible. Use your safeword when it's something arising from the scene that isn't working. All right?"

He ducked his head, nodding. "Yeah."

"Good." I stroked my thumb across his lips and led him to the cross.

CHAPTER TWENTY-FOUR

Geoff

Robin anchored me to the cross as he had to the bench, by the rings on my bindings. He clipped my sleeves to the eyebolts along the struts. Not just near my wrists, but up my whole arm, taking the pressure off any single point. He even affixed them so that they pulled on the binder in opposite directions, keeping it from riding up my arm.

It felt far more complicated than cuffs would have. I was torn between resenting the special concessions and being grateful that Robin had considered these things.

"Try to squirm again," he instructed me when he was done, and I tugged obligingly. "Harder. Like you're really trying to get away."

As I pulled, it became apparent that if I moved too much, my arm would slip down in the binder until it caught on my hand.

"I was concerned that might be the case. If you feel it putting too much pressure on the joint at the base of your thumb, let me know." He pressed close, his clothes rough against my back as he reached around to grasp my cock and work it up again, until I groaned and wriggled, trying to push into his grip. "That's it. That's good, baby. Think about how hard you're gonna come when I'm done with you. But not yet." He stepped back, and I moaned, bereft. "Not until after I've whipped you."

I jerked against the restraints wrapped around my arms and legs, my head snapping around to follow him as he opened a cabinet and withdrew two floggers—one made of a shiny Mylar-looking material, the other of leather—and a paddle. Then he pulled out something else. It appeared to be a plastic handle with a glass tube that curved and ended in a flared head.

He laid the paddle and floggers on a table and plugged in the other item.

"Violet wand," he explained, extending both his arms before him and bringing them together slowly. When the one holding the wand approached the other, the wand glowed purple and static electricity crackled. A tiny lightning bolt leaped from the wand to Robin's forearm. "The zap gets more intense the farther from the body it is. This is a relatively low setting. It feels quite pleasant."

I couldn't help but flinch when he reached behind me, and then I felt my skin tingle gently. It was nice—not quite ticklish, but not painful either. An effervescent fizz zinging along my flesh. I twitched, trying to squirm away whenever the shocks got more intense, but I was held securely in place. When he brought the wand into actual contact with my skin, the sparks stopped. He drew it away again, and they resumed.

As I quickly acclimated to the sensation, I let my head fall forward, sinking into it, moaning softly each time a particularly sharp zap jolted me. He ran that flared wand over my back and down my ass and legs, making me jerk and shiver.

"There's some electrical play we probably won't be able to do. Certain forms of electrostim, stun guns, and cattle prods make the muscles seize quite hard, which wouldn't be a good idea. But static is perfectly safe—and a hell of a lot of fun."

I nearly came out of my skin when he slipped it between my legs, brushing it over my taint and balls.

"Jesus!" My gasp ended with a groan, my hands fisting above the close-fitting sleeves. My dick tightened and jerked with each shock, pre-cum dripping from the tip in cool droplets. I wriggled; I couldn't help it. It felt good, but it was intense enough that my body kept trying to flinch away.

"That's it. Dance for me, baby. Let me see that ass move." His teeth scraped lightly on my hip bone, and then another round of tingling zaps traveled over my nuts and behind them. "There are insertable attachments for this, you know. I could send these shocks right up your ass, or even along a sound up your cock." His murmur was soothing, contrasting with the stimulation of the wand. "And there's one that's like a cock ring, with two prongs running down to rest against your balls. It's designed not to ground out when it comes into contact with you. Someday, I'm going to strap you into the swing and introduce you to those attachments, but not today."

I moaned, uncertain whether I should be relieved or disappointed not to have that particular experience yet. I was so fucking hard, each jolt seemed like it was going to push me over the edge, but I remained hanging there on the precipice, groaning and alternately trying to writhe away and hump something.

"At higher settings, and with narrower attachments, it gets a bit harder to take." He did something behind me, and the sparks intensified. My groans turned to sharp, barking cries. He paid attention to my balls and taint for a moment, then wandered away, down my legs or over my back, only to return once I'd had a breather.

The next time he turned up the intensity, my sounds verged on screams.

"With an attachment with a fine point, at a high enough setting, you would swear you were being sliced with a knife. You can burn brands—temporary or even permanent—into the skin with the right tools."

I went still, whimpering, and Robin chuckled behind me. "I thought you'd like that idea." He turned it up again, and I screamed.

By the next time he offered me a reprieve, I was shaking, sweat popping out of my pores in beads to soak my skin and hair. I was out of my head, higher than I'd ever been before, so fucking turned on and exultant and quaking with the memory of pain.

Robin pressed close, caging me between his body and the cross. He embraced me, and if I'd been unbound, I would have clung to him, unconcerned with how needy I was being, full of adoration for him and feeling damn near worshipful. My chest ached with the enormity of it. It was too big for my ribs to contain.

"You're doing beautifully." Robin kissed the wet skin along the side of my neck, the line of my jaw. He even knelt behind me and kissed the sensitized flesh of my back, running his hands up and down every inch of bare skin he could find. Then he wrapped his arms around me and simply held me. He was hard once more against my ass, rubbing his fly along my hip, but he made no move to fuck me. "I love the sound of your screams. I love the way you move when you can't handle any more, and then the way you go still and sag when you give in and just *take* it. So beautiful. So strong. I want you so much. Every minute I'm with you makes me want you more."

Something suspiciously like a sob erupted from my throat, and all I could do was hang there in my bindings, limp against his body. I would have done anything for him in that moment. *Anything*. He could have flayed me alive, and I would have thanked him and begged for more.

I think I might have said something, but I have no idea what. He stepped to my side and turned my head, kissing me slowly and with incredible tenderness. I yearned for the kiss, trying to move closer, trying to bury myself in him.

"We're not quite done yet." He nipped at my lips and drew away, despite my dismayed sound. "I promised you a whipping."

I could barely open my eyes to see what he was doing as he plugged a cord into the violet wand and then tucked what looked like a small probe into the waistband of his jeans, against his skin. He took up the Mylar flogger, and I realized what was going to happen only a second before he trailed the silvery ribbons over my back, igniting a chorus of zaps each time it approached and moved away. He'd turned the intensity down, I think, but I knew he could easily crank it back up—and would.

"This one grounds out when it touches you, so we won't use it for long. Just enough for you to get the idea. The paddle and other flogger, though, are designed not to do that. You'll be able to feel them through the entire stroke."

The Mylar was light. The sensation it evoked had nothing to do with its weight impacting my skin, and everything to do with the eruption of charges from each fall. They got more powerful as he turned the violet wand up higher, the sparks leaping from the falls to my flesh from a greater distance, the zaps getting sharper. I began to moan and writhe again, both sounds and motion becoming more energetic the higher he dialed up the intensity.

Then Robin stopped. He took the small probe out of the waistband of his jeans and wedged it inside one of the sheaths on my calves. On the next stroke, the sensation changed. The sparks leaped from my body to the whip instead of the other way around. I could feel them surging from inside my flesh, ripping through my skin to find a route of escape. After only a moment of that, he turned up the intensity again, and I began to howl.

When he stopped, it seemed like there should have been some remnant of heat to my skin, a memory of the impact. It was hard to remember it had all come from a flogger that had the heft of a child's toy. I was shaking again, but Robin didn't give me a chance to catch my breath. He quickly switched out the Mylar flogger for the paddle, and then he was beside me, stroking my cock with one hand and swinging the paddle with the other.

He didn't swing it hard. He didn't have to. The static electricity charging my body jumped from my skin into the metal contacts somewhere inside the paddle, adding far more sting than the force of the blows themselves could account for. Now, though, even with these light swats, my skin did begin to heat up, blood rushing to the surface, no doubt turning my ass pink. It sensitized my nerves, made the zaps hurt more. My moans quickly turned into wails, and once again I found myself wriggling my ass in a futile effort to evade the pain.

"Beautiful. Keep dancing for me," Robin murmured, his hand pumping and curling and twisting on my cock.

Every so often the edge of the paddle would connect with the plug holding my asshole open. Thankfully the silicone of the plug prevented sparks from transmitting around my asshole, but the impact itself jolted the muscles and even my prostate, making me moan for a different reason.

"Love this. Keep moving, baby. Let me hear you. So gorgeous."

Time lost any meaning. I don't know how long he continued to paddle me, raining gently warming blows that hurt far more than my mind could make logical sense of. My head fell back, rolling from side to side, my throat vibrating with moans. My ass felt like it was on fire.

And then it ended, and his hands caressed my heated, tingling skin, nails gently scraping to ignite a burn.

"Almost done now." Robin embraced me from behind again,

hugging tightly, kissing my neck and shoulders. I melted into it, whimpering in exhaustion and the memory of pain. How it was possible to feel so damn good when something hurt so much, I couldn't understand, but I was flying. Somewhere on the very edges of awareness, I realized he must have shut off the violet wand, because zaps didn't leap from my skin to his.

I moaned when he left me, needing the press and warmth of his body and the comfort of his nearness. His voice washed over me as he crossed the room to retrieve the heavier, leather flogger, then came back. "Just a little more. We won't do much; I want to see if this is something we'll be able to use in the future."

Through heavy-lidded eyes, I watched Robin swing the flogger experimentally at the wall, first landing isolated blows, and then finding a rhythm. He twisted his wrist so that the falls traveled in a single, continuous motion, moving in a circle, the tips brushing the wall on each trip down before they came up from the opposite direction and over the top to descend again. The result was a nearly continuous rain of blows stroking down the wall.

After a moment of that, he swung it on the diagonal, crisscrossing his target with strokes that moved his arm in a sort of figure eight. I could see his breath pick up with the effort. When he stopped, he stripped off his shirt and approached me bare-chested. He was damp with sweat when he pressed against me again, kissing my shoulders.

He was going to hit me with that. Holy God, this was what I'd dreamed of for years. What I'd wished for and known I could never have when I watched those porn videos. The snap and fall of leather against my skin and the agony that would follow.

It was going to happen.

That flogger could be deadly for me, but he was going to hit me with it anyway. And I was unconcerned. Not because I was suicidally willing to accept that risk, but because I knew he would keep me safe somehow.

His hand stroked down my spine, and with just that touch, I knew he could do anything he wanted to me. I must have said as much, because his lips brushed my shoulder again. "Thank you."

Then he stepped away and swung the flogger.

It had far more weight than the Mylar one had, naturally, but he didn't swing it hard, and he swung from a distance, so I caught only the tips instead of the full thud of the falls. The first few times they flicked lightly against my shoulders, just the very ends swiping down my back. He didn't have the violet wand on; the sensation was pure impact, with none of the zaps that felt like they were sizzling through my muscles and piercing my skin from the inside out. Even without a heavy swing, the snap of the tips hitting my skin generated the same sort of heat that still burned the flesh of my ass. Warmth blossomed through my skin—not quite painful but with a bit of sting. My head fell forward, and I gave myself over to it.

When my skin felt fevered, he added the charge of the violet wand, and even at a low setting, the prickling zaps made those light strokes *more*. The blows began to land rapidly and continuously, flicking and stinging and shocking with each pass, and I realized he must be doing the same circular motion he'd done against the wall. The sensation was nonstop, except when he paused to turn up the charge on the violet wand.

Then the impact crossed my back, sweeping from the top of my shoulder to the bottom of my ribs on the opposite side, before crossing back the other way. The figure-eight swing he'd practiced. The speed with which the blows landed left me no opportunity to absorb each stroke before the next one fell.

Another adjustment on the violet wand gave me only seconds of reprieve, and then the pain was worse than ever.

Moans quickly became cries, which crescendoed to screams that escalated to breathless shrieks and sobs. I twisted in my bonds, trying to find a way free, begging him to stop.

"I can't!" I gasped, my spine bowing and my head thrown back in a futile effort to arch away from the blows. There was nowhere to go, though. My face was wet, and I had no idea if it was from sweat or tears. "Please, I can't!"

"You can," he growled, his breathing harsh behind me. The rhythm of the strokes paused. When it resumed, he'd turned up the intensity of the violet wand again. I shrieked once more. "That's it, baby. Give in to it. Ride it."

I continued to scream and struggle for several minutes more, and then all resistance abandoned me. I could only slump against the cross, moaning. Finally the blows tapered off and eventually disappeared.

Then Robin's body was against mine again, skin sweat-damp, sliding wetly along my own. He kept an arm around me, holding me up as his hand sought the carabiners clipping the rings on my wraps to the eyebolts on the cross. My knees wouldn't support me at first, and he had to steady me until I could get my legs beneath me.

I was still hiccuping intermittent sobs, shaking like I never intended to stop. With Robin's arm around my waist, I staggered the few steps to the pillowy nest in the corner and sank into it, curling up there with a whimper.

All the while, Robin murmured praise and reassurance. He told me over and over how beautifully I'd taken that, how proud he was of me, how much he wanted me. I tried to press closer to him, would have crawled inside his skin if I could have managed it. Time passed with me in a strange, semi-aware place, exhausted but too wired to fall asleep, drifting somewhere between consciousness and oblivion.

"Stay here," Robin instructed after an indeterminate amount of time. "I'm going to get you something to drink and clean you up."

I'm not sure I even acknowledged him, but he didn't press me for a verbal response this time. I felt abandoned when the warmth of his arms was gone, but he was back in no time, tipping a bottle of sports drink up for me to sip. I lay there passively while he wiped my arms and legs down with a wet cloth, only then realizing that he'd removed the sleeves and calf sheaths. He bathed my chest and finally my ass, slipping the hollow-cored plug out at last.

I'd forgotten its presence, but the reminder brought my flagging erection back to attention.

"Please," I whispered, rolling toward him, reaching for him. My hand found the bulge at his fly easily, and I palmed it. "Fuck me."

"You're not too exhausted?" I moaned softly, his hips pressing against my hand.

I shook my head, pulling at his zipper. "No. Want what you promised me. Please . . ."

It took only the barest maneuvering for him to roll me to my stomach and get his jeans down around his hips. Then he was spreading me, stretching me, filling me. The crisp hair on his sweaty chest rubbed against the hypersensitized skin of my back, and his strokes gave me the friction I'd lacked the last time.

I groaned gratefully. "Yes. Please . . ." I pushed up with my hips, trying to get him in deeper. I wanted him to pound me through the cushions and into the floor, sparing me nothing. After a moment of struggling, I got my knees beneath me, though my elbows would have nothing to do with supporting me. Instead I simply hugged a cushion under my chest and knelt there, ass up, rocking to meet his thrusts.

The press of his body, sweaty and sticky against mine; the ache of his cock stretching me; the tight pressure in my balls begging to erupt; the jarring impacts of his hips against my ass—I loved it all, loved everything to do with him. I don't know how I kept from blurting out an ill-timed confession he could have written off as me being out of my head. Instead I moaned and shouted my encouragement, begging "more" and "harder" and "faster" and "deeper" and "please-God-fuck-me-give-it-to-me-now."

I went into meltdown at the merest stroke of his hand, pumping into his palm with endless surges of pleasure so keen they were agony. The spasms went on and on until it felt like my nuts had wrung themselves dry. Only then did I feel the wet pulse of him inside me, pouring into my body what his diabolical game had denied me before.

I collapsed into the cushions, still twitching. On the edge of awareness, I sensed him cleaning us up and wrapping himself around me. But neither my muscles nor my powers of speech seemed to have any strength left. And so I dropped off, sinking rapidly into a weary sleep.

CHAPTER TWENTY-FIVE

Robin

Autumn spun on as Geoff and I settled into a comfortable routine. I was still enjoying the novelty of having a full kitchen to cook in, and it turned out Geoff had spent a couple of years tending bar at a banquet hall when he was in art school. The allure of my freshly stocked, crystal-paned liquor cabinet proved as strong as my cooking. It gave him a chance to brush up his skills on the nights we weren't planning to play. Those nights, we wouldn't have so much as a single beer. On the other days, it could be dinners with martinis, brunch with mimosas, or late nights in the hot tub with a pitcher of sangria.

The evenings we didn't play were spent in the sort of cozy domesticity that seemed to puzzle Geoff. I doubted it was something he'd ever envisioned for himself during all those years of holding people at arm's length. He'd sit and sketch designs while I worked on my bookkeeping. Then he'd lie on the sofa with his head in my lap while we watched the evening news, an endeavor that more often than not ended in a blowjob or with Geoff bent over the arm of the sofa.

I had well and truly fallen for him. Jesus, I was getting downright sappy. I found myself smiling during random moments of the day when I thought about him, found myself yearning to be with him when we weren't together. And it wasn't just the sort of vulnerable, needy way he clung to me at the end of a scene, when I'd broken him down and laid him bare, that had me feeling that way.

By the end of the second week after I moved in, the number of nights he'd stayed at my house outnumbered the nights we'd spent at his apartment. By the end of the third week, his overnight bag always contained enough clothing for several days. A stash of factor became a permanent fixture in my refrigerator, because that was easier than hauling it back and forth.

Sundays became our day to play, the day we could go all night, exhaust ourselves with pain and pleasure, then sleep until noon.

On the fourth Monday at my house, I stood in the doorway of the bathroom that connected the bedroom and the playroom, watching Geoff crane his neck to peer at the dark purple welts that crisscrossed his back and ass, and even the backs of his thighs. Last night had been our first time trying a single-tail whip. I hadn't broken the skin and wouldn't for some time, if I ever did, but he'd been sobbing and incoherent by the time we were done. Then I'd bound him to the straps of the swing and fucked him until he damn near passed out. And today . . . today he had the thing he'd craved most since we'd begun playing.

Marks. Welts. Bruises created deliberately, with aforethought, not as a result of some mishap relating to his clotting disorder.

Trophies, in other words.

I thought seeing those sorts of marks on him would bring back unpleasant memories of Kyle, but it was not even remotely similar. There was a simple, innocent joy to Geoff's pleasure in being marked that Kyle had never had.

He looked triumphant, twisting to see them better. They were livid against his pale skin, and spread wider from the line the whip had traveled than perhaps they might have in someone who wasn't a hemophiliac. But not dangerous. Not life-threatening. No deep-muscle damage along his spine or in his pelvis to threaten the nerves and blood supply to his lower body.

And the *sounds* he'd made when I fucked him with those lines of molten fire still blazing on his ass and thighs . . .

"Preening?" I couldn't help asking with a smirk.

He peered up at me, still sleep-tousled and utterly delectable. He scrubbed a hand through his sandy-brown hair, which was flattened on one side and stood in wild clumps on the other.

I wanted to eat him with a spoon. And maybe some whipped cream.

He gave me a slow smile and twisted to admire my handiwork again. "Not preening. Just—"

"Anticipating how I'm going to make sure from here on out that you're never without marks of some kind on your back?" I stepped close, pinning him between my body and the bathroom counter. My morning wood pressed against my stomach, and he gasped as the cold edge of the counter rubbed against his welts. His dick palpably decided it liked this state of affairs just fine. "Thinking of ways to thank me for giving you those marks?"

My lips found his ear, and my nails raked lightly down his back to reawaken the memory of pain from the whipping.

"Mmm, God, yes." He practically purred.

I captured his mouth, and he grabbed me by the hips and jerked me closer, in no way passive this morning. He took control of the kiss, deepening it, seizing my hair to hold me still while he tried to suck the breath out of my lungs.

I was panting and flushed when he pulled away, and it was Geoff's turn to smirk.

"Shower?" I drew him by the hands toward the glass and tile stall with its dual shower heads. He nodded eagerly, stepping inside and leaning against the wall while I adjusted the water temperature. When I turned back to him, he shoved me out of the stream against the opposite wall and dropped to his knees.

He hissed when the water hit his welts, but it didn't stop him from licking the rivulets that trickled down my abdomen. "You said something about thanking you?"

I groaned. "Fuck, yeah." I threaded my fingers through his damp hair as he ran his lips up and down the side of my cock, stroking me with his wet hand from root to tip before he sucked me into his mouth and all the way down his throat.

After that first lunge, he took his time with it, drawing it out as long as possible for me. I moaned and gasped appreciatively, thrusting into his mouth until I came down his throat.

Afterward he knelt there, catching his breath, as I stroked his hair and shoulders.

"You okay?" I smiled down at him.

"Never been better," he answered with absolute sincerity in his eyes, and accepted my hand to help him to his feet.

All the caution in the world can't guard against a random accident. I didn't realize his knees were stiff from kneeling on the tile—maybe Geoff hadn't either—but he wobbled and slipped. I grabbed for him, but my hands and his skin were wet, and in the end he hit the wall anyway.

It wasn't a hard hit. It didn't have to be. Horrified, I heard his skull knock against the tile with a solid *thud*. Dread settled on Geoff's face, along with a sort of annoyed resignation.

"Ow. Fuck!" He rubbed his scalp, scowling.

"Are you all right?" I steadied him, running my hands uselessly over his body to assess him for injury. I reached for his head but then pulled back, not sure I should touch.

Shit. He hadn't missed that quick withdrawal. His eyes narrowed, and he grabbed my hand, pressing it against his head where it had struck the tile.

"I won't break," he growled.

Shit.

"I know. I'm sorry. You *are* all right?"

"Yeah, probably." He mustered a smile, trying a bit too hard to project a nonchalant attitude. "It's probably not a big deal. We just need to be on the lookout for a brain bleed."

"What do we need to watch for?"

"Um, headache, dizziness, nausea, blurred vision, irritability, disorientation, lethargy . . . The list goes on, but I think those are the major points. They can be slow bleeds, so it might not show up right away." He tried for another smile, but it still looked forced. "Really, it'll be fine. I'll infuse once we're out of the shower, and we'll watch how things progress for the next day or two."

"Let's do that now."

I knew he was taking this seriously when he didn't argue. I turned off the water and hustled him into the bedroom, still dripping wet.

"Can you get us some towels and breakfast?" he asked, shivering as he gathered his factor and supplies.

"You don't want me to—"

He shook his head emphatically. "Not this time. Just . . . let me do this myself. Don't hover, don't make a fuss, just get us some damn breakfast, okay? Will you do that?" Annoyance was creeping into his tone despite his obvious attempts to rein it in. "This is no one's fault. It was a stupid fucking accident, and I really don't want to let it fuck everything over."

I nodded uncertainly and went for towels as he began to prepare a larger-than-usual dose of factor. "Enough to get my levels up near a hundred percent," he explained without making me ask. I left him to it and ran downstairs in a pair of sweats to hunt up breakfast.

"Okay, should I read this as you being irrationally irritable, or are you just pissed off about something?" I demanded that evening, after the third or fourth time Geoff had snapped about something inconsequential in less than an hour.

He growled, folding his arms over his chest. Then he sighed and dropped them. "I don't know. I guess I'm rational enough to admit that I really won't be able to tell if I'm being irrational. I have a headache and my mood is shit, and maybe that's a sign of a bleed. Or maybe my head just hurts because I bumped it against the mother-fucking wall or because I'm stressed out. And I'm annoyed because this isn't how I wanted to spend my day."

I nodded soberly, studying his eyes to detect any changes in his pupils. But I kept my distance. He likely would have torn into me if I'd tried to be snuggly. Never mind that six hours ago we'd wanted to spend the day being snuggly. It was a bit of a quandary because we both knew I needed to monitor him, but he clearly wanted to be left the fuck alone. I wasn't going to try his temper further by being oversolicitous, but neither was I going to let his irritation push me so far away that I missed something I needed to be looking out for.

"This won't affect how I see or treat you," I murmured. I saw the doubt flicker in his eyes and knew that was at least some of what was worrying him. His jaw flexed, but he didn't answer.

I let him mull that over for a while until I saw the slight twitching of his eye that said his head was hurting badly enough to make him wince.

"Do you want me to get you your pain medication?"

"What?" His head came up sharply, and he winced again and glowered.

"I said, do you want your pain meds? For the headache?"

"No." His lips tightened, and he tried to walk that bit of pissiness back. "Can't. Need to keep an eye on what the pain is doing."

"All right." I got a grip on my own irritation, reminding myself that this was hitting several buttons for him and he didn't handle his illness gracefully on the best of occasions. "Okay, I'll tell you what. I'm going to fix dinner and do some work in my office, and I'll check back with you every once in a while."

"Yeah, okay." He frowned and blew out a breath. "I'm sorry I'm being such a bitch about this."

"Thanks. It's okay." Wow. He really was trying.

I brought him a plate of stir fry that he hardly touched, and retreated without a word. Geoff stretched out on the sofa to channel surf idly.

When I emerged, he had dozed off. My first gentle attempt to wake him up didn't accomplish anything, so I took the opportunity to call the number of the Hemophilia Treatment Center hotline without pissing him off again. Ten minutes later, I shook his shoulder and called his name. Geoff tried to bat me away, his brow furrowing as though his headache was worse.

"Come on, baby, up you go," I urged, trying to help him sit.

He blinked at me with bleary eyes and tried to lie back down. "Lemme sleep."

"Didn't you say something about drowsiness being a symptom to look out for?" I won the battle to keep him upright. I don't think he even realized he was groaning softly.

"It's also a symptom of I-didn't-get-enough-fucking-sleep."

"Well, let's at least get you upstairs to bed."

"Anything to get you to shut the fuck up and let me sleep," he muttered, but he allowed me to tug him to his feet, then promptly swayed against me.

I caught him, making an effort to keep my voice calm and even. "Okay, that's it. I'm going to take you to the hospital in Holland."

"Just call the HTC. They'll tell you it's all good. I put the number in your phone."

"Yeah, I called them ten minutes ago when you wouldn't wake up the first time. They said if I saw anything else that gave me concern, get you to the hospital. Better safe than sorry and all that. Now come on."

I watched him struggle with that, part of him clearly wanting to tell me to fuck off. Luckily there seemed to still be a rational corner of his mind that suggested maybe getting checked out wasn't such a bad idea.

Nodding and grumbling, he let me escort him to the car.

CHAPTER TWENTY-SIX

Geoff

After a CT scan, the hospital admitted me for observation overnight. By the time we were done in emergency and I had a room, visiting hours were already over, and they made Robin leave. He promised to return in the morning, and despite my earlier irritable mood, I was not happy to see him go. From the moment we entered the hospital, I had a bad feeling about the whole thing. The emergency nurse was professional, but I didn't think I had imagined the way her mouth tightened when she saw Robin stroke my hand. It brought back to me the fact that, whatever the sexual minority demographics that made up the Saugatuck area, we were in ultrareligious, ultraconservative West Michigan. The politics in Saugatuck didn't hold true for the rest of the county, much less the whole region.

With that single grimace from the nurse, the sense of safety that should have come with being in the hospital was gone. I would have felt better with Robin at my side, so that we could deal together with whatever bullshit they might try to give us.

For all my weariness earlier, that vague sense of alarm made it difficult for me to get to sleep once I was in my room. I dozed fitfully and woke up in the wee hours of the morning to hear a murmured conversation near my door.

"Did you see his back?" It was a woman speaking. A nurse? One had introduced herself to me when I was admitted, but I wasn't familiar with her yet.

The woman she was speaking to—another nurse?—made a derisive sound. "He came in with a man. Who knows what those guys get up to?" I was sure only the fear of losing her job kept the woman from substituting "fags" for "guys."

"No one deserves that sort of treatment, no matter who they are. I'm going to call a social worker and the police. That man he's with has to be stopped before he kills him."

Shit.

I spent the next several hours cursing myself for being so stupid. I'd been in such a lather for kinky thrills that I hadn't even considered the potential consequences for Robin. I *knew* better. I knew parents and partners of hemos were sometimes suspected of abuse when people misinterpreted the bruises and bloody noses. It was one of the things we were warned about when beginning adult relationships.

I debated calling Robin to come get me and checking myself out of the hospital AMA before anyone had a chance to cause trouble for us, but the fact was I knew I needed to be there. If I had a brain bleed, it had to be monitored. If I left, I might save Robin legal difficulties, but only at the expense of my own safety.

By the time a woman arrived the next morning—her gentle, sympathetic bearing screaming *crisis counselor*—my headache was beginning to recede and dismay had been edged out by anger. When I refused to speak to her, she left.

I tried to call Robin. It went to his voice mail. I didn't hear back from him within the next couple of hours, at which point a cop showed up to talk to me. Typical middle-aged, white, overweight, doughnut-eating cop. It was all I could do not to roll my eyes at the predictability of the whole dog and pony show.

"Look, man." He settled into a chair by the bed with a world-weary sigh. Oh, yay. This was where he'd try to do the "straight talk" approach. "I get it. You're used to people discriminating against you, not listening to what you have to say, not believing you. No one wants to think a guy can be the victim of abuse, and half the people around here probably think a gay guy deserves what he gets. But I'm not one of them. So why don't you tell me about those bruises on your back?"

Well, hallelujah! My good buddy, Officer Straight-Able-Bodied-Privilege, was here to tell me he wouldn't dismiss me. The day was saved.

I shrugged and offered him a somewhat vacant smile. "I gave myself those bruises."

"I don't care what he told you. You weren't asking for it."

"No, I mean I put those bruises on myself. Performance art. I'm an artist. Went to art school and everything. I'm working on this act that uses a whip, and I just keep hitting myself." My smile got toothier, and I held out my hands in a helpless, *What can you do?* shrug.

His eyes narrowed. "You smash your own head into the wall too?"

"Slipped in the shower." I fluttered my eyelashes. "Should've been more careful getting up after sucking my boyfriend's dick."

He flushed and looked away, squirming. I felt a savage stab of satisfaction at having discomfited him. It took him a moment to regain his composure enough to level that no-nonsense gaze at me again.

"You realize impeding a criminal investigation is a crime, right?"

I blinked, suddenly all wide-eyed innocence. "I know some performance art can be edgy, but *criminal*? Would it make a difference if I said it was for charity?"

"You wanna end up dead?" I could see his patient, tolerant, understanding act wearing thin. "I'm not your enemy here. I want to help you. Doesn't matter to me who you screw. I just don't want this guy killing you or anyone else. Next time you might not be so lucky."

"Robin had nothing to do with it." I didn't have to feign sincerity. "I'm a hemophiliac. Accidents happen, and accidents are a little more dangerous for me than for your average guy. It's no big deal. I know you mean well, but you've made the wrong assumption here, Officer."

"Would it make a difference to you if I told you your boyfriend has done this before?" He pulled a notepad out of his inner jacket pocket. "I did some checking. Seems Mr. Brady's last boyfriend filed a complaint against him for domestic abuse not long before Mr. Brady moved here from New York. He'd been beaten with a cane."

I went still, a shiver rippling through me. "So he claimed. It was awfully convenient that the accusation happened to cast suspicion on the credibility of Robin's testimony against him for embezzling."

The cop's eyes gleamed, and he pushed a business card into my hand. "You decide you're tired of being his next victim, give me a call. Let's just hope it's not too late by then. Guy with your medical condition's got to be careful."

I remained mute, my eyes burning as I waited for him to leave. Then I grabbed the phone and dialed Robin, who thankfully answered this time.

"You okay?" he asked anxiously.

I nodded, even though I knew he couldn't see it. "Yeah. They don't think it's serious enough to keep me here. They're going to release me this afternoon, probably. I just need to be really conscientious about keeping my factor levels up until we're sure, and not risk any more injuries for at least a few weeks."

I could hear Robin digesting that. "All right. I'll close the gallery early and come get you."

"Okay." I fell silent, trying to figure out how to bring up what had happened. Finally I went for broke. "Um, I got a visit from a guy from the Saugatuck-Douglas Police Department today."

Robin's sigh crackled through the speaker of the phone. "Me too. We can talk about it when I pick you up."

I nodded, closing my eyes wearily. "Got it. I'll see you this afternoon."

"Right. See you."

Damn it all, that wasn't good enough. With his history, Robin needed to know I trusted him. He'd never done a thing to me that I hadn't wanted, and I wouldn't let myself doubt him.

"Robin?"

"Yeah?"

Suddenly I couldn't breathe. My pulse pounded in my temples, and my lungs felt like they were in a vise. I knew what I had to say, and I was terrified.

I said it anyway.

"I, um— I love you."

He was silent for several heart-stopping seconds, and when he released it, his breath sounded shaky.

"Thank you." His voice was barely a whisper. "I love you too. I'll see you this afternoon."

My hand trembled when I turned off my phone, but in spite of everything, I was smiling.

THE CAR RIDE was filled with stilted courtesies, as though neither of us wanted to commit to a serious conversation while Robin was driving.

"Do you want me to take you home?" he asked softly as we drove into downtown Saugatuck.

"Would you mind if we went to your place?" I hadn't realized until that moment that I was more at home in his house than I was in my own little room above my shop. "I mean, I'd understand if you'd rather not have me there."

Robin shot me a surprised look before turning his attention back to the road. "Why wouldn't I want you there?"

"I should've considered this. I think I mentioned to you that people sometimes draw the wrong conclusions when they see bruises on hemophiliacs. It just never occurred to me what it might mean for *you* specifically if someone suspected you of domestic abuse."

Robin barked an incredulous laugh. "If you think that's bad, try researching some of the court cases involving people charged with assault for completely consensual BDSM play. If anything, I should have warned you."

"Seriously?" I blinked as he drove up the hill and turned into his driveway.

He nodded, parking the car and running his hands up and down the steering wheel with a sigh. "Yeah. It'd be hilarious if it weren't so fucking infuriating. Most courts have upheld that under the law, you can't consent to being assaulted. Unless you're doing MMA or something, of course. Come on. Let's get you inside."

While he herded me into the house, Robin regaled me with a story about the bust of a BDSM party in Massachusetts. "It was, like, ten years ago or so. I think I was in college, just starting to explore the scene, but I've heard the Old Guard talk about it. Cops raided a play party in Attleboro. One woman was charged with assault with a weapon. Wanna guess what the weapon was?"

I didn't really need help settling in on the sofa, but after what had happened that morning, I was uncharacteristically okay with letting him hover and coddle me a bit.

"I'm almost afraid to ask."

"A wooden spoon. They charged her with assault for spanking another woman, and they said it didn't matter if the other woman was consenting, because you can't consent to assault. The whole debacle became known as Paddleboro." He shrugged. "It eventually got dropped, and *Lawrence v. Texas* has made it a lot harder to prosecute anyone for what they do in the bedroom. Guess that's one good thing about kink going mainstream. Maybe now some of those laws will change with the times."

I snorted. "Right. We're in a country where it takes a ruling by the Supreme Court to nullify laws prohibiting blowjobs."

"True." Robin's smile faded as he sat down beside me and took my hand, lacing our fingers. "You believe I never abused Kyle, right?"

"I do." And I did.

He nodded, leaning back and drawing me against him. I rested my head on his shoulder and let him hold me.

It took me a long while to muster up the will to say what I had to say. "I think we need to give up any play that could leave marks. No more whippings or that sort of thing."

Robin sucked in his cheeks. "I understand. It probably isn't safe enough for you to risk it."

"Me? Pfft, I'm fine. It's not safe for *you*." He gave me a startled look. "What would have happened to you if I'd had a serious brain bleed? If I'd been left comatose, or a vegetable, or if I'd died? No, don't even try to argue. *It could happen*. It could have happened *this* time. This is *not* a far-fetched possibility. Brain bleeds are a very common way for hemos to die. They would have thought you had something to do with it, and you would have been facing a manslaughter charge. If I get seriously sick and they see marks on me, even if they believed you that I consented, it wouldn't matter. Like you said, they'd just claim that consent was no defense."

"That's ridiculous!" Robin pulled back, the set of his jaw stubborn. "I'm not going to give up something we both obviously want and need just because of some outdated laws! Jesus, I mean, would I stop fucking your brains out if *Lawrence v. Texas* hadn't invalidated anti-sodomy laws? They want to try to charge me? Bring it on. I can afford a great lawyer, and I'm sure the ACLU, Lambda Legal, and the National Coalition for Sexual Freedom would have a field day with it."

"That's not what you said the night we met. I didn't get it then, but your irritation over me putting you in a situation where you might be held legally accountable for injuring me—that was all about the charges Kyle had brought against you, right? Because that could have been really bad for you."

He gave a short, jerky nod. "But things were different then."

"How?"

"I was in a bad place emotionally over it all. And the whole thing with Kyle hadn't been completely dismissed yet."

"Obviously not 'completely' if Officer What's-His-Name can pull up the record so easily." I frowned. "I'm not willing to take the risk."

"It's *my* risk to take!"

"Funny, I said that to you that first night and you didn't buy it any more than I'm buying it now." My head was starting to ache again. "A minute ago you were willing to stop for my safety. Why can't I be willing to stop for yours?"

"Because your safety is a valid concern, and this—"

"—is *also* a valid concern, whether you choose to admit it or not." I grabbed both his hands and squeezed until he met my eyes. "If things had played out differently today, you could be in handcuffs right now."

"Maybe." His eyes narrowed, his gaze challenging me. "Or maybe you're just looking for another way to let this thing keep you from living the life you want to live."

I jerked my hands away and stood, storming over to the stairs. "*This thing* has ruined the lives of everyone I've ever cared about. Maybe I don't want to see it ruin yours too."

I turned to mount the stairs, but his voice followed me.

"Would they say it was worth it?"

With my hand on the banister, I paused to face him.

"These people whose lives you say your hemophilia has ruined. If I could poll them, would they agree? Or would they say every minute they spent with you was worth whatever difficulty they might have faced?"

I didn't have an answer for him, and I was too tired to argue about it any longer. I went upstairs and crawled into bed alone, where I failed to sleep despite my exhaustion. It was a long time before Robin joined me, spooning against my back and drawing me close.

His lips pressed against the nape of my neck.

"Do me a favor?" he whispered. "Let's table the discussion for now. You said we'll have to take it easy for a while anyway, right?"

I nodded mutely.

"Okay. Then let's decide then what we want and what we feel is safe. Give ourselves time to back away from the knee-jerk reactions and consider. Can we do that?"

"Yeah." I rolled to face him, and his kiss was the softest, most tender thing I could possibly have imagined. It made my chest ache. "Yeah, we can do that."

CHAPTER TWENTY-SEVEN

Geoff

My reluctance to begin playing again—at least in ways that would leave marks—surprised me as much as Robin's *lack* of reluctance. For a guy who'd been keen on taking things slowly, he wasn't fazed at all by the idea of getting back into it. But it was too big a risk, and I was content without it. That was something I wouldn't have imagined a year ago. I'd been so fixated on what I felt I'd been deprived of my whole life: the roughness and the pain. Sex had always been about seeking a thrill, not intimacy.

Falling in love with Robin changed all that. Between my mother's death in the spring and the approaching holiday season, my life had taken so many unexpected turns that I had given up trying to predict anything further out than the next weekend's plans.

I couldn't bring myself to regret a minute of it.

By the end of November, I was living with Robin on a de facto basis, even if I never bothered to change my mailing address from the little apartment above my studio. It wasn't anything we discussed or planned or made official. It just . . . happened. I don't think either of us realized it until Thanksgiving, when I spoke to Ling, trying to decide what our holiday plans would be. Since Robin had already promised his guest room to Jace, I offered Ling my apartment without a second thought.

"You know, you should consider renting it out," she remarked.

"Why would I do that?"

"Um, because you don't live there anymore?" She didn't quite tack the *well, duh* onto her response, but the tone carried it well.

"Huh."

That evening after the last client left, I went upstairs and looked around. There was a layer of dust on everything except the refrigerator, which was the only feature I used during the workday. The closet was mostly empty and a cobweb stretched between the bathroom ceiling and the showerhead.

When he picked me up that evening, Robin found me up there, pulling the rest of the clothes out of the closet to take with me.

"What are you doing?" he asked, draping himself across the bed.

I shrugged. "Just grabbing some stuff I need."

He rolled onto his side, propping himself on an elbow. "You should consider renting this place out."

"Yeah, I'll give it some thought." I hid my smirk, glancing at him out of the corner of my eye. "It's nice to be able to offer Ling someplace to stay when she comes to visit, though. Doesn't matter if the bedroom is soundproofed. It would still feel weird having sex if my little sister were downstairs."

"Mmm, especially since I've thought of some great ways to celebrate the holidays." He caught my hand as I passed and tugged me gently toward the bed. "I want to make you scream again. Think it's safe to do that now?"

I groaned, and everything in my body went taut. My skin felt tight, too snug to contain the pounding of my blood and the flush of heat that washed over me. I let him roll me under his body, achingly hard for him. I hugged his thigh between mine, grinding against him.

"I want that." I dragged my open mouth along his jaw toward his lips. His tongue thrust deep into my mouth, and I latched on to it, sucking hard.

Robin seized my hands and pinned them up over my head. He straddled my hips, the rising bulge in his slacks pressing against my own. His lips traveled down my neck, threatening a bite that would never materialize. Merely the threat was enough to make my pulse trip. The knowledge he would never do it couldn't quell the instinctive surge of adrenaline.

"I want to leave so many marks on you, you'll be seeing them for a month."

It was like a blast of snow sweeping in from Lake Michigan, chilling me. "We can't."

Robin lifted his head, his pale-blue eyes sober. "Can't because you don't want to, can't because it's too dangerous for you, or can't because you're afraid for me? Only two out of those three are answers I'm going to accept."

I jerked my wrists out of his grasp and pushed him off me. "Well, that's too fucking bad, because the one you won't accept is the only one I'm not going to budge on." I drew my knees up to my chest, hugging them. "It's not worth the risk."

I wished I were better at expressing my feelings. I wished I could tell him how much I valued what he'd helped me explore, the dreams and fantasies he'd made real for me. He'd unlocked things I'd never imagined possible, and if some of it wasn't exactly what I'd wished for, it was close enough that I could be more than content with it.

The families of hemophiliacs could counter accusations of abuse simply by explaining the truth. But there was a hostile society outside Robin's door, waiting and willing to condemn him if they got the wrong idea—or worse, even the right one. No amount of explaining could keep them from going after him if they chose to. The law—well-intentioned to protect victims of true abuse—made no allowances for us.

"Baby." Robin sighed and sat up, his lips brushing the back of my shoulder. "I'm not going to live my life afraid that ignorant people won't understand. You of all people should respect that. How many times in your life have you been ostracized because of ignorant assumptions?"

I swallowed, shaking my head against the image of panicked parents yanking their children out of my vicinity on the playground. Such scenes formed some of my earliest memories. Even now, people asked me how I "caught" hemophilia and if I could infect others.

I turned to look at Robin, letting him know he had my attention.

He offered me a tight smile. "Call it an act of civil disobedience. I don't care if the law thinks we don't have the right to decide what we do in the bedroom. If they come after me, so be it. I'm willing to take that fight on."

"I just—" I sighed, plucking at a loose string on the bedspread. "My medical issues are mine to deal with. I have to live with them and all the ways they affect every aspect of my life. You don't. And you certainly don't have to take risks because of them."

He caught my hand. "Yeah, I do. What, you think after how far we've come the last six months, I'm going to decide I've had enough inconvenience and write you off as a bad investment? That's not gonna happen." He pressed closer behind me, his lips ghosting along the back of my neck. "There are things we haven't done yet, things I know you want, and I'm going to make sure we do them all. I want to give you everything you ever dreamed of."

There was something so ardent about his whisper that my throat tightened. It felt like a vow. I wasn't sure I could handle pursuing that line of thought at the moment; my emotions were too raw and confused. Self-doubt assailed me. What was I doing? I didn't know how to be in a relationship, how to cope with someone loving me. I wasn't prepared for that.

I drew a deep breath and redirected the conversation to something that at least seemed safer. "Like what?"

"What do I want to do?"

I nodded. "Yeah."

"Remember that video you shared with me?" The edge of his fingernail traced an imaginary slice down my shoulder blade. "I want to give you that. Not the heavy impact play—I know that's out of the question. But the rest."

I tried not to whimper, but I'm not sure I succeeded. Everything dissolved in a dark, nearly suffocating surge of *wanting*. What did you do when everything you ever wanted was being offered to you on a silver platter, but the only way to take it was to endanger someone you loved?

The problem was, I didn't think I was being alarmist this time. I'd done a lot of research over the last month since we'd had this discussion, and none of it had contradicted my primary concern.

If Robin did what he had promised me that morning after he whipped me—if he saw to it that I was never without marks of some kind—it was only a matter of time before I was hospitalized again and those marks were once more called into question. And if it ever went to court, the fact that Robin's ex had so much as murmured an allegation of abuse would be sufficient to send Robin to jail.

That, I realized, was the real sticking point. My health and issues of consent could be dealt with, but the stigma from that false claim would condemn Robin no matter what. Kyle had fucked things up for us but good. *That* was where my concerns stopped being alarmist and became a serious consideration.

Robin nudged me when my silence had drawn on too long. "If you don't want that anymore, just say so."

"It's not a matter of wanting." I leaned into him. "The problem is, no jury on this side of the state is going to sympathize with a fag who has a dungeon next door to his bedroom, especially a fag who has been accused of abuse before. I've done my homework on this. People have lost their jobs, their children—"

"I don't have kids—not yet, at least—and I'm self-employed." Robin shrugged, looking down at me with a cocky grin. I jerked out of his arms and jumped to my feet.

"And you also have this fucking arrogant idea that nothing can touch you! You told me from the beginning that you know your life has been charmed, but apparently you've never considered that it might not always be that way. Well, I'm here to tell you, baby, that sometimes life fucking *sucks*, and it's not fair or just, and there's no reasoning with it and no way to get out of it. If you can't accept that idea, then I'm the last person you should be involved with, because life with me is going to suck even harder than average."

Robin stared at me, his grin fading. Finally, he appeared to be taking this seriously. "You're really that worried about this?"

I gave him a tight nod.

"But why? It's *my* risk."

"Gee, I think we've played this song before." I rolled my eyes. "What if it's not just yours?"

"What do you mean?"

I swallowed, folding my arms over my chest and looking away. "I was thinking of asking if you'd mind if I authorized you to make medical decisions for me. That way if something happens and Ling can't be here right away . . . But what if I'm incapacitated and you can't act on my behalf because you're accused of being the one who put me in that condition to begin with? Or what if . . ."

"What if what?"

I kept my gaze fixed on the carpet. "What if someday you do have a family to lose?" I thought of Ling and her insistence that someday she wanted a niece or nephew, even if she had to carry the baby herself. I didn't say that part, though. It was a presumptuous concern, yet I couldn't help but court it.

For once, Robin sounded flummoxed. "I didn't— I hadn't—" I heard him take a breath, as though bracing himself. I did likewise. "You're right. Those are things I definitely need to consider." My eyes flew to his, and he gave me a warm smile. "If you want help with the paperwork for the medical issues, we can talk to my lawyer, see what needs to be done."

And just like that, with no muss, fuss, or dramatic pronouncements, we committed to a future together.

Robin held out his hand, and I let him draw me back to the bed. His fingers crept under the ends of my hair to stroke my neck. "Okay. That's that, then. No whippings that will leave marks." He leaned in and kissed below my ear, and his voice dropped to a low growl. "I'm assuming needle play is still all right? It would be a lot harder to paint those marks as nonconsensual. I can still make you scream."

I started to melt again, but something felt like it was missing, or off. Regret scratched at the back of my mind, taking some of the shine off the understanding we had reached. Temptation kept whispering two words in my ear.

Just once.

A consolation prize, for both of us. One chance to taste something I yearned for, to refuse to let fear dictate my every choice. Then we'd do the smart thing, the wise thing, the safe thing, the responsible thing. But for just one time, I'd be unafraid.

Was I being self-serving? Reckless? Possibly. I didn't know anymore.

I swallowed. "Just once."

"What?" Robin drew back to stare at me.

"One last time to leave marks."

He studied me for a long moment, then dragged me in for a hard kiss. "Guess I'd better make it count."

WE DECIDED to wait until after the holidays, after Jace and Ling left. Jace wouldn't be concerned if he saw the marks, but Ling might, and I didn't want to try to explain to her. The four of us rang in New Year's with a pitcher of sangria and hot tubbing outside in the snow.

Then, on the second of January, Robin and I were alone once more in his house—in our home. We started the day off right, with Robin herding me to the sex swing—he wasn't going to take the chance of anything going wrong with my joints that day—and fucking me until I nearly blacked out when I came. Aching, and with his cum still seeping out of me, I sat passively while he infused me with a large enough dose of factor to get my levels close to one hundred percent.

I showered while he made brunch. As I took a piss, I felt, as always, the sting of self-consciousness, of being controlled, of being *possessed*, at nothing more than the sight of the open bathroom door.

Robin didn't need grandiose ceremonial gestures to assert dominance. He didn't need collars or trappings. All he needed were the little things, like an open door denying me the possibility of privacy.

After we ate, we went to the playroom. He hadn't even done anything to hurt me yet, but I was entranced as he zipped me into my arm and leg bindings and clipped me to the rings on the cross. Maybe it was because I was already letting go, making my mind blank, shutting everything out except for him. For this one time, this one perfect day, I refused entry to the fears that plagued me every day of my life. I put it all in Robin's hands. He would take care of it. The only thing I had to do was trust in him.

I also trusted that I had done everything I could to shield him on the off chance that something went awry. In Robin's safe, and in the hands of his lawyer, were both a video recording and a testimony I'd written, affirming that I had consented to everything Robin would do to me today. And Robin would be recording our play, to prove that I never withdrew consent, or that if I did safeword, he heeded it.

It might not protect him if something happened and a really aggressive prosecutor decided to go after him, but it would go far.

Now it was out of my hands. So I let it go.

Bare-chested, in nothing but a pair of jeans, Robin pressed

against my back, pinning me to the padded cross and covering my body with his. His lips were warm on my shoulders.

"Do you want this?"

I nodded, too spacey for words.

"Speak," Robin growled in my ear, reminding me that verbal acknowledgments weren't optional. Especially today.

"Yes!" I moaned as his hand slipped around my hip and seized my cock, stroking me until I was on the brink.

"Tell me what you want."

I whimpered as he released my dick, and cleared my throat, trying to find words.

"I want you to whip me."

"Is that all?"

"No. I want—I want you to leave marks. Bruises. Even break the skin." I drew a shuddering breath. Already it seemed I could feel the lighter strokes with which he would warm me up, escalating toward the ones that would burn or even slice. Fear and a sweet, sweet rapture jockeyed for position in my chest. And that was just from anticipation. "I want you to make me bleed."

He was silent for a while then, pressed against me, warm and sheltering. After a moment, though, he stepped back, and the cord of a dressage whip tickled as he dragged it across my skin.

"What's your safeword?"

That had to be a formality for the sake of the video. He knew I wouldn't be able to relax and enjoy this unless I was sure we had covered all the bases multiple times.

"Bodysuit."

"And that's the only thing I'll stop for, right?" he clarified—again, for the sake of the video. "You can beg and scream and tell me no, but unless you use that word, you don't actually want me to stop."

"Yes." I laid my head against the padded wood. "I don't want you to stop. Please."

"Tell me again. One last time. Do you want this?"

I arched my back, offering it to him as a target. "Yes. Please. I want it."

"I love you," I thought I heard him whisper, and then he let the whip fly.

There was no real comparison to describe the pain of that thin bit of knotted leather cord biting into my skin. "Heat" was too mild. It was like being lashed by lava. It stung from the first, but long after the blow fell, the burn continued to mount and spread, radiating out from that narrow line.

The first dozen strokes, I was sure I wouldn't be able to take it. It was too much. They *never* stopped hurting, nor hurt less. The next dozen were still agony beyond description, but I had lost the ability to process and react to it the way I had in the beginning. It still felt like I was being flayed alive, but that incredible swell of euphoria cushioned me from it. I screamed and eventually wept, with nothing more than a vague awareness of my own responses. I was sobbing, shaking, and if those black twill sleeves hadn't been holding me to the cross, I wouldn't have been able to support myself. Robin's chest was like an open flame against my back, igniting all those criss-crossing stripes.

"Six more," he murmured, his lips against the back of my neck. "I'm going to try to draw blood this time. Okay?"

I nodded weakly, then managed to recall that I was supposed to give audible responses. "Okay," I said on a hitching breath. "Six more."

I shrieked when the first one landed. The pain was immense; surely I had to be gushing blood from a wide-open fissure down the back of my shoulder. But my skin was dripping sweat—if I was bleeding, I couldn't feel it. The next one was, if anything, even more brutal, and the one after that harder still.

Then I felt it—the smallest trickle of something wet down the flesh covering my ribs.

Three more followed, precisely placed rivers of molten agony running down my skin.

I had no memory of him releasing me from my bindings and moving me to the cushions in the corner. Lying with anything touching my back was unthinkable; I sprawled on my front, hiccuping sobs still punctuating my breaths.

The touch of a wet cloth made me cry out in both pain and relief. Even Robin's expensive, soft-as-down washcloths grated like sand-paper. But blessedly cool sandpaper.

Robin was murmuring a steady litany of gentle praise and reas-surances, which I kept tuning in to and then drifting away from. ". . .

took that beautifully. So proud . . . little bit of antibiotic ointment on these . . . amazing . . . Drink for me?"

The movement to reach the straw was almost more than I could do. But my mouth was parched and the water sweet and cool. Then Robin eased me back down and that was all I could remember for some hours. I didn't quite fall asleep, but I was way the hell out of my head, drifting in an insensible, semiconscious haze.

God, I felt fantastic. The pain—and, oh, there was plenty of it— was a negligible concern.

Robin sat next to me, tending to anything I needed. I think maybe he was reading in between stretches of solicitude. It never occurred to me to mind him making a fuss over me.

Sometime in the evening, I came down to earth enough that he managed to get me on my feet and into bed. Carrying me wasn't a possibility with my back so welted. He kept the room warm enough that I didn't have to have the covers touching my back. We lay together in the dark, his fingertips lightly tracing my shoulders and hips. Anywhere but my back.

"I don't think once is going to be enough," I muttered with bitter-sweet resignation, my face half-buried in the pillow. "That was too incredible. I don't know what to do."

He kissed the shell of my ear. "It's okay. We'll figure it out."

"Aren't you afraid at all?"

"No, and you don't need to be either." More butterfly-light kisses wherever he could reach on my face. "Rest. We have as much time as we need to work things out."

Six months ago, I wouldn't have accepted that. I wouldn't have been able to leave it alone, wouldn't have really bought into the idea that I didn't have to have every experience and all the answers right that moment.

But now?

Now I believed him.

While the Dunes Resort in Douglas, Michigan, is a real place, the Buns & Baskets fundraiser for the Mr. Michigan Leather event usually happens in March, not in June. Hopefully they'll pardon me for taking liberties.

ACKNOWLEDGMENTS

I want to thank the hemophiliac gay men who took the time to answer my questions as I researched this book. While there is a great deal of information out there about hemophilia and even about sex and hemophilia, there's not much about gay sexuality and hemophilia.

Particularly I would like to thank J, who spent time with me on Skype answering questions about incredibly personal things. It was a pleasure working with him, and I very much appreciate his willingness to help me get it right. We were both flying blind when it came to BDSM and hemophilia, though, so while I tried to get a feel for hypothetical issues that might come up, any errors there are entirely my own.

THANK YOU FOR READING!

If you enjoyed this book, please be sure to support authors so we can continue to write the books you love. One great way to do this is to recommend the book to your friends on social media. Another is to review it at Goodreads and/or whichever site you purchased it from. Thank you!

Gea Change

SAUGATUCK BOOK 1

AMELIA C. GORMLEY

SEA CHANGE

SAUGATUCK, BOOK 1

One Summer Can Change Everything...

Topher Carlisle's always been the black sheep—literally—in his middle-class family. Biracial, gay, and genderfluid, his family doesn't think he'll amount to much, and he just might believe them.

After a bout of severe depression has put both his academic and financial prospects in danger, he accepts his best friend's offer to stay in her family's summer home while he works to make up the shortfall of his athletic scholarship. But his tendency for self-sabotage is strong and soon a terrible mistake in judgment leaves him homeless.

From the moment he sees Topher, artist Jace Sieger knows that this is someone he needs to capture on canvas. He's no stranger to poor life choices, and he sees something in Topher worth nurturing.

The challenge, though, is chipping through Topher's prickly defenses to reach the sensitive, traumatized soul beneath. With the help of his friends Geoff and Robin, maybe, just maybe, they can convince Topher he's worth something after all, and that a few mistakes don't make him irredeemable.

What starts as a casual vacation fling grows into something that will change both of them forever.

STRAIN

In a world with little hope and no rules,
the only thing they have to lose
is themselves.

AMELIA C. GORMLEY

STRAIN

THE EROTIC, POST-APOCALYPTIC THRILLER!

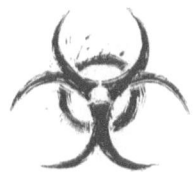

In a world with little hope and no rules, the only thing they have left to lose . . . is themselves.

Rhys Cooper is a dead man. He's spent years hiding from the virus that wiped out most of the human race, but an act of futile heroism has him counting down his remaining days. The timely arrival of superhuman soldiers offers some feeble hope—but only if Rhys can reconcile himself to doing what is necessary to take advantage of it.

Sergeant Darius Murrell has seen too much death and too little tenderness, seeking out survivors only to put the infected out of their misery, or send the uninfected to a safe haven he and his fellow Juggernaut troops can never enjoy. Rhys's situation is different, though. Not only is there an improbable chance that Darius won't have to put a bullet in Rhys's head, but he has somehow managed to get under Darius's skin.

The virus Rhys must infect himself with is sexually transmitted, and optimizing his chance of exposure requires him to submit as often as possible to Darius—and the other soldiers. Though the boundaries of morality have shifted in this harsh new world, what they must do has them asking if their humanity is too high a price to pay for Rhys's survival.

ABOUT THE AUTHOR

Amelia C. Gormley published her first short story in the school newspaper in the 4th grade, and since then has suffered the persistent delusion that enabling other people to hear the voices in her head might be a worthwhile endeavor. She's even convinced her hapless spouse that it could be a lucrative one as well, especially when coupled with her real-life interest in angst, kink, feminism, and pretty men.

When her husband and son aren't interacting with the back of her head as she stares at the computer, they rely on her to feed them, maintain their domicile, and keep some semblance of order in their lives (all very, very bad ideas—they really should know better by now.) She can also be found playing video games and ranting on Tumblr, seeing as how she's one of those horrid social justice warriors out to destroy free speech, gaming, geek culture, and everything else that's fun everywhere.

Blog: http://ameliacgormley.com
Tumblr: http://ameliacgormley.tumblr.com
Facebook: http://facebook.com/ameliacgormley
Twitter: http://twitter.com/ACGormley
Goodreads:
http://goodreads.com/author/show/6445292.Amelia_C_Gormley